2 3 OCT 2020

MURDER AT BLACKBURN HALL

MURDER AT BLACKBURN HALL

SARA ROSETT

MURDER AT BLACKBURN HALL

Book Two in the High Society Lady Detective series

Published by McGuffin Ink

ISBN: 978-0-9988431-7-9

Copyright © 2019 by Sara Rosett

Cover Design: Alchemy Book Covers

Editing: Historical Editorial

Map Illustration by Hanna Sandvig: bookcoverbakery.com

Newsletter sign-up for exclusive content: SaraRosett.com/signup

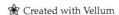 Created with Vellum

ACKNOWLEDGMENTS

Thank you to Jim Honderich for helping me get the golf right and to T.C. Milton, proofreader extraordinaire.

A huge thank you to my Patreon supporters:

Carol S. Bisig
Margaret Hulse
Carolyn Schrader
Connie Hartquist Jacobs

Thank you so much! I'm a blessed author to have such wonderful readers.

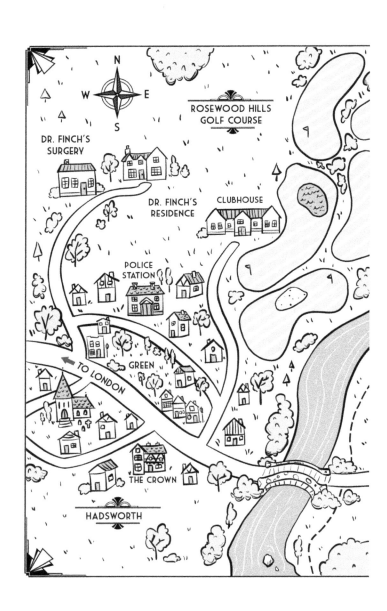

TO SIDLINGHAM

EAST BANK
COTTAGE

RIVER PATH

BLACKBURN HALL

THE Village of Hadsworth
& Blackburn Hall

CHAPTER ONE

*M*adame LaFoy gestured to the chair across the desk from her in the small office at the back of her hat shop. "Please have a seat, Miss Belgrave."

I perched on the edge of a chair upholstered in pale peach and folded my hands in my lap as Madame LaFoy gave my hat a critical look. I'd done my best to freshen up the cloche with two feathers and a new ribbon, but her lips turned down. She didn't bother to suppress a sigh as she transferred her attention to her desk, where she searched among the ledgers, scraps of fabric, ribbon, and flowers. She extracted a letter from under a cluster of peacock feathers. She skimmed the wrinkled pages. "Gwen Stone has given you a character." Her attention switched from the letter to my face. "A relative?"

I shifted on the chair. "Yes." I'd hoped with the difference in our last names, that fact would be overlooked. It seemed rather sordid to rely on family connections for an entrée to the working world, but jobs were extremely hard to come by. I'd had to swallow my pride and ask my cousin for a reference.

Madame LaFoy nodded. "I see the resemblance."

That would be a first, I thought but kept silent. My tall,

1

elegant cousin Gwen had dark eyes and blonde hair. I was shorter with dark blue eyes and bobbed brown hair. Not to mention the differences in our temperament. I liked to be on the move, while Gwen was quiet and steady.

"Something about your bone structure," Madame LaFoy murmured, then added, "Miss Gwen Stone has excellent taste, and she's a good customer." She dropped the letter onto the desk. "You *do* understand the position is a hat model?"

"Yes."

"And you'd be able to . . . fulfill the requirements of the position, Miss Belgrave?"

Daughters of the gentry, even impoverished gentry, weren't supposed to work. Madame LaFoy might have hoped employing me would draw in some customers from my set. Unfortunately, many of my friends had also landed in situations like mine, finding themselves among the *new poor*, as the newspapers called us.

Madame LaFoy said, "Most likely, some of my patrons will be friends of yours or of your cousin. It could be awkward—"

"It won't cause a problem," I said. "I'll be very professional."

A frown wrinkled Madame's forehead. "Do you have any experience?"

I smiled. This question had always tripped me up in my previous job interviews. For once I could answer in the affirmative. "Yes, I've worn hats all my life."

Madame LaFoy's frown deepened. "Do you have any experience working in a *shop*?"

So Madame LaFoy was not the lighthearted sort who laughed at little jokes. I rearranged my features into a serious expression. "Well, no, but I'm a quick learner."

The downward curve of Madame LaFoy's lips became more pronounced.

I sat straighter. "I can start as soon as you'd like. Even as early as tomorrow." It was Friday afternoon, and I knew the millinery was open on Saturday. I doubted Madame had more interviews lined up today. If she really needed someone, then she might take a chance on me if I could start right away.

Madame LaFoy stood, and the silk of her skirt whispered around her calves as she moved to the office door. "I'll give you a week's trial, beginning tomorrow morning. Eight o'clock sharp. Not a moment later."

My heels sank into the rug as I walked to the door, weaving through peach-colored settees and occasional tables topped with fresh roses. I couldn't quite believe it had come to this, applying for jobs again. After what had happened at Archly Manor, I'd been so sure I was on my way.

I'd taken a job and completed it successfully. I was the first to admit the route to the conclusion had taken a few unusual turns—hairpin turns, to be completely accurate. But I'd done it. And I'd been paid too. I'd returned to London with enough money to pay the rent on my poky room and even repair my motor, a dear little Morris Cowley, and garage it at the edge of Belgravia, not far from my boarding house.

But my funds were dwindling at a rapid rate. My choices were to either go back to the job search or return to live in Tate House with my father and Sonia. I'd rather model hats for every snobbish high society matron in London than live under my new stepmother's thumb.

I stepped out of the shop into the lingering summer heat and made my way across Mayfair toward the Savoy, where I had an appointment with Jasper Rimington for tea. He'd sent me a message yesterday. He was back in London after a trip and wanted to hear how my new venture was going. Jasper was an old family friend. We had gone for years without seeing each other, but a few months ago we'd met again by chance. It was before the Archly Manor incident, and my financial situation had been rather dire. Jasper had spotted it straightaway and suggested tea, which I'd desperately needed.

My bank balance wasn't as grim as it had been then, but I wasn't about to turn down tea at the Savoy. I didn't even consider the extravagance of hailing a taxi. I walked.

Jasper was lounging in a chair in the opulent lobby, looking dapper and slightly bored as he surveyed the room with his hooded gray eyes, a book held loosely in his hand. When he spotted me, he tucked the book under his arm, then came my way, drawing the attention of two women strolling through the lobby. Jasper didn't notice. "Hello, old girl." He removed his hat, revealing his blond hair. He was fastidious about his clothing and fussed over every seam, but that attention to fashion didn't extend to his wavy fair hair.

"Hello, Jasper. Given up on hair tonic?"

"It's a losing battle. I've conceded to the curl."

"I'm sure the ladies are thrilled." I'd heard more than one deb rhapsodize about Jasper's hair.

A hint of grin turned up the corners of his mouth. "I couldn't say. Grigsby, however, is mortified. Looks as if I've personally run him through with a saber every time I leave my rooms."

"Your valet does have rather strong opinions." He disapproved of me and didn't bother to hide it. "Can't say I agree with him." I tilted my head. "It suits you." I tucked my hand through his arm. "It is good to see you."

"Missed the old mug, did you?"

"Actually, yes. I'm glad to know you're back in town. Where were you again?"

He waved his walking stick as we set off toward the restaurant. "Here and there. Too boring to recount."

"Really? I'd think Bebe Ravenna would be rather entertaining." I'd glanced over a woman's shoulder on the Tube a few weeks before and had seen Jasper's picture in the newspaper. The willowy blonde actress had been draped over his arm.

Jasper waved a languid hand. "I met her at a party where I'd been invited to make up the numbers, nothing more."

I didn't doubt the truth of the statement. With so many young men lost in the Great War, hostesses had to scramble to balance their tables and dance floors. "Well, Miss Ravenna looked pleased to have you there."

"She was a pleasant companion," Jasper said in an offhanded way. "But I'm sure my activities are nothing as exciting as what you've been doing."

"Hardly."

Once we were seated and our tea arrived, Jasper said, "Now, don't puncture my bubble. During my dull sojourn to the continent, I passed many a tedious train ride picturing you having the grandest of adventures. I refuse to believe you're living the quiet life. Found any more stray murderers?"

"Nothing is as exciting as that. Far from it, in fact."

"No commissions from your newspaper advertisement?"

"A few. So far, the inquiries have been from elderly ladies with missing pets."

"Pets?"

"In the last fortnight, I've recovered a pug, a tabby, and a rather high-strung Chihuahua."

"Aren't all Chihuahuas high-strung?"

"My experience is limited. This one certainly was."

Jasper set down his teacup. "So, not what you were expecting?"

"Not at all. I've decided I must draw the line and refuse any more of these animal cases. Otherwise, I'll become known as the pet detective. Yes, I know it's funny, but it's not at all what I hoped for."

"Of course. I'm sorry I laughed, but you do have to admit there's a certain humor there."

"I'm sure I'll think it's hilarious—years from now. It's to the point that I've become one of the gainfully employed."

Jasper paused, teacup halfway to his mouth. "You've found a regular job?"

"You don't have to sound so shocked," I said.

"It's not a slight against you, old thing. It's just that there are so few jobs to be found."

"I realize that. I'm fortunate to have found an opening," I said. "I have a week's trial at Madame LaFoy's Millinery."

"Mayfair. A good address."

Trust Jasper to know the best hat shops in London, I thought as I savored my peach Melba.

"So you have no other prospects?" Jasper asked.

I shook my head. "I had to tell Mrs. Forsyth there was really no hope of tracking down her parakeet. It flew out of her drawing room window last week."

Jasper cleared his throat. "I can see how that would be an impossible case."

"Quite. And since that's the only other inquiry I've had—"

"Thus, the hat shop. I understand." Jasper looked away for a moment as he drummed his fingers on the table, then he took a card from his waistcoat pocket. "If you're not interested in pursuing a future in millinery, you should consider telephoning Vernon." Jasper placed the card on the table in front of me. "He's in a spot of bother."

Vernon Hightower, Owner was printed under the words *Hightower Books.* I ran my finger over the embossed letters. "My. You do have friends in high places." Copies of mystery releases from Hightower Books were on display in bookstalls all over London. "Is this the source of your lurid fiction?"

"Some of it. Speaking of that . . ." Jasper reached for the hardback book he'd been carrying. When we'd been seated, he'd placed it on the seat of one of the empty chairs at our table. "I promised I'd share my library of crime fiction with you. This one isn't from Hightower Books, but I think you'll enjoy it."

I read the title aloud, *"The Secret Adversary.* The cover is . . . interesting." It featured a bear dressed in a suit, removing a theatrical mask of a man's face. "You're sure this is a mystery?"

Jasper laughed. "Yes. Mystery and adventure and a love story."

I ran my hand over the cover. "If only that were my life instead of hat shop girl working to make ends meet."

Jasper raised his eyebrows as he tilted his head toward the business card. "Then give Vernon a call."

I placed the book to the side of my place setting. "What's his spot of bother?"

"It's not my story to tell. Hightower mentioned it at the club—only the barest outline and in strictest confidence, of course. A delicate matter. It's not really in my line, but you might find it of interest. That's all I can say about it. I floated the idea of you taking it on."

"Your Mr. Hightower sounds interesting, but I have a job lined up." Jasper didn't press the issue, and we moved on to other topics.

Jasper and I had a lovely tea. We parted at the door of the Savoy, he to go to his club, and me to my room at Mrs. Gutler's. On my way, I passed a telephone box, and my steps slowed. I'd tucked the business card and the book away in my handbag as I left the Savoy.

During tea with Jasper, I'd dismissed the idea of calling Mr. Hightower, but perhaps I *should* contact him. After all, Madame LaFoy was only giving me a week's trial. If she wasn't satisfied, I could be looking for work again next week. It couldn't hurt to telephone Mr. Hightower.

I did an about-face and retraced my steps. I telephoned Hightower Books and was put through to Vernon Hightower's secretary, who seemed reluctant to let me speak to his boss until I mentioned Jasper's name.

A few seconds later, a smooth masculine voice came on the line. "A friend of Jasper Rimington's, are you?" The accent wasn't as polished or exact as someone's from the high society set, but it wasn't a rough working-class accent either.

"Yes. Mr. Rimington didn't give me any details. He only said I should contact you about a delicate matter, as he phrased it. I might be of help to you."

"What's your name again?"

"Olive Belgrave."

The line was silent for a few beats. "Be here tomorrow morning, eight o'clock."

I hesitated. Did I want to become a hat shop girl—steady employment and a measly paycheck, but a paycheck nonetheless—or did I want to take a chance on something else, something I knew absolutely nothing about?

"Are you still there?"

"Thank you, sir." I tightened my grip on the earpiece. "I'll be there."

I ended the call, then asked to be connected to LaFoy's Millinery. Madame herself answered.

I swallowed, then plunged in. "This is Olive Belgrave. I've had a change of circumstance. I'm terribly sorry, but I'm afraid I cannot be there tomorrow morning."

Madame LaFoy's voice managed to convey the iciness of a winter breeze. "I see."

"Again, I'm very sorry. Perhaps Monday—"

"No, Monday is out of the question. In the future, I'll be delighted to receive you as a customer but not as a job applicant. Goodbye, Miss Belgrave."

Heart beating fast, I replaced the receiver. Well, I'd done it now. Either I was embarking on a new adventure, or I had a bright future as a doggie detective.

CHAPTER TWO

*a*t half past nine that evening, I was pressed into the crush of a Mayfair townhouse, looking for my finishing-school chum, Gigi, more formally known as Lady Gina Alton. It was her birthday, and Gigi was having a little party. I was glad I had the party to attend. Otherwise, I'd have spent the whole evening wondering if I'd done the right thing when I cancelled with Madame LaFoy.

I'd returned from the Savoy and changed out of my day dress into one of my cousin Gwen's cast-off evening gowns, a sleeveless, V-neck frock in black that fell in a straight line to my calves. The simple lines of the dress emphasized the beautiful scalloped beading that spread across the material in a blooming silver sunburst.

I danced with Monty Park, a man who'd been at Archly Manor. So far, I'd managed to avoid another of the guests from that party, a man I knew as Tug. He tended to overindulge in drink and become too friendly. Dancing was going on in one room, cards in another, and a spread of food was displayed buffet style in a third. I stared at the tables piled with salmon, sponge fingers, tiny frosted cakes, and puff pastry.

What a pity Gigi's party fell on the same day as my tea with Jasper at the Savoy. If the party had been on another day, I could have indulged in scrumptious food on *two* separate occasions. I normally dined on threepenny buns and weak tea in the evening as a matter of economy. The sight of all the luscious food made me wish I'd brought a larger handbag. The salmon was out of the question, of course, but the sponge fingers were a definite possibility. If I could tuck a few of them in my handbag, they'd make for a decadent teatime tomorrow.

"Olive! It's been positively forever since I've seen you."

"Hello, Gigi. Happy birthday."

"Thank you. I'm so glad to see you." Gigi's midnight-black hair was cut in an Eton crop. Trimmed short in the back like a boy's cut, the sides barely skimmed the tips of her ears. On someone else, the hairstyle might have been boyish, but with her long lashes and delicate features, she oozed femininity. A cigarette smoldered at the end of a holder, which was clamped against the edge of the cocktail she held. She was even shorter than I was and popped up onto her tiptoes to survey the area behind me. The fringed hem of her dress danced as she moved. "Did Gwen come with you?"

"No, she and Violet and my aunt have gone on holiday to the South of France."

"And no wonder. After what happened at Archly Manor." Her scarlet lips split into a smile. "Scandalous . . . but so thrilling too!"

"It sounds that way, doesn't it?" This was especially true in the case of the articles written immediately after the arrest of the guilty party. Some of the stories had been so far from the truth that I'd given another finishing-school chum, Essie Matthews, an interview. Essie was a society reporter for *The Ballyhoo*, and I expected to see her tonight. "Is Essie here?"

Gigi waved a languid hand, sloshing her cocktail and

leaving a trail of cigarette smoke floating upward between us. "Somewhere about."

I stepped back from the smoke. I'd always had issues with asthma. It had been much worse when I was younger. As I'd grown, I'd had less frequent episodes, but I'd found breathing cigarette smoke directly could bring on one of my attacks. So far, the high ceilings of the townhouse's rooms along with the open windows and doors had kept the air fresh.

Gigi's gaze, which had drifted over my shoulder, sharpened. "Oh, I must fly. There's Daphne, and I haven't seen her in an *age.*"

Gigi flitted off, and I moved away from the food, deciding to raid the table immediately before I left.

I ran into Monty in the hall, and he asked, "Care to dance again?"

"Yes, that would be lovely."

The townhouse didn't have a formal ballroom, but the furniture had been removed from one of the large drawing rooms, and the rug had been rolled up. The musicians played the first chords of a foxtrot, and Monty extended his arm. "It seems like all anyone wants to talk to me about is what happened at Archly Manor."

I stepped into his arms. "I know the feeling."

"I had no idea it would make me such a celebrity." He maneuvered us to the left, deftly avoiding a rambunctious couple headed our way. "Haven't dined at home in weeks, but I'm finding the questions tedious. I enjoyed it in the beginning. But, I say, there's only so many times a chap can answer the question, *what's it like to know a murderer?*"

"I completely agree, but I think your popularity is directly related to matchmaking mothers."

Monty laughed. "It's not that. I'm not even a second son. Third, you know. Hardly an outside chance at the old family pile, not to mention the family funds. No, they don't want me for their daughters. They only need me to make up the numbers."

It was a shame young women were not as in demand for dinner parties. While I'd rather avoid the questions, it would be nice to have a good dinner every once in a while.

Monty pulled my hand to his chest as another couple twirled by. "Now I refer them to your interview. Nicely done, by the way."

"Thank you. Essie did a good job with it. Since it's a topic that you and I are tired of, let's talk of something else. What are your plans for the autumn?"

"Am I going hunting, you mean?" Monty shook his head. "No, not my line. I do have a little golfing holiday set up. I depart in a few days to visit some of the best courses. Do you golf?"

"No, I haven't tried it."

"You should. It's a jolly good game."

As the dance ended, a couple next to us jostled Monty. They turned to apologize, and the young woman squealed then clamped her hand onto Monty's arm. "Monty! I haven't seen you since you came to dinner. Where have you been hiding yourself? We simply must dance." She looked back at her former partner. "You don't mind, do you?"

The other man exited with a gracious bow. Monty gave me a look I imagined a drowning man would give to a passing ship. "Olive?"

"Oh, I mustn't get in the way, and I want a breath of fresh air. Enjoy." I gave him a wink as I moved on. So perhaps being on duty to fill out the numbers at dinner parties did have a downside after all.

I inched through the crowd at the edge of the dance floor. The room was becoming crowded and stuffy. A pall of cigarette smoke now hung over the whole room, and I moved toward the windows as my chest tightened. As I neared one of the windows, a man passing by me pulled his cigarette out of his mouth and exhaled a puff of smoke directly into my face.

The weight pressing against my chest increased. I waved the smoke away and made for the door that stood open to the garden. *Slowly. Breathe slowly and evenly*, I lectured myself as I walked at a steady pace out of the room. Frantic movements only made it worse, although I was itching to break into a run to get into the fresh air. I reached the door and went to the edge of the steps that dropped down to a garden with a towering chestnut tree that blotted out the stars.

I leaned against the coolness of one of the stone pillars that framed the stairs and supported the townhouse's next story. I concentrated on breathing slowly in and out. After a few moments, the noise and lights of the party, which had receded as I focused entirely on my breathing, came back to my awareness. The band around my chest eased, and I took a few deep breaths without pain.

"Olive?"

Essie Matthews stood at my elbow. Her always ruddy cheeks were now flushed a bright red. "Are you all right?"

"Yes, I'm fine." I knew I'd be okay now, but I shouldn't go back into the party, or I might have another episode.

Essie fanned her face with her hand, ruffling her short brown bob. "It's so close in there. I couldn't stand it anymore either." She reached into her handbag. "And I just absolutely must have a ciggie."

She took out a cigarette and lighter. The flame danced, she drew in a breath, then she exhaled toward the garden. She grimaced and examined the end of the cigarette. Even though she was breathing away from me, I still took a step back. She noticed my movement. "I'm sorry. I forgot they set you off." Essie had seen me struggle with my breathing a few times during finishing school, in particular on the ski slopes. "But don't worry," she continued. "These are asthma cigarettes." She held out the cigarette. "Want a puff?"

"Thank you, but no." I'd heard about asthma cigarettes, and once I'd asked the doctor in Nether Woodsmoor about them. "Can't see how they'd help," Dr. Miller had said. "From what I've seen, smoke irritates, doesn't soothe. Probably do more harm than good." Since Dr. Miller suffered from asthma in a worse way than I did, I'd taken his advice and avoided regular cigarettes as well as the medicinal asthma ones.

Essie drew on the cigarette with a frown. "Not like a real cigarette at all." She waved it, the red tip jumping in the darkness. "You're sure? It's a new brand that'll be out soon. One of the reporters at the newspaper wrote a story on it and gave me a few." With the cigarette tucked between two fingers, Essie opened her handbag and dug around with her free hand. She pulled out a small package and thrust it into my hands. "Here, you can have the rest of these. They don't do the trick for me."

I tilted the package toward the light from the open door. "Breathe Easy," read the biggest line. "For relief of the paroxysms of asthma. A unique blend of herbs. Effective for treatment of asthma and hay fever as well as diseases of the throat. Not recommended for children under six."

I held the box out and felt the remaining cigarettes shift inside. "I won't use them."

She pushed my hand back. "Keep them. You might change your mind."

Essie was one of those determined people who were difficult to sway from their chosen course of action. The easiest thing would be to keep them and throw them away later. I tucked the cigarettes into my handbag. Essie stubbed out the cigarette on the balustrade, then scanned the crowd at the door. "I must find someone who has a real cigarette."

She took two steps away, then spun back. "If you have any more juicy stories, let me know. I'll be there in an instant."

"Of course." Essie's society column was never far from her thoughts.

She hurried away. "George, you always have a cigarette. Might I have one?"

I left the party by way of the buffet and managed to tuck some sponge fingers and two cakes into my purse.

One should not have cake for breakfast. I tried to ignore the slightly seasick feeling as the lift swept me to the top floor of the building where Hightower Books was located.

I'd intended to save the purloined cakes for tea, but their lure was too strong. I'd eaten one before I set out for my appointment with Mr. Hightower. Now I wished I'd exercised more self-control. I wasn't used to such a blast of decadence so early in the morning, and it had soured my stomach.

I flexed my fingers in my gloves, which felt too tight. It couldn't be that I was nervous. I'd trooped back and forth across the city, meeting with all sorts of people in my search for a job. If Mr. Hightower turned me down, it would be nothing new. I'd just have to return to applying to dress shops while searching for lost pets.

I assumed I'd have to wait, which would have given me time to tame the butterflies in my stomach, but I was immediately ushered into Mr. Hightower's office. I suppose I'd expected his office would look similar to a solicitor's office—a spacious room, a weighty desk with lots of polished wood, and rows of leather-bound volumes. But Mr. Hightower's office reminded me of my father's untidy book-packed study, where I'd often spread out on the rug before the fire with a book or a notebook while Father scratched away on his commentary.

Mr. Hightower's office was a small space, barely larger than his battered desk. I'd been right about the books, though. They were everywhere, tilting higgledy-piggledy on the shelves, stacked on the carpet at the corners of the room, and balanced on the corner of Mr. Hightower's desk. However, the books weren't leather-bound volumes. Row upon row of popular fiction with the Hightower Books logo of a stone tower filled the shelves. The bright colors created a rainbow effect and gave the room a cheerful atmosphere. My stomach settled. I felt at home in the book-stuffed room.

Mr. Hightower came around the desk, and I shook his hand. "Pleased to meet you," he said, indicating a chair in front of his desk. He was around fifty, I imagined, with a dark horizontal slash of bushy brows and a receding hairline on either side of a widow's peak.

I took a seat, and he returned to his chair, which squeaked as he dropped into it. He linked his hands on top of a stack of typewritten pages centered on his desk. The paper crinkled under his cuffs. "So, Miss Belgrave, tell me about yourself."

"Do you want the short version or the long?"

"Let's say, give me the short story, not the novel."

"Very well. I grew up in Nether Woodsmoor, a small village in Derbyshire where my father was a vicar before he inherited a legacy that allowed him to retire and work on a commentary. I attended boarding school and had a year at a finishing school in Switzerland. My mother, who was American, died when I was younger. She set up a fund for my education. Her wish was that I would return to her alma mater, a university in the United States, and pursue a degree from there as she had. I went to America last year but was called home when my father became ill. Thankfully, he's recovered, but I've decided to stay on."

It wasn't my choice to stay in England, but I wasn't about to tell Mr. Hightower about my shock on discovering my father had married his nurse or the fact that he'd lost all the funds for my education when he invested the money in a fly-by-night operation. I realized I'd fisted my hands in my lap. I relaxed my fingers and smoothed my skirt. "But that's not really of interest to you. I imagine the incident at Archly Manor is why I'm here."

"Yes, that *is* the reason I wanted to speak to you. Mr. Rimington told me about it. He also said you're as tenacious as a terrier after a rat."

"Hmm, yes, that's true, I suppose. Although I'm not sure that's a flattering comparison."

He chuckled. "And he said you have a sense of humor as well as the ability to be extremely discreet."

"Well, that's better."

Mr. Hightower stared at me for a moment, then reached for a pair of spectacles and hooked them over his ears. "Miss Belgrave, I may not look like it, but I'm a bit of a gambler. I'm sure I seem to be the very picture of a staid city man to you, but I do love to take a chance. Not on horses or cards, you understand. In business. One has to like risk to be a book publisher. I thrive on hunches. And my hunch is you can help me. I'd like to hire you. Are you interested?"

A tingle of excitement raced along my skin. This was so much better than modeling hats. "Yes. Very much so."

"Good. I'm about to share some information with you. If it were to go outside the walls of this office, it would cause a considerable amount of distress at Hightower Books. It's a delicate situation. Do I have your solemn promise you will keep this information to yourself?"

"Yes. I won't mention it to anyone else."

"Excellent." Mr. Hightower gave a flicker of a smile. "Because you're a vicar's daughter, I know I can trust your word." He pulled a folder from under the stacks of typed pages and removed a photograph from the file. "That's Ronnie Mayhew. Our readers know him as R. W. May, one of our most popular authors. He's missing, and I'd like you to find him."

CHAPTER THREE

I examined the photograph Mr. Hightower handed me across the desk. It was a studio portrait of a man with curly hair and a full beard. With his abundant hair and flowing beard, he resembled the illustrations of Moses in Father's religion books.

R. W. May posed stiffly in a chair, one arm propped next to a stack of books on a table beside him, his bearded chin in his hand. The image itself was dark, which gave it the feeling of a daguerreotype from the last century. "If Mr. Mayhew—or is it Mr. May . . . ?"

"Mr. Mayhew is who you'll be searching for, so let's use that. It's how I think of him."

My excitement fizzled. I wasn't the right person for Mr. Hightower. He didn't need a quiet inquiry. He needed someone more official than me. "If Mr. Mayhew is missing, this is a matter for the police, not me." I handed the photograph back.

"That's where the delicacy comes in. Hear me out, then you can turn me down if you like."

A frisson of interest bubbled up again. "Sounds reasonable."

Mr. Hightower returned the photo to the folder, then picked up a stack of four hardcover books from beside the piles of paper. He came around the desk and handed them to me as he sat down in the matching visitor's chair next to me. "Take a look at these."

The cover on the first book depicted a young brunette with red lips in a bright sleeveless dress. A rope of pearls swayed to the side as she raised a candle high and peered around the corner of a dark tunnel. "Oh, I recognize this one. *The Mystery of Newberry Close*. The Lady Eileen mystery series. My aunt read it and quite enjoyed it." The next one on the stack was *Intrigue on the Scotch Express* and featured a train speeding through the countryside. The third one was titled *Murder at Castle Colfax*. Its cover was more abstract. A feminine hand hovered over a gun against a bright red background. "I must admit I'm not a connoisseur of detective fiction. Mr. Rimington tells me it's a wonderful escape."

"I highly recommend it." Mr. Hightower said. "But, of course, I would." He gestured to the bookshelves lining his office.

I turned the books in my hands, skimming the back covers as well as the front and back flaps. Many books featured authors' photographs on the back covers, but these only had text, no images. "You didn't put Mr. Mayhew's picture on these books."

"No, a marketing decision." Mr. Hightower reached over his desk for the folder. He took out the photograph, examined it for a moment, then tapped it against the arm of the chair. "When we took on Mr. Mayhew as an author, all the arrangements were made through the post. I haven't met him in person. Once the contracts were signed and we were preparing the manuscript for printing, we asked for a photograph." Mr. Hightower held up the photo. "Mayhew sent this one along. The publicity department was appalled."

"Why? Mr. Mayhew looks respectable."

"And that's the problem. Since you haven't read any of Mr. Mayhew's books, you wouldn't know it, but the books are about Lady Eileen and her set, Bright Young People doing exciting and interesting things, like becoming involved in murder and mysteries."

"Yes, I can see that from the covers. So the author's image doesn't match the tone of the books?"

Mr. Hightower pointed the photograph at me. "Exactly. I had an instinct about you, and this proves I was right. We thought we'd bought a book from one of the Bright Young People. Turns out, we had bought a book from a middle-aged man who could write with the *voice* of a Bright Young Person. We told Mr. Mayhew there wasn't enough room on his book jackets for his photograph. He never mentioned it again after the first book, and we didn't bring it up again either. You're probably wondering why I'm telling you about his photograph?"

"No, you tell a fascinating story. I'm intrigued, and I'm sure this story has a plot."

"Yes, that was merely the opening act. Now we come to a turning point. Mr. Mayhew has missed his deadline. The manuscript for his next book, *Murder on the Ninth Green*, has not arrived."

"I thought authors were late with their manuscripts all the time?"

"Oh, yes, they are. Constant problem." Mr. Hightower adjusted his tie. "Except for Mr. Mayhew. He's never missed a deadline. *Never.* In fact, his manuscripts have always been early. Mr. Mayhew's deadline was two weeks ago. I received a letter from him last week. He apologized for the delay and said I'd absolutely have the manuscript by Friday of last week. The manuscript still hasn't arrived." Mr. Hightower drummed his fingers on the folder.

After a few seconds of silence, I asked, "And you've

contacted him?" It was an obvious question, but Mr. High-tower's flow of words seemed to have dried up.

"That's the problem. I have no way of getting in touch with Mr. Mayhew."

"Surely you have a postal address?"

"All his correspondence is handled through his solicitor. I have contacted him. Unfortunately, the solicitor had a bad fall. Took a hit to his head and was unconscious for a few days. He's come around now, but he isn't his usual self. He's still confused and forgetful. In short, he's in no shape to run his office or answer questions. He's recovering but must take it slowly—complete rest at home for now. His doctor has forbidden him from returning to his office. I've been in touch with his secretary, who looked through the files, but he didn't find any mention of Mr. Mayhew."

"But you've had correspondence from the solicitor regarding Mr. Mayhew?"

Mr. Hightower cleared his throat. "Not on legal matters. Mr. Mayhew signed a five-book contract and used a different solicitor to handle those negotiations. Shortly after it was signed, I received a letter from Mr. Mayhew asking that all correspondence be sent to his new solicitor in Hadsworth, but nothing of a legal nature has come up since then. The solicitor sends the manuscripts to us and forwards our correspondence to Mr. Mayhew."

"So he's essentially a post office."

"Correct."

"Seems strange."

"Which exactly describes Mr. Mayhew. He's an odd one. From the very beginning, Mr. Mayhew insisted on this manner of doing business. I've attempted to entice him to London, offered to take him to dinner and a show, introduce him around the office, but he always refuses. He's intensely private. In fact"—Mr. Hightower hunched forward—"I wouldn't be surprised to discover Mr. Mayhew had some sort of agreement with the solicitor to handle his matters off-book. I believe that's why the secretary can't find a record of Mr. Mayhew as a client."

"So you have no other way to contact your author except by post through the solicitor?"

"That's correct, but I do have an idea where Mr. Mayhew might be," Mr. Hightower said. "Mr. Mayhew and I have had a small exchange of personal correspondence through the solicitor. Christmas cards, that sort of thing. One year, Mr. Mayhew mentioned enjoying an unusually heavy blanketing of snow. A large storm had unexpectedly dumped several inches in Kent at Christmas, and I remember thinking at the time, *Mr. Mayhew must live in Kent.* The solicitor's office is in Hadsworth, which is a small village in Kent. I can't imagine Mr. Mayhew traveling a long distance to engage a solicitor simply to handle the transfer of his manuscript to me and receive our checks. Now, I'd go down to Kent myself and look around Hadsworth, but I'm afraid I'll cause a stir if I do that."

He glanced toward his closed office door. "What I haven't told you about Mr. Mayhew is . . . well, Mr. Mayhew's books have become the backbone of our sales for the last three years. The success of *Mystery at Newberry Close* was . . . well, phenomenal. We've never seen anything like it. We've been doing print run after print run. Even now, it still sells at a steady pace—a *brisk* steady pace. The other R. W. May books have done just as well. Our company is rather dependent upon Mr. Mayhew for its future success."

"So you're afraid that if word gets out that his manuscript is late or that it's—umm—perhaps not coming . . ."

"Yes. I don't want to worry anyone here, but I must do something."

Mr. Hightower might own the publishing company, but he was an excellent storyteller in his own right. He'd captured my interest, and I was itching to delve into the mystery, but I couldn't in good conscience barrel along, no matter how intriguing I found the situation. I pushed the words out of my mouth. "I still think this is a matter for the police."

"That *is* my next step if Hadsworth doesn't pan out," he said quickly. "I want you to . . . get the lay of the land, you might say. I can't do it myself—it would raise red flags all over the office, and with our investors as well if word got out. If I hire a private detective, I'm sure he'd stick out in Hadsworth. It's a small village, and a stranger staying at the local inn asking questions about a man named Mayhew would certainly be noted. But that's not what I propose."

He put the folder on the desk and picked up a letter written on thick cream stationary. "Lady Holt of Blackburn Hall, which is located near the village of Hadsworth, has been pestering me to publish an etiquette guide. She writes a column for *The Express* about the proper fork to use and how to address invitations. She thinks her guide would be a best seller."

Mr. Hightower's tone indicated he thought that sort of book would stick to the shelves rather than fly off them. He tossed the letter on the desk and settled back in his chair, his gaze fixed on me with a definite speculative air. "If a young woman of your class and status were to visit Blackburn Hall on my behalf to examine Lady Holt's manuscript, it could be done with a minimum of fuss. I can arrange for you to stay at Blackburn Hall for a few days, during which you can make some discreet inquires and find out if Mayhew lives in Hadsworth and what's happened to his manuscript. If the original is lost in his solicitor's office—well, Mayhew seems to be a cautious sort of chap. I imagine he's got his own copy of the manuscript."

"So you want me to find out if Mr. Mayhew lives in Hadsworth. If he does reside there, then you want me to find out what's happened to the manuscript."

"Exactly."

Mr. Hightower's assumptions about Hadsworth sounded

as if they'd be correct, but what if they weren't? "What if I can't find any trace of Mr. Mayhew?"

"Then you'll have had a well-paid holiday in the country."

"And what if Mr. Mayhew was in Hadsworth, but he's gone when I get there?"

Mr. Hightower said, "My, you do like to cover all the possibilities, don't you?"

"I need to know exactly what you expect from me."

"That's fair. All right, if Mr. Mayhew was living there but has done a bunk, try and find out where he's gone. I imagine he's been called away unexpectedly—that's what I hope, anyway. If you can't get a line on Mr. Mayhew, I *will* contact the police." He ran a hand over his forehead. "And then all hell will break loose here at Hightower Books."

A short rap sounded, the door opened, and a man leaned in, a swath of his dark hair falling forward over his brow. "Vernon, I need to speak to you about—I'm sorry, I didn't realize you were in a meeting."

Mr. Hightower stood and picked up a typewritten stack of pages from his desk. "I suppose you're after the Brittenham manuscript." He walked across the room and handed it to the man. "It's going to need a lot of work."

"I was afraid of that." The younger man looked from me to Mr. Hightower, clearly waiting for an introduction. I gripped the arms of my chair to stand, but before I could move, Mr. Hightower pushed the manuscript into the young man's hands. "I'll chat with you about it in a minute." He closed the door, forcing the man to step back.

Mr. Hightower returned to the seat beside me. "My executive editor, Busby. Leland Busby. He has no idea about Mr. Mayhew's manuscript. I've been putting Mr. Busby off, telling him it's on the way." Mr. Hightower hunched forward in the seat, hands on his knees. "I'll pay you forty pounds to go to Blackburn Hall and make some quiet inquiries. Twenty pounds now and twenty pounds after you complete the visit.

You must report back to me directly. No one else in the office."

Mum taught me a lady does not gape, and I managed to keep my mouth from dropping open, but just barely. Forty pounds was extremely generous. And a trip to visit a country home on top of it? I didn't need even a moment to think it over. "I can do that." I stood, we shook hands, and then I held out the stack of R.W. May's books.

Mr. Hightower waved them back to me. "Keep them. We have a few copies to spare. A little light reading for you. Perhaps you'll run across something that will help you find Mr. Mayhew."

CHAPTER FOUR

wo days later, I left for Blackburn Hall after Mr. Hightower finalized arrangements with Lady Holt, which gave me time to pack and read the first R.W. May book. I'd taken the book with me to the park the day before I left, intending to read a few chapters. My small bag was packed, and I'd informed my landlady, Mrs. Gutler, I would be leaving town for a few days on a visit to Blackburn Hall. I had nothing else to do for the rest of the day, so I picked up the first book, *The Mystery of Newberry Close,* and left for Kensington Gardens. It was much cooler in the park than in my stuffy room.

I settled on a bench in the shade and opened the book. A piece of paper folded in thirds lay between the cover and the end paper. The typed letter was dated three years ago and addressed to Mr. Hightower. It contained a list of potential titles, and the signature at the bottom was *R. W. Mayhew.* It was interesting to see that Mr. Mayhew had proposed *Death on the Train,* but someone—Mr. Hightower or an assistant, presumably—had marked through the words and written, *Intrigue on the Scotch Express,* which was a much better title.

I refolded the paper. Since the list only contained three

SARA ROSETT

titles and those books had already been released, I didn't think I needed to rush the letter back to Mr. Hightower. I turned to the first chapter and began to read. The clever whodunit featured plucky Lady Eileen and her faithful—and besotted—chauffeur. I became so immersed in the story that I didn't move for several hours. I picked up some buns on the way home and returned to reading, finishing the novel in bed that night.

I'd enjoyed it so much, I stacked it with the other R. W. May books and stowed them in the Morris Cowley with my suitcase to take with me to Blackburn Hall. These country house affairs could either be delightfully fun or dreadfully dull. If Blackburn Hall turned out to be the latter, at least I'd have something to pass the time.

It was a beautiful late summer day as I drove out of London. It had rained heavily during the night, but the day was clear, and the countryside sparkled with a green vibrancy, a last burst of lush color before the more somber tones of autumn. The village of Hadsworth was located in the rolling Kent countryside, where thickly wooded hills were interspersed with patches of emerald fields.

I reduced my speed as I approached the village. Homes, shops, a church, and a prosperous-looking half-timbered pub, The Crown, lined the road. A couple of smaller lanes crossed the High Street like crosshatches, but they petered out not far from the main road. As I reached the end of Hadsworth, I slowed even more as a group of men in plus fours with golf bags on their shoulders crossed the road. The man in the lead touched his flat cap. I waved my fingers over the steering wheel, then let the motor roll on as they turned in at a large sign labeled *Rosewood Hills Golf Course.*

Following the instructions Mr. Hightower had relayed, I left the village, crossed over a small stone bridge, then watched for the gates that marked the entry to Blackburn

Hall. I spotted them, turned in, and drove through a dense thicket of chestnuts.

The lane came out of the trees, and Blackburn Hall, a well-proportioned seventeenth-century red brick mansion, sat in a clearing of the rolling hillside. A river bounded the left side of the house, and beyond the gleaming curve of water, wide fairways of the golf course showed through the trees. Gardens in the formal style stretched out in front of the house, their rectangular outlines echoing the squared-off shape of the house.

Blackburn Hall hadn't been built along the same lines as the grand estates like Parkview Hall and Archly Manor. Acres and acres of parkland surrounded those homes. Blackburn Hall—both the house and the grounds—was on a smaller scale with the house set closer to the main road, but it was a charming house with the formal gardens and the swath of river alongside it.

The lane forked in front of me. One branch went to the front door and the other disappeared around the side of the house. I hesitated, foot on the brake. What was the status of an emissary from a publisher? Was I a guest, who went to the front door, or was I the help, who went to the back?

Under an arch of Palladian glass, the front door opened and a tall woman came out. She stood by the door, hands clasped at her waist. I could see from the cut of her gown she was a lady. But even if I hadn't been able to discern her status from her clothing, her ruler-straight spine would have announced it. She had the best posture of anyone I'd seen since finishing school.

It had to be Lady Holt. A flutter of nerves swept through me. I was about to deceive this woman. I doubted Mr. Hightower had a real interest in publishing her book. My "looking over it" was a ruse to get me in the door, a fact I hadn't let myself dwell on until now.

I drew in a breath, prepared my best smile, and let the

motor coast forward along the branch of the lane that took me to the sweep at the front door. I shut off the motor and heard the low-level hum of the river in the distance. Lady Holt crunched across the gravel, her hand extended. "Miss Belgrave, such a pleasure to meet you. I'm Lady Holt. Welcome to Blackburn Hall."

The current style of tubular dresses with straight lines suited Lady Holt, who looked to be in her late thirties or early forties. Her blonde hair was touched with gray on either side of her narrow face. In fact, everything about her was long and straight, I realized as I shook her hand. Her narrow fingers were chilly, but her grip was strong. "Thank you for having me," I said. "It's a pleasure to be here."

She waved a long arm as she turned to the door. "Come, I'm sure you're fatigued from your journey."

"No, not at all. It was only a short drive from London," I said as we crossed the parquet floor of the entry hall, which was open to the story above. The soaring room was paneled in dark oak, and an oak staircase with hefty ornamental carvings on the banisters and spindles rose along the right-hand side.

"Excellent. Then perhaps you'd like to join me in the drawing room? We can have tea, and then you can see the etiquette guide."

"Oh—I suppose that would be fine." I wasn't sure if looking at the manuscript right away was a good idea. I'd hoped to draw out the examination of it a bit to give me time to make inquiries about Mr. Mayhew, but I couldn't turn her down. Perhaps I should've said I was tired and retreated to my room for a few hours, but that wouldn't have done any good either. I couldn't ask about someone while I was supposedly resting in my room.

A wrinkle appeared on Lady Holt's forehead. "Unless—"

"No, it's fine. I'd love to see it now." I handed my gloves, handbag, and hat to a hovering servant and followed Lady

Holt into a sitting room furnished in pale green and gold, which felt light and open after the weighty oak entry. A set of French doors at the far end of the room were open, and the scent of roses and freshly cut grass wafted in on the light breeze.

"Come in, Miss Belgrave, and meet my sister, Serena Shires."

A woman who looked to be about six or seven years younger than Lady Holt came across the room and nodded a greeting. "I'd shake your hand, but mine are smudged. If I'd known we were having guests, I would have tidied up." Her figure was more padded than her sister's, and no gray showed in her unruly brown curls, which were short and dark and sprang out around her face. Unlike Lady Holt's fashionable dress, Serena wore a cotton smock over her plain dress. The smock was smeared with dark patches of what looked like dirt.

"I told you this morning." Lady Holt's clipped words didn't seem to impact Serena.

"I forgot," she said lightly and turned to me. "So sorry. I tend to get lost in my work." Serena and I exchanged greetings—minus a handshake.

A frown creased Lady Holt's long face. "And you haven't even changed out of your work clothes, Serena." Lady Holt looked to the writing desk at the side of the room. "I hope you haven't ruined my manuscript."

"I know better than to go near your manuscript. I popped in for a moment to look for the note I made last night after dinner." She said to me, "I find ideas always come to me at the most inconvenient times. If I don't write them down, they're lost. I jotted it down on a scrap of paper. Maybe I took it upstairs after all."

"I haven't seen it," Lady Holt said. "You should have written it directly into a notebook."

"You're right as always, Maria." Serena looked at me sideways. "My sister is never wrong. Life goes so much more smoothly if you agree with her."

"Serena! What will our visitor think? I must apologize, Miss Belgrave. My sister is irrepressible."

A small grin had been teasing at the corners of Serena's mouth, and now she smiled fully. "Maria's upset that I don't follow her etiquette rules—although I don't know anyone who follows them to the letter. And I can't imagine anyone needing an etiquette book nowadays."

Lady Holt's mouth flattened into a long straight line as she pressed her lips together. She reminded me of someone I knew, but I couldn't place the person. Lady Holt drew in a breath through her nose. "You know how many letters I receive. People constantly write to me for clarification on the finer points of proper behavior." Lady Holt gestured to a large stack of envelopes beside the manuscript on a writing desk. "These arrived during the last few days." She shifted her attention from her sister to me. "I'm delighted Mr. Hightower has finally realized the need for a modern etiquette guide. It's gratifying that Hightower Books will publish my guide. The times are changing, but certain things"—Lady Holt shot a look at Serena— "like good manners never go out of style. As I'm sure you agree, Miss Belgrave."

I didn't have incredibly strong views on the need for a modern etiquette guide, but I wasn't about to confess that. I was here in the guise of a publisher's assistant, and I had a role to play. "Yes, Mr. Hightower is interested in the possibility." I emphasized the last word because Lady Holt seemed to think Mr. Hightower had already decided to publish her guide.

My subtle accent on the word went right by her. "Well, then, let's have tea. Afterward, I can show you the manuscript, and Serena can go back to her amusements." Lady Holt sat down, her straight spine not touching the back of her chair, and began to pour our tea.

Serena said, "My work, you mean."

I asked, "What are you working on, Miss Shires?"

"Serena, please." She flicked a look at her sister. "Formalities tend to complicate things to an absurd degree. My motto is *make everything as simple as possible*." She settled back into a chair with her teacup. "I research rates of decay."

I hadn't expected that answer at all. "How interesting."

"Right now, I'm working with fabric. I completed a study on cotton, tricot, flannel, linen, wool and silk recently. I've moved on to a new set—velvet, tweed, canvas, chintz, leather, and felt—to test their decay rates."

"And how do you do that?"

"I bury swatches of fabric and observe the changes. I have a temperature- and humidity-controlled case. You'll have to come up to my workroom and see it. I presented a paper on the first round of tests—"

"Really, Serena," Lady Holt said. "I'm sure Miss Belgrave is only being polite. Your research isn't an appropriate topic for general conversation."

"Decomposition is a part of life."

Lady Holt shuddered. "Serena, please."

It was a shame Mr. Hightower had sent me to read Lady Holt's etiquette book. Her sister seemed a much more interesting character. Perhaps Serena's studies might make an intriguing topic for a book.

I gave myself a mental shake. I wasn't *actually* a publisher's assistant. The whole thing was a façade. I needed to rein in my enthusiasm for my imaginary job.

Serena reached for a sandwich. "If I have to talk about my work, Maria would prefer I discuss my other interests."

I stirred my tea. "You're working on something else?"

Lady Holt said, "The question is, what *isn't* she working on?"

Serena waved the sandwich. "I dabble in all sorts of things." She reclined comfortably in her chair, an easy smile on her face. "Everything interests me. This morning I was working with a new sort of pen." She put the sandwich on her saucer and wiggled her stained fingers. "One that wouldn't have to be refilled. It's the tip that's giving me problems. I tried a bit of sponge, but that was unwieldy." Her gaze drifted up to the ceiling. "Perhaps a fabric would work better. Not cotton . . ." She snapped her gaze back to my face. "It needs to be absorbent but able to control the flow of ink, something I haven't figured out yet. And then there's the vacuum cleaner experiment. I want to make a quieter one. They make a great deal of racket, you know."

"Someone talking about me?" A sturdy, broad-shouldered young man of about eighteen or nineteen walked in through the open door. He had sandy-colored hair, a tanned faced, and his mouth was set in the same flat line as Lady Holt. "Hello, Mother," he said, then nodded at Serena. "Aunt Serena."

He turned to me as Lady Holt began, "Miss Belgrave, this is my son—"

"Zippy!" I finally remembered who Lady Holt's flattened mouth reminded me of—the Honorable Edward Brown, more casually known as Zippy. Lady Holt's lips thinned practically to the point of nonexistence. I quickly amended my greeting to the proper form. "Mr. Brown, I mean. It's a pleasure to see you again."

Zippy and I had shared a few dances when I was a deb, but he'd been an acquaintance, not a close friend. I did remember a couple of friends ragging him, asking why he spent all his time in London when Hadsworth was only a short drive away. "I like the London air, old chap," had been his reply. Other than the fact that he enjoyed golf, that was about the only thing I remembered about him.

As she looked at me, Lady Holt's expression wasn't as open and welcoming as it had been. It didn't take a genius to work out that she was less than pleased her son knew me and that I'd called him by his nickname. I felt I should explain Zippy was an acquaintance and I had no designs on him that ended with me in white satin and him in a morning suit. Before I could say anything, Zippy said, "Nonsense. You must go on calling me Zippy. Everyone does."

"Edward, Miss Belgrave is from Hightower Books. She's here to see my etiquette guide."

Zippy, who had reached to shake my hand in greeting, held it a few beats too long. "Brilliant to see you here."

Lady Holt's eyes narrowed as she focused on our linked hands.

I extracted my hand. "Delighted."

Lady Holt reached for the teapot, but Zippy said, "Don't bother, Mother. I can't stay. I'm meeting Tommy for a round of golf."

"You won't be late for dinner, will you? We're a small party this evening."

"No, of course not. I must be off." He gave his mother a quick kiss on the cheek, whisked a sandwich off the tea tray, and said to me, "I'm sorry I can't stay to chat, but I'm sure we'll be able to catch up later."

Lady Holt's gaze followed Zippy as he left the room, then she said to me, "I've planned a small dinner party for this evening. I thought you might enjoy meeting a few of our local families."

Her manner had cooled several degrees, and I imagined she wished she could retract those invitations and cancel dinner. I'm sure she didn't want to do anything else to throw me and Zippy together socially. She needn't have worried. Zippy hadn't caused a single twinge in my heart, and I knew from the short conversations I'd had with him that his first love was sport. Unfortunately, Lady Holt didn't seem to realize that.

We finished our tea, and Serena's easy flow of conversation smoothed over Lady Holt's chilliness. Her gaze kept straying to the writing desk with its stack of paper. After discussing the weather and my journey from London, I set my teacup down. "Perhaps you'd like me to take a look at that manuscript now?"

Lady Holt unfolded her angular frame as she stood. "Yes, I have it laid out for you."

Serena uncurled her legs where she'd tucked them up on the cushion and headed for the door. "I'll leave you to it."

Lady Holt pulled out the chair of the writing desk for me and moved a slender book bound in tan leather to one side. She turned to the Table of Contents in the manuscript. "As you can see, I've arranged it so the first section covers introductions, then I go into invitations, and so on. Before you begin, I must show you a special touch." She flipped through several pages to a sheet with a pen-and-ink illustration. It depicted a man holding a woman's hand as she stepped over a puddle of water. "I've commissioned a series of drawings to illustrate some of the trickiest points," Lady Holt said. "They give it a new aspect, don't you think? I don't know of any other etiquette guide with illustrations."

"I can't say I've heard of any." But then my study of etiquette books had, thankfully, been quite brief.

"This visually shows how a man should step across the puddle first, then extend his hand and hold the woman's hand—*never* her arm—while keeping the umbrella over the woman. She's protected from the rain and able to move easily across the water."

"Yes, I can see that." Although why she couldn't hold her own umbrella and step across the puddle herself, I didn't know.

I bit back those words as Lady Holt continued, "This is the first of several illustrations." She looked at the clock on the mantelpiece. "I sent the rest to Anna yesterday so she could type the captions on them. She assured me that she would have them back to me before tea."

"There's no rush. I'll start with the manuscript now. You can show me the illustrations later."

Lady Holt scowled. "I suppose we'll have to. Although I do wish you could read it with the illustrations. They add so much. I'll ring up Dr. Finch."

"Dr. Finch?"

"Anna's father. She took a typing course, and—"

"Here I am." An auburn-haired woman with a smattering of freckles across her nose and cheeks came across the room. She removed her beret as she said, "I told Bower there was no need to announce me. I knew you'd be waiting for these." Her long necklaces of bungle beads clacked against the buttons of her dress as she walked.

She held out a portfolio to Lady Holt. "I'm sorry for the delay. I had to drop Dad at Russell Farm. One of the boys broke an arm, and Dad wanted to get out there as quickly as possible."

Lady Holt opened the portfolio and flipped through the pages. "Understandable, I suppose."

The young woman, who must have been in her early twenties, turned to me. "And you must be from the publisher?"

Lady Holt was so absorbed in looking through the pages, she didn't realize she'd missed a chance to introduce us. For someone who was an etiquette expert, she was certainly lax on performing introductions herself. "Yes, I am." I held out my hand. "Miss Belgrave."

"I'm Anna Finch. If your publisher ever needs any typing done, I'm available. I can pop up to London in a moment."

"I'll let him know. Do you have a card?"

Anna patted the pockets of her dress. "No. How unprofessional of me."

"It's fine. I'm not going back to London for a day or two." I shot a look at Lady Holt out of the corner of my eye. She didn't contradict me. Mr. Hightower had arranged for me to stay three days, but at the pace Lady Holt was moving, it seemed I might be shuttled back to London tomorrow, preferably with the manuscript in tow and my recommendation a given. "You can get it to me later. I'll hand it off to Mr. Hightower when I return."

"Thank you. I appreciate that. I was working in London at an insurance office, but they reduced their staff, and I couldn't find anything else." Anna leaned toward me and lowered her voice. "I'm simply dying to get back to London. Hadsworth is dull—dreadfully so."

"I'd think you'd get quite a few visitors because of the golf course. It's close enough to London that people could drive down for a round of golf."

"Oh, golf." She waved her beret. "Don't *talk* to me about golf. I'm sick of golf. That's all anyone wants to talk about, and I have no aptitude for it at all. Believe me, I've tried."

Lady Holt snapped the portfolio closed. "I'll leave these with you, Miss Belgrave." Lady Holt placed the illustrations on the desk with the reverence that someone might use to handle a valuable medieval manuscript. "Anna, come with me. I'll write you a check."

Anna followed Lady Holt, then turned and walked backward for a few steps. "It was a pleasure to meet you, Miss Belgrave. Perhaps we'll see each other again before you leave Hadsworth."

"I hope so," I managed to say before Anna disappeared through the door after Lady Holt. I looked at the thick manuscript and sighed. Anna seemed to be a young woman looking for a friend. She might be a good person to ask about Mayhew, but Lady Holt was adamant about her manuscript. I flipped to the last page and let out a deeper sigh. Four hundred fifty pages. I knew how I was spending the rest of my afternoon.

CHAPTER FIVE

J'd hoped to skim the etiquette book and then slip away and ask some questions about Mr. Mayhew in the village, but Lady Holt kept me busy all afternoon. By the time the dressing gong sounded, I'd read over one hundred pages, admired thirty illustrations, and discussed— or rather listened to—Lady Holt's concerns regarding the publication of the book. I'd done my best to answer her questions. Unfortunately, I'd had to tell her most of her concerns would have to be taken up after the book was formally accepted for publication. She didn't seem to grasp the fact that Hightower Books hadn't yet decided to publish the book. In her mind, publication was a *fait accompli*.

I went upstairs to dress, anxiety gnawing at me. Perhaps I should telephone Mr. Hightower and let him know he needed to make a slot on his spring calendar for an etiquette book. Lady Holt was a dominant personality. I was sure she'd get her book published either through Hightower Books or some other publisher.

I'd managed to ask exactly one question, trying to work my way around to asking about Mr. Mayhew, but Lady Holt wasn't to be distracted. I'd asked if anyone else in Hadsworth wrote—perhaps they traded manuscripts or discussed their writing? Lady Holt looked at me as if I were delirious. "No, I'm the only one with any literary interests."

The maid, Janet, a slip of a girl with thin brown hair and close-set eyes, helped me into the sleeveless pink dress with a deep V-neck and diagonal ruffles across the skirt. It was another hand-me-down from my cousin Gwen, who had excellent taste. Even though she was several inches taller than me, most of her gowns fit me with a few adjustments to the hem. Thank goodness I was shorter than her. If I'd been taller than Gwen, none of her lovely gowns would have fit me— well, I suppose I could have worn them, but they would have hit me at the knee, and that would have been scandalously too short. Hemlines had risen to above the ankle, but anything above the calf was risqué. A dusting of powder, a dash of lipstick, and a bit of mascara, and I was ready. Lady Holt probably wouldn't approve, but I put on the makeup with a light hand and thought it was flattering rather than garish.

I planned to visit Hadsworth tomorrow. Surely Lady Holt wouldn't insist on focusing on her manuscript *all* day. I should be able to visit the village. But for now, I'd focus on what I could find out here at Blackburn Hall. I went down to dinner, determined to work a mention of Mr. Mayhew into conversation. I entered the drawing room, and Lady Holt introduced me to Lord Holt. After meeting him, I knew Zippy had gotten his broad-shouldered build from his father, but Lord Holt was carrying quite a bit more weight around his middle than his son. Lord Holt had a booming voice, a thick white mustache, and an intense love of golf. "Couldn't believe my luck when they opened the course a few years ago," he said as we sipped our cocktails.

I asked, "Do you golf often?"

"Never miss a day on the links."

"An acquaintance of mine lives in the area, I believe, a Mr. Mayhew. Have you met him on the course?"

"Mayhew? Sounds familiar but can't place him." At a signal from Lady Holt, Lord Holt excused himself and moved to join his wife.

I was happy to see Anna was one of the guests along with her father. Dr. Finch also had auburn hair but a lot less of it than his daughter. He seemed friendly in a mild sort of way but didn't have the same outgoing personality of Anna. She was chatting with Serena, and I moved to join them. Zippy strolled in, and Anna stiffened like a bird dog scenting its quarry. Zippy greeted the three of us, giving Serena, Anna, and me a quick "good evening," then he moved on to speak to his father.

Serena went back to talking about the difficulties of creating a quiet vacuum, but I could tell Anna was only half listening as her gaze tracked Zippy's progress across the room. I could hear snatches of conversation from Zippy and Lord Holt as they discussed the relocation of a sand trap on the ninth hole of the course, something I didn't think interested Anna at all, but she never managed to give Serena her full attention after Zippy's entrance.

Dr. Finch joined our group, handing off a fresh cocktail to Serena. "Thank you, Robert," she said. "I heard Don is back in his office?"

"I cleared him to work a few hours each day," Dr. Finch said.

"I'm sure Emily is grateful," Serena said. "Last week she was at the end of her rope. Don is a terrible patient. Even in the short time we've known them, I can see he's naturally short-tempered. I can't imagine how much more irritable he is confined to bed."

Serena turned to me. "Our local solicitor fell down the stairs."

"How awful." It had to be the solicitor Mr. Hightower had

mentioned, who acted as Mr. Mayhew's intermediary. I was glad to hear he was recovering. The solicitor would be my first stop in Hadsworth tomorrow. I hoped I could catch him during his shortened office hours.

Bower, the butler, announced dinner was served. By the time the ladies retired to the drawing room and left the gentlemen in the dining room, I knew exactly why Zippy spent so much time in London and so little at Blackburn Hall. Lady Holt controlled the conversation around the dinner table in the same way I imagined a general carried out a military campaign. I hadn't been able to raise one question about Mr. Mayhew while we dined.

In the drawing room, Lady Holt suggested bridge, but Serena waved off the idea. "No, we did that last night. Let's have something different."

I scooted across the room to a table covered with jigsaw puzzle pieces and sat down by Anna. If Lady Holt insisted on bridge, I didn't want to be her partner. I imagined she'd play with a drive to win and be unforgiving of mistakes. Serena held firm on not playing bridge and read a scientific periodical instead, so Lady Holt played a game of patience while Anna and I gradually fitted together the pieces of an alpine meadow.

I slotted a piece of green dotted with white flowers into place. "How did you decide to become a typist, Miss Finch?"

"Oh, call me Anna, please. Everyone assumed I would become a nurse to help Dad, but I can't stand the sight of blood. I faint straightaway at a single drop. I'm quite useless. Training to be a typist was a way to help Dad and gain a little experience working for him at the same time. I eventually moved to London, but when my position at the insurance company was eliminated, I couldn't find another job. Unfortunately, it's more about who your connections are than what your qualifications are."

"That's been my experience as well." I'd worked for Aunt

Caroline when I couldn't find work anywhere else, and I was only at Blackburn Hall because Jasper had put me in contact with Mr. Hightower.

"At least I found a little work around here to keep me busy," Anna said.

"So you still work for your father?"

Anna nodded. "There's also the Women's Institute. They have bits and bobs that they need typed up—minutes and the like. I'm so much faster than Henrietta." She grinned. "More accurate too. And I have my own typewriter. I don't have to use the one at the Institute. Then there's the golf course. Occasionally, they need extra help during the busy season. But Mr. Mayhew keeps me busy most of the time."

I resisted the urge to swivel fully toward her and merely took a sip of my coffee. "Mr. Mayhew? What do you do for him?"

"I type his manuscripts."

"He's a writer? Lady Holt said there were no other writers in the village."

Anna dropped a puzzle piece, a flush creeping into her cheeks. "Surely you know . . . don't you? I mean—" She lowered her voice as she leaned down to pick up the puzzle piece from the floor. "You're with Hightower Books. I assumed you knew Mr. Mayhew is . . ." Her voice dropped to a whisper. ". . . R. W. May."

"Well, yes. I was aware of that."

"Oh, good." She sighed and brushed her hair away from her cheek.

I couldn't believe my good luck at having Mayhew's name dropped in my lap during a conversation after dinner. Was it really going to be that easy? "I didn't know anyone else here in Hadsworth knew Mr. Mayhew wrote novels."

"No one knows he's the novelist R. W. May. Everyone in the village knows he has some sort of writing job. Everyone *thinks* he writes technical manuals, and they think I type them."

"You must see a lot of him."

"Actually, no one does. Because of his . . . well . . . you know."

"No, I don't. I'm new to Hightower Books." A true statement if there ever was one.

"I didn't realize." Anna glanced around the room. "It's no *great* secret, so I don't suppose it will hurt to tell you. He wears a tin mask."

"Oh, I see." Many men had returned from the Great War with facial disfigurements, and specially designed masks hid their injuries. "I can see why he might want to keep to himself," I said, but my thoughts were racing. The photograph Mr. Hightower had shown me of Mr. Mayhew was one of a man without any disfigurement or injury. I'd seen veterans on the streets of London in their masks, which were quite lifelike. They were painted to match the soldier's skin tone, but one could usually see the edges where the mask ended. The man in the photograph hadn't been wearing a mask.

"He mostly keeps to his cottage," Anna said.

"Where's that?"

"East Bank Cottage, near the river that separates Blackburn Hall from the golf course." She pointed vaguely in what would be the direction of the golf course. "It was an old workman's cottage. Lady Holt had it converted and completely modernized. She even had electric run from the plant here at Blackburn Hall for it. She had planned to lease it to holiday people—golfers, I think. But then Mr. Mayhew took it. That was several years ago."

"But *you've* met him?"

"I work for him, but I don't talk to him."

"I don't understand."

She tried to fit a piece into the puzzle, then removed it.

"He leaves me his handwritten manuscripts outside his cottage in a basket by the door, and I type them up. I drop them through the post slot at his cottage a few chapters at a time. If he has changes, he leaves those for me in the basket. I retype everything and drop it off again."

"Interesting system. Surely you've seen him out and about occasionally?"

"Only a few times, and that was from a distance. He does like to walk in the evenings. Sometimes I see him walking on the paths around the village, but he's usually a good distance away. I only know it's him because he always wears a bright tie and matching pocket square. His tweeds blend in with the woods, but that bit of bright purple or yellow catches your eye."

"I understand he has a new book coming out soon." I leaned forward, doing my best imitation of someone fishing for inside information. "Do you know all the details?"

Anna abandoned the puzzle piece and picked up a new one. "I'm sorry, but I can't talk about anything like that. Strictly hush-hush, you know."

"Too bad he's such a recluse. I'd love to meet an author, especially one we're publishing at Hightower Books."

"I don't think that would be possible even if he were here." She lifted a shoulder. "But it doesn't matter. He's left."

"Left?"

"He's on holiday."

"That would be lovely." I tried to infuse wistfulness into my tone, despite the fact that my jaunt to Blackburn Hall certainly felt like a holiday. "Did he go to the seaside?"

"Haven't the faintest. It was a bit unexpected, I think." The skin between her brows crinkled. "He hadn't mentioned anything about it. He sent me a note last week with instructions to carry on."

Serena dropped her scientific journal onto a side table and came across the room to us. Anna made room for her on the sofa. "I've been meaning to ask you, any progress on your whisper vacuum?" Anna said to me, "Serena is incredibly brainy. She's going to come up with a quiet vacuum."

"Not yet, I haven't. My last attempt failed miserably," Serena said. "I have such a difficult time concentrating when it's noisy. I think people are much more productive in a peaceful, quiet environment." She moved a couple of puzzle pieces around. "Do you play golf, Olive?"

"No, I've never tried it. I wouldn't know how to begin."

"Oh, you must come play a round with me. It's not that difficult. I can show you the basics."

Anna let out a sharp laugh. "Not difficult? Don't let Serena fool you, Olive. Golf is one of *the* most frustrating pastimes."

Serena said, "Don't listen to her. You'll love it, I'm sure. I'm already part of a foursome tomorrow, but what about . . . let's see . . . I have a tee time on Friday. Would you like to go with me?"

"I may not be here on Friday," I said.

"I'm sure Maria will keep you captive here until Mr. Hightower consents to publish her book," she said with a grin. "Let's tentatively plan on Friday morning."

The men joined us at that point, and Zippy suggested a game a charades, which made asking more questions about Mayhew impossible. After everyone retired for the evening, I went upstairs, changed into a pair of jodhpurs and sturdy shoes, and pulled on a blouse and cardigan. I hadn't known what activities would be on the agenda at Blackburn Hall. I'd been sure to bring appropriate clothes for every activity, including riding. Dressing appropriately was a sign of good breeding, and I hadn't wanted to get off on the wrong foot with Lady Holt by having to ask to borrow clothes if riding was planned.

I wasn't planning on riding that night, though. I wanted a look at the cottage. I didn't expect to find Mayhew had suddenly returned, but I did want to locate East Bank Cottage and see what sort of place it was. And if I noticed a way inside . . . well, I might duck in for a few moments and look about for a note or discarded map or train schedule. Any information that I found, I'd pass on to Mr. Hightower.

I hadn't brought a torch, but I thought there might be one in the closet under the stairs near the Hall's telephone table. The door of the closet was paneled and blended seamlessly with the board and batten pattern of oak paneling on the wall under the stairs. If the door hadn't been open when I went down to dinner, I wouldn't have known the closet was there. A servant had been putting away a set of golf clubs. It looked like the sort of place that would collect miscellaneous odds and ends like sporting equipment, boots, umbrellas, and perhaps a spare torch.

The entry hall was dark and deserted. I trotted down the stairs and hunted along the wall beside the telephone table and a conveniently placed chair until I found a notch in the oak molding. It swiveled when I prodded it, and the door opened. A mishmash of tennis rackets, croquet mallets, and golf clubs sagged along the inside wall beside boots, umbrellas, and a few boxes. On a shelf, I found a mix of mittens and scarves as well as a torch. The light was a bit dim when I switched it on, but I wouldn't need it for long.

I dropped the torch into my pocket, then slipped out through the sitting room's French doors. I was halfway across the terrace when I paused. The lights in the drawing room were still on, and I assumed some of the family were still awake, but I didn't want to be locked out of the house if everyone retired before I returned.

I found a flat piece of bark in the garden, returned to the house, and wedged it in the latch of the door against the strike plate so the door closed but didn't lock, a handy trick I'd learned at boarding school. Essie Matthews had used a coin when she'd shown me how to make sure the door didn't lock behind us when we snuck out at night, but since I hadn't thought to bring change with me, the bark would have to do.

I walked through the sculpted hedges and circular flower beds to the curving path that followed the river. On the other side of the swiftly moving water, the golf course was an expanse of blackness. Overhead, the wind whistled through the trees. Except for the swooshing sound of the water and the hoots of an owl, the night was incredibly quiet until thunder rolled in the distance. I picked up my pace.

I left the ambient light coming from Blackburn Hall and moved into the thick blackness of the countryside, where I had to switch on the torch. The path ran through a belt of trees near the river and was wide and easy to follow, except for a small crumbled portion near a towering chestnut tree at the edge of the riverbank. Some of the earth around it had fallen in a cascade down to the river, which flowed several feet below the path. As I walked on, the path curved away from the river, and the ground rose steadily. I kept going until I spotted a square structure set a few yards off the path. A sign attached to a gate read *East Bank Cottage*.

The building was completely dark and looked deserted. The hinges moved soundlessly as I opened the gate and stepped through it. I turned off the torch and walked carefully down the track to the cottage. My eyes had adjusted to the night, and I made out curtains covering the windows, but not even a chink of light showed around the fabric. The air stirred, and a stronger gust of wind buffeted the cottage, heavy with the scent of rain. Thunder rumbled again, closer this time.

I padded quickly back to the path and returned to Blackburn Hall. I didn't want to get caught in a downpour and leave sopping footprints on the stairs as I returned to my room. At least I'd located East Bank Cottage. I'd be an early bird the next day and take a morning walk before Lady Holt could corral me into reading the rest of the manuscript.

CHAPTER SIX

$\mathcal{I}$ wrapped my cardigan tighter around my waist as I walked along the path to East Bank Cottage the next morning. I wished I'd brought a coat with me to Hadsworth. The storm had moved through during the night, and the air had a chilly edge, a reminder that autumn wasn't far off.

The distant *thwack* of golf clubs connecting with balls drifted through the air from the other side of the river, along with occasional snippets of conversation and laughter. Pounding rain had fallen during the night, accompanied by thunder and winds that had rattled the windowpanes. This morning, ragged patches of clouds scuttled across the sky, and wind whipped through the tops of the tree branches. The path was spongy, and the river, swollen with rain, tumbled over the rocks, filling the air with the sound of its rush and burble.

The path turned, and I halted. The earth that had formed the path along the riverbed had sheared away, taking with it the large chestnut tree I'd noticed last night. The massive tree had toppled into the river. Water gurgled over the leaves and swirled among the barriers of the branches. The tree's roots had formed part of the bank that dropped down to the river, but now the root ball was exposed, extending into the air above my head. Mud clung to the gnarled roots and water dripped from the fine hair-like offshoots. I gave the area around the fallen tree a wide berth, moving across the squishy wet leaves of the forest floor, testing the ground as I walked.

Once I emerged from the grove of trees into an open area, the ground firmed up, and I moved back to the path as it arched away from the river and climbed to higher ground. I turned off down the track to East Bank Cottage and passed through the gate.

The cottage looked as quiet and deserted as it had last night. The curtains were still closed, and no smoke wafted from the chimney. It certainly didn't look as if anyone was home, and Anna had said that Mr. Mayhew was on holiday, but after I'd returned to Blackburn Hall last night, I'd lain awake in bed listening to the rain battering against the windows.

Was Anna *sure* Mayhew had left Hadsworth? Perhaps he'd intended to leave, notified Anna of his departure, but then something had happened . . . and no one realized he hadn't actually left. Did he have someone who came in to clean or deliver food? Had Mayhew also contacted them and told them he was leaving? If he had, then no one would have visited the cottage since last week.

Of course, Mayhew might be sunning himself on the veranda of some seaside hotel or trekking along a path in the Lake District, but Mr. Hightower had said Mayhew was conscientious and didn't miss deadlines. Mr. Hightower hadn't received the manuscript. Mayhew didn't sound like the type of person who would ignore that sort of obligation. The more I thought about it, the more I felt I had to take a peek inside the cottage to make sure nothing was amiss.

But now as I approached East Bank Cottage in the bright

sunshine, my determination slipped. It looked so idyllic and tranquil. The daylight picked out details that had only been fuzzy in the dark. Flowers and ivy trailed from window boxes on either side of the front door, and there was a shiny brass mail slot in the lower panel of the door. Water dripped from the flower boxes, leaving muddy trails down the stone exterior. The basket Anna had described sat beside the front door, protected from the rain by a small outcropping of roof. The basket was empty.

I approached the door and knocked briskly. When no answer came after a few moments, I considered heading back to Blackburn Hall. I could telephone Mr. Hightower, tell him Mayhew was away, and collect the balance of my forty pounds.

I stepped back from the door. No, it was no use. I couldn't walk away. I needed to know the cottage was empty, then I'd contact Mr. Hightower. I knelt down and pushed on the mail slot. All I could see was more of the same metal. The mail slot must be fixed with a hood on the other side to prevent someone from doing exactly what I was—looking directly inside.

I made a complete circuit around the cottage. Herbs and vegetables filled a square of earth in the back. The plants in the kitchen garden were leggy, and weeds poked through the soil in between the neat rows of vegetables. I'd hoped one of the curtains would be open an inch to give me a view inside, but all the curtains were pulled, and when I tried the handle at the back door, it didn't budge.

I didn't want to return to Blackburn Hall without at least a peek inside, but I drew the line at breaking in. I couldn't do that. My father's training had instilled certain precepts I just couldn't bear to break. So smashing a window was out, but I could search for a key.

I returned to the front door and lifted the mat, but there was nothing under it. I danced my fingers along the doorframe, then felt around the edges of the window boxes. Nothing. I shook the moisture from my hands, then traced my fingers along the window frame. At the end of one of the windows, I felt something cool and flat. I pulled the key down from the ledge and inserted it into the door, my heart pounding fast.

I pushed the door, but it stuck, leaving a gap of only a few inches. I shoved, and the door fell back. I poked my head inside. A pile of large envelopes rested on the rug inside the door. I pocketed the key, closed the door, then picked up an envelope. It was sealed and had no address, just a note written in a sharp-cornered blocky style with a date from last week and the words *Chapter Seven*. These must be Anna's typed chapters.

I replaced it where I'd found it and surveyed the single open room that made up the entire main floor of the cottage. It was dim and stuffy in the small space, and the acrid smell of ashes lingered. I wished I could throw open one of the windows and let in the cool air.

A single upholstered chair was positioned by a fireplace next to a side table with a lamp. On the opposite side of the room, a desk sat in front of one of the curtained windows that looked out onto the path to the cottage. At the back of the room, a sink, a dresser, an electric cooker, and a round wooden table formed a kitchen area. The curve of a cast-iron tub showed through a half-open door off the kitchen.

A ladder in the main area of the room disappeared into an opening in the ceiling. I took a few steps up the ladder. The attic space had been converted into a bedroom, which contained a single bed, neatly made, and a deal dresser. A set of doors, a built-in wardrobe, filled one wall of the sloped-ceiling room.

I climbed down the ladder, relief washing over me. I hadn't wanted to put it into words, but I'd been afraid I'd find Mayhew either sprawled unconscious on the floor or perhaps terribly ill and incapacitated, but the cottage was empty. I stood for a moment, hands on my hips. I was inside and nothing horrible had happened to Mayhew. I might as well look around and see if I could find a trace of where Mayhew had gone—or perhaps a copy of the manuscript.

I went to the desk and twitched open the curtain a few inches to give me some natural light. A Remington portable typewriter sat at its center. A stack of blank typing paper rested beside it along with a monthly calendar, which was blank except for a note in curling handwriting on last Friday's date, *Book due!* The note was circled, and an exclamation point at the end of the letters spilled over into the squares above and below.

Other than a few pencils, the rest of the desktop was clean. I reached for the top desk drawer, then paused at a twinge of guilt. I felt like a sneak. Who was I to go through Mr. Mayhew's desk? I fisted my hand and remembered what Mr. Hightower had said. The welfare of the employees of Hightower Books rested with Mr. Mayhew. If I could find an indication of where Mayhew had gone, then Mr. Hightower could continue the search instead of contemplating a balance sheet with red numbers, which would eventually mean cuts at Hightower Books. I hated to think of anyone being put out of their job, and I wanted to discharge this job successfully so Mr. Hightower would recommend me.

I shook out both my hands, worked my shoulders around a bit, and then gingerly pulled out the top drawer of the desk, which contained pens and more paper. Well, so much for being a snoop—nothing to worry about there. The next drawer held a stack of empty envelopes as well as a pile of typed manuscript pages. I riffled through them. They were typed notes on a story with mentions of plotlines, characters, and clues. The rest of the drawers contained files and folders labeled with things like *Ideas, Revisions, Contracts,* and *Research.* The research folder was fat with clippings from newspapers and took up most of the space in the drawer. The rubbish bin under the desk was empty.

I turned away from the desk and surveyed the rest of the room. My eyes had adjusted to the low light, and I noticed a few details I hadn't taken in at first glance. A blanket hung over the arm of the chair near the fireplace, and the corner of a book stuck out from underneath it. I twitched the blanket back and tilted my head to read the title of the book that lay splayed open, facedown. It was the same book Jasper had given me, *The Secret Adversary.* Eyeglasses, the arms unfolded, sat on top of the book as if Mayhew had taken them off and laid them down, intending to return and read another chapter.

An uneasy sensation prickled along my spine. I replaced the blanket and caught a whiff of a foul odor from a decaying arrangement of flowers in a vase on the side table as the wind whistled in the fireplace. It was much cooler on this side of the room.

I stooped down by the fire. I inhaled the acrid scent of ashes as I closed the flue. I stepped back, the familiar band around my chest tightening. *Slowly. Breathe slowly.* Hand on my chest, I worked the air in through my nose and out through my mouth until the sensation of pressure on my chest eased.

I moved into the kitchen, troubled and edgy. No dirty dishes rested in the sink, but a plate, glass, and some silverware were turned upside down on a towel. A partial loaf of bread sat in the breadbox. It was hard as a brick. I closed the breadbox, and I went back into the main room, my uneasiness intensifying.

This was not the cottage of someone who'd left for a holiday. It felt like someone had stepped out for a short time and would return at any moment. I also hadn't found one bit of information that might indicate where Mr. Mayhew had gone —no jotted train times, maps, guides to walking holidays, or travel books. Of course, something could have happened to draw Mr. Mayhew away unexpectedly. Perhaps he hadn't had much time to prepare to leave—but would he go off and forget his glasses and leave the flue open? And what about the bread in the kitchen? Surely he'd throw it out along with the fresh flowers that would turn putrid within a few days?

A worry that I didn't want to name pushed me to climb to the top of the ladder and look around the bedroom. I peeked in the wardrobe, which had an empty space on the floor, clear of dust. A suitcase would have fit perfectly there. Shirts, heavy suits, and an overcoat only partially filled the rack.

The top drawer of the bureau wasn't closed. In the two-inch gap, I expected to see socks, ties, and undershirts, but instead my heart jerked at a partial face staring up at me. In the next instant, I recognized it was a tin mask, painted in such a lifelike manner that it looked like a bit of cheekbone, nose, and chin had been discarded in the drawer. I pressed my hand to my chest and felt the thump of my heartbeat. I told myself not to be silly. It was only a mask. No need to jump like a child hearing a scary story.

The mask was designed to cover the nose, the right side of the cheek, and the chin. Eyeglasses attached to the top of the nose would hold the mask in place. The mask was well used. Scratches marred the paint and some of the color had faded. The rest of the drawer was filled with ties and pocket squares neatly folded and arranged in a rainbow of vibrant colors from cool purple to warm tangerine.

Despite my firm lecture to myself to calm down, I slid the drawer closed with shaking fingers. This was not good—not good at all. Why would Mayhew leave his mask? I suppose he could be tired of wearing it. Or perhaps he was traveling home and didn't wear it around his family? But if that were the case, wouldn't he have wanted it for the journey?

I peeked in the next drawer, which contained socks, ties, and a few collars. The bottom drawer stuck, and I tugged on it. It flew open, and a bundle of pastel fabric puffed up. The drawer was stuffed. Mayhew must have pressed the fabric down to be able to close the drawer. I ran my hand over soft silks and satins and stiffer cottons. "Curiouser and curiouser," I murmured. I couldn't resist examining the fabric bulging over the edge of the drawer. I shook out a silk gown in the style of about ten years ago with a nipped-in waist and a full skirt.

I dropped it over my arm and pulled out the next item. It was a cotton dress, also in an outdated style. The simple lines and tiny waist would suit a young girl. A cotton chemise, a brassiere, and stockings were shoved to one side on top of two pairs of dainty shoes. I refolded everything and pressed it down so I could close the drawer. Perhaps they belonged to a sister or female relative? But then why did Mr. Mayhew have the clothes in his bedroom?

I went back down the ladder and gazed around the room. The only place I hadn't checked was in the bathroom, and since I'd looked everywhere else, I might as well have a look in there too. It had obviously been added when the cottage had been remodeled because everything in it—the commode, the bath, and the mirrored medicine cabinet over the pedestal sink—was new. A pink silk dressing gown hung from a hook. Behind the mirrored door, the medicine cabinet contained aspirin, tooth powder, a toothbrush, and a familiar rectangular box. I turned it around so I could read the label. *Smith's Towels, the best innovation for ladies. Comfortable, convenient, and a necessity to health.*

I stood there for a couple of long moments, staring at the box, then opened it. One sanitary towel remained. The little clock on the mantelpiece chimed, and I nearly dropped the box.

Breakfast—breakfast at Blackburn Hall, and Lady Holt and her manuscript. I had to get back.

I replaced the box and hurried to the front door. After I

locked it, I replaced the key over the window frame, then took off at nearly a run down the path back to Blackburn Hall, my thoughts in a whirlwind. Everything I'd thought I'd known about Mayhew had been turned upside down. It didn't appear he'd left on a journey, and yet it did—some of his clothes and his suitcase were gone, but there was no indication of his destination, and the cottage looked as if someone had only stepped out for a moment.

And then there was the astounding fact that it appeared Mayhew was actually a woman.

What should I do with that information? From the way Anna had spoken about Mayhew last night after dinner, it seemed he—or should it be she?—had fooled all of Hadsworth. Could I possibly be wrong? I didn't think so. The interior of the cottage had several feminine features—the flowers, the ruffled curtains, the pink dressing gown, the lack of a razor for shaving . . . and then there was the box in the medicine cabinet, the indisputable evidence of a female living in the cottage. My cheeks heated. I couldn't imagine actually speaking to anyone about such a thing.

The chatter of dirt and small pebbles bouncing down the riverbank sounded as I neared the river, and I slowed, pausing in the shade of the pine trees. Serena clambered up the riverbank and gained the path. Breathing heavily, she braced her hands on her knees. She wore golf clothes, a sweater, a pleated skirt, and patterned stockings. Both her stockings and shoes were covered with mud, and the hem of her skirt was soaked.

"Serena—"

She jerked upright, her hand pressed to her chest, and scanned the path. I stepped into the sunlight.

"Oh, Olive—I didn't expect anyone to be on the path." Her complexion was washed out with a gray tinge.

"I'm sorry I startled you," I said. "Are you all right?"

Serena scrubbed her hand through her hair. "I'll be fine in

a moment . . ." She drew in another breath. "Bit of a shock, coming on it like that, but fascinating nonetheless."

"Coming on what?"

"A body." She gestured at the bank. "Down in the riverbed, where the tree tumbled over."

"Oh no. Did someone fall into the river?" It didn't seem extremely deep, but with all the rain, I supposed if someone had fallen and injured themselves, they might not have been able to climb out of the swiftly moving water.

Serena shook her head. "No, that's not what happened."

A shout carried through the air. Serena and I turned. Across the river, two women, also in golfing clothes, stood in a small clearing at the edge of the riverbank, their attention focused on us. One of them cupped her hands around her mouth. "Should we come over as well?"

Serena shook her head in an exaggerated motion and yelled, "No, it's too late."

The other woman shouted back something about the club-house, and the pair departed, carrying an extra bag of clubs, which I assumed were Serena's. She turned back to me. "I overshot the putting green. I was looking for my ball along the edge of the river when I saw a flicker of red on this side, which is odd at this time of year."

"I can see how that color would catch your eye." The browns, golds, and reds of autumn weren't in evidence yet. The leaves, pine needles, and flashes of meadow through the trees were a bright green while the underbrush around the trees was a muted brown, the same shade as the tree trunks.

Serena took a deep breath before she continued. "It was fabric—a man's tie. Muddy, but the garish color showed through. Then I made out the shape in the shadows and could see it was an outline—a figure of a person on the riverbank among the roots of the overturned tree. I have excellent distance vision, and I hoped I was wrong, but I decided I better come across to be absolutely sure. I wasn't—wrong, I mean. I thought it was a man. The clothes—" She scrubbed her hand through her hair again. "It doesn't make sense . . ." Her voice trailed off, but I could still hear her as she said, ". . . the figure was feminine." She repeated the word more firmly. "Definitely feminine."

My stomach plummeted, and my heart began to thud. "It's a woman dressed in men's clothing?"

Serena's arm dropped to her side. Her gaze fixed on me. "How did you know?"

"A hunch."

CHAPTER SEVEN

I went as close as I dared to the verge where the earth dropped down to the riverbed. Clods of dirt under the fringe of grass at the edge broke away and thumped down the steep incline, landing with soft plops on the tangle of moist earth, rocks, and tree roots. The body was in the mound of earth that had once surrounded the tree and had been heaved up when the tree had fallen.

The sodden tweed jacket and dark trousers pressed against a curvy body. The rain must have washed away the mud from the fabric. The red tie drew my eye up to the face, which was turned away from me. Even at a distance, I could see an indention on the temple. I looked away. It reminded me of a spongy dark spot on an apple going bad. A square shape half buried in the mud a little distance away was a leather suitcase. Something glittered in the sun. I inched closer and sucked in a breath. A face was half buried near the suitcase, no—not a face—a mask. It was a tin mask, a cheek-bone, nose, and chin with eyeglasses attached to the nose, their empty lenses reflecting the sunlight. Mayhew must have had two masks. The other mask, the older scratched one, was at East Bank Cottage in the bureau drawer.

I swallowed hard and stepped back. "We should go back to Blackburn Hall and contact the police."

Serena jerked her gaze away from the body. "Oh—yes. Yes, of course," she said. After I turned away, she lingered a few moments, staring at the body, but once she joined me, she set a brisk pace. "That area of the riverbank has been weak," she murmured more to herself than to me, I thought.

"It has?" I asked.

She started and looked at me as if she'd forgotten I was walking beside her. "Yes. In fact, I noticed last week a bit of ground near the tree had collapsed."

We walked the rest of the way back to Blackburn Hall in silence. I was thinking furiously, trying to work out what I'd say to the police. Serena cut through the gardens at the back of the house. "Let's go in through the drawing room. Shorter that way." She rang for Bower and instructed him to contact the police, then went up to change out of her muddy clothes.

I perched on the edge of a chair and focused on my clasped hands. I didn't want to think about the body, how long it had been buried in the cold earth, or how it had gotten there, but I couldn't harness my imagination, and I'd run through several awful scenarios by the time Serena returned. She didn't sit but walked back and forth in front of the French doors, her hands braced on the back of her hips. "It's got to be Mayhew."

"Could it be someone else from the village?"

She shook her head. "No, can't be. No one is away from the village, and all the servants are here at Blackburn Hall." She stopped walking and gave a quick smile. "It's insular here, and we do know all the comings and goings of everyone."

"You don't have to explain that to me. I grew up in a small village. Anna mentioned Mr. Mayhew last night," I said. "She said he kept to himself. Did he go into the village often?"

"No. He had food delivered. Mrs. Henley went in once a

week to clean for him, but she's told me he always went for a long walk when she came."

Bower stepped into the room. "Police Inspector Calder has arrived. He's gone down to the river but says he will be with you shortly."

Serena opened an enamel box on the side table and took out a cigarette. "Show him in here when he returns."

"Very good." Bower closed the door.

Serena said, "I'll try to get as much out of Calder as I can. It shouldn't be hard. He's a rabbit."

Within a few minutes, Bower escorted Calder and an accompanying constable into the room. Once I'd been introduced, Calder asked me a few questions about my movements that morning, then turned his attention to Serena. Calder hadn't said he wanted to speak to Serena alone, so I'd moved to the side of the room, out of his line of vision.

Calder shifted on the delicate chair covered in striped silk. He had flat facial features, except for his eyes, which protruded, a combination that reminded me of a pug I'd found a few weeks ago for a society matron. After his initial round of questions, Calder circled back to when Serena found the body. "Why did you examine the body, Miss Shires?"

Serena drew on her cigarette, then blew a puff of smoke toward the chandelier. I took a step away from the dispersing haze.

"I've already told you," Serena said. "I saw what looked to be a figure—a body—and went across to investigate."

Calder blinked his bulging eyes. "No, I meant why did you study the form itself? What made you examine it further?"

Serena stabbed the cigarette into the ashtray. "Oh, you mean why didn't I run screaming when I realized it was actually a human being?"

"No, I—" He moved again, and the little chair creaked.

SARA ROSETT

"You stated you noticed it was a woman. But the person is in men's clothes. How did you know it was a woman?"

"The clothes are wet and plastered to the body. Surely you noted that? The cleavage is obvious." She traced an hourglass shape in the air, the cigarette clamped between two fingers. "Small waist and a swell around the hips. Do I need to go on?"

Calder's cheeks turned pink, and he bent over his notebook. "No, that's—er—fine." He cleared his throat. "Did you touch the body in any way?"

"Of course not. Once I realized there was no urgency, that he—I mean *she*—was beyond help, I stepped back. I'm sure you'll be able to confirm that from my footprints in the mud. I didn't need to check for a pulse. She'd been dead for several days."

Calder's head jerked up. "Several days?"

"Without a doubt. Marbling had set in, and the body was beginning to swell around the abdomen. Despite the swelling, it was clear she was a woman. It's been cool lately, and the earth covering the body would have buried it deep, which explains why putrefaction was limited."

Calder's eyes narrowed. "You know quite a bit about dead bodies, do you?"

"I'm a scientist. I've studied decomposition, Inspector Calder, and recognize it."

Calder stared at her a moment, then seemed to give up on his attempt to come up with a reply. He turned his goggle-eyed gaze on me. "And you, Miss—er—Belgrave? You walked the path and passed directly by there. What did you notice this morning?"

"I didn't go close enough to see down to the river at that point. When I came to the fallen tree, I circled around and went up into the woods."

Serena took another cigarette from the box and tapped it against her thumbnail. "Who was it, Inspector Calder?"

64

He cleared his throat again. "Well . . . can't really say at this point . . . haven't made a formal identif—"

"It's Mayhew, isn't it?" Serena's flat statement cut across Calder's equivocation.

Calder blinked, tugged at his earlobe, then glanced out the window. "It does appear to be the person who inhabited East Bank Cottage."

"You found something identifiable?"

Calder hesitated.

"Oh, come now, Inspector Calder. Who else could it be? Everyone else in the village is accounted for. If anyone had left or gone missing from Hadsworth for several days, it would be common knowledge."

"Could be someone from the golf course." Calder's tone was almost belligerent. "We get a lot of holiday people."

"But they rarely cross the river, carrying a suitcase. If it were a golfer, I would expect a bag of clubs to be buried with the body, not a suitcase."

I silently applauded Serena's logic and her clear statement. I didn't think it could be anyone else either, especially after seeing the state of East Bank Cottage.

"You are accounted the brainy one, Miss Shires," Calder said in a tone that was far from complimentary. "Yes, the suitcase labels as well as some papers inside it indicate it was Mayhew."

Serena lit the cigarette and leaned back against the chair. "So Mr. Mayhew was a woman," she said, not with surprise or shock, but as if she were contemplating how to work out a complex equation.

"It appears so."

"Why dress as a man? She lived here for years and no one knew."

"Too soon to say—can't make any assumptions now—"

"Did you find his tin mask?" Serena asked.

Calder scowled. "Yes, it was near the suitcase."

Now was the time to speak up. I drew a breath to tell Calder what I'd seen in the cottage, prepared to confess my snooping, but before I could continue, Serena said, "The mask was a disguise." Serena turned, angled her arm along the back of the chair, and said to me, "Could you see her face when you looked?"

"No, it was turned away. Well, except for the temple."

"Yes, took rather a knock there, by the look of it. But I could see her face when I came across the river. It was undamaged." She shifted back to Calder. "The mask must have been a blind to get people to leave her alone. The question is, why did she want to be left alone?"

"Since she met with an accident, we may never know," Calder said.

I moved to the sofa and took a seat. "Then you think it was an accident?"

"That section of the path has always been hazardous. It should have been cordoned off long ago." He turned his attention back to Serena. "How much contact did you here at the Hall have with Mayhew? Let's call her that. It makes it simpler."

Serena tapped ash from the cigarette. "None. No contact at all. I rarely saw . . . Mayhew. Once in a while, I'd catch a glimpse of . . . her. She took long walks around the countryside. But those were only fleeting glimpses, usually from a long distance away. We never stopped to chat."

"And when was the last time you saw Mayhew?"

"Oh, I don't know." She lifted the cigarette to her mouth. "Several days ago, I suppose. I was buying stamps in the village. I remember it because I didn't see her around the village much, only occasionally, but everyone has to buy stamps at some time or another, I suppose. Let's see—that would have been late Tuesday afternoon, I think. I turned away from the counter, and Mayhew was behind me in the queue." She stilled, her arm suspended in the air as she focused on the plaster medallion above the chandelier. "No, that's wrong. A friend came down from London to discuss my paper on decay rates for *The Journal of Forensic Studies*. She stayed overnight, then we played a round of golf the next morning before she returned to town. We made up a foursome with two ladies from Yorkshire who were on holiday. It was early on Wednesday morning last week when I saw Mayhew."

Calder leaned forward. "Mayhew was on the golf course?"

"No, across the river, on the path. The fairway drops down from the trees and takes you right up to the edge of the riverbank. No trees at that point, and the view is open to the river. A movement caught my eye. Mayhew was walking along the path, holding his hat. It was breezy that morning. He waved, and I waved back. I knew it was him because I saw the flash of that cheery red tie." Her words slowed. "That same tie I saw today. I must have seen him right before . . ."

Calder asked, "Did you hear any noise or see him fall?"

Serena put the cigarette down on the edge of the ashtray and rubbed her scalp, causing her already disarranged curls to stand out around her head even more. "No, we played through to the next hole. I never looked back." She cleared her throat and sat up a bit straighter. "Mayhew favored bright ties and pocket squares—red, yellow, and even purple. I didn't see Mayhew often, but the few glimpses I did catch of him—er—*her*, she always had a brightly colored tie and coordinating pocket square."

"What else did you notice about Mayhew that morning?"

"She wore a tweed jacket." Serena closed her eyes. "A flat cap and dark trousers."

Lady Holt swept into the room. "Bower informs me there's been an accident near the river."

Calder stood. "Good morning, Lady Holt. Yes, your ladyship, it seems a few days ago, an unstable portion of the path collapsed and a—er—person went down with it. A further collapse—a landslide, if you will—covered the body, burying it until this morning, when an uprooted tree shifted the earth, exposing the body." Calder paused to draw a breath.

"It was Mayhew," Serena said.

Lady Holt looked at her blankly. "Mayhew?"

"The person who lived in East Bank Cottage," Serena said. "And he was a she. Mayhew, I mean."

Lady Holt blinked. "I'm afraid I don't understand."

Serena said, "The wounded man—the one with the mask. Surely you saw Mayhew on the estate grounds or in the village occasionally. Mayhew was a woman dressing as a man, and she didn't need a mask either. Her face was completely normal—well, as normal as it could be after being buried for several days."

The color drained from Lady Holt's face. Her perfect posture didn't change, but she sank into a chair. The constable approached and murmured something to Calder, who didn't see the change in Lady Holt's complexion. The constable retreated, and Calder said, "Lady Holt, what can you tell me about Mayhew?"

"Nothing," she said, her words as precise as her posture. "I've never had any interaction with her."

"No?"

"No, all the details about letting the cottage were handled through the estate steward. I don't have anything to do with that sort of thing—a lady shouldn't involve herself in trade or investments, you know. Both Lord Holt and I leave all that sort of thing to our estate steward."

"I'll need to have a word with your estate steward later."

Was now the time to mention Mayhew was a well-known novelist writing under a pen name, or should I keep quiet? How far would the investigation into this death go? Having just been involved in the incident at Archly Manor, I knew if the police thought Mayhew's death was suspicious, they'd probe into every aspect of Mayhew's life. But it didn't appear Calder would look too deeply into Mayhew's death.

Calder seemed to think it was an accident, but he'd have to check Mayhew's cottage. Would the police find my fingerprints there? I'd never been to Hadsworth, so I couldn't be considered a suspect in the death—if it turned out to be foul play—but having my fingerprints found at East Bank Cottage would be embarrassing. Snooping was incredibly bad manners. It was just not what one did when one visited a country home.

Lady Holt's color was returning to normal. "I expect your people to finish by lunch, Inspector."

"Yes, my lady, but we have to investigate the death."

"Investigate?"

"Determine what happened, if it was accidental or . . ."

"Of course it was an accident. This person was found beside the river in a landslide of some sort, you said?"

"Yes, my lady."

"Then it *was* an accident. Unfortunate and terribly sad but an unpreventable occurrence. I'm sure you'll find that's what happened."

"But we must determine—"

"Nonsense. We can't have a hint of anything disreputable going on at Blackburn Hall, or we'll have those horrible gossip sheet reporters down here, clamoring to get in. And neither I nor Lord Holt want that sort of attention. Is that understood?"

Calder seemed to shrink under Lady Holt's gaze. "Yes, my lady. But we do have to investigate, and there will have to be an inquest."

"Oh, an inquest. As long as it takes place in Hadsworth and the verdict is death by misadventure, it will all be fine. Just keep Blackburn Hall out of it. Make sure you describe the incident as taking place near Rosewood Hills Golf Course, not Blackburn Hall." Lady Holt stood, which meant Calder had to rise as well. Lady Holt said, "I know you will do all you can to clear this up with as little fuss as possible."

Lady Holt rang for Bower, and Calder was shown out. Calder had barely left the room when Zippy came striding in through the French doors. "What's all the commotion down at the river?" Zippy took a cigarette from the box. "I just came off the course, and everyone's saying there's a dead body."

"For once, the gossip is correct," Serena said. "It's the person who lived in East Bank Cottage—Mayhew. And that's not all. Mayhew was a woman."

Zippy spoke around the cigarette as he lit it. "You don't say." Zippy closed the lighter with a snap. "Well, that will set the gossip mill churning."

"Apparently, no one knows who she was or why she was masquerading as a veteran with a mask," Serena said.

He dropped onto the opposite end of the sofa from me, reclining back and crossing one leg over the other. "Obviously, she wanted to be left alone."

"But why?" Serena asked. "There has to be a reason."

"Aunt Serena, you're far too analytical. Not everything can be traced back to a reason—or, at least, we can't always find out the reason." Zippy rested one arm along the back of the sofa. "Besides, it's nothing to do with us, you know."

"Very true," Lady Holt said. "But it will be a great inconvenience, I'm sure. All of these people tramping back and forth. I instructed Calder to clear up everything this morning. I expect that to be the last of it." She turned to me. "We must get on with the manuscript. Are you ready to continue, Miss Belgrave?"

"Yes, of course," I said as I realized that I hadn't even thought about how Mayhew's death would impact Hightower Books. I needed to contact Mr. Hightower.

But not even a death could distract Lady Holt from our review of her manuscript. Two hours later, Lady Holt straightened the edges of the pile of paper in front of her. "I think we've done quite well for today. I have an appointment this afternoon and won't be able to continue going over the manuscript. We should be able to finish tomorrow."

I eyed the remaining pages. "Yes, I think that will be possible." I'd had a difficult time focusing on Lady Holt's concerns. My thoughts were taken up with Mayhew's death and my visit to East Bank Cottage. I should have spoken up immediately and told Inspector Calder I'd been inside the cottage.

But Lady Holt was so forceful, and she'd been clear that she expected the incident to be considered an accident and wrapped up quietly. If the police never checked the cottage for fingerprints, they'd never know I was there. Why bring it up and endure all the embarrassment it would cause? Not to mention it would mean I'd have to confess that the examination of the manuscript was a ruse. When Mr. Hightower offered me the job, I envisioned being long gone before Lady Holt learned of the duplicity. A slightly seasick feeling hit me at the thought of what her reaction would be to that news.

No one else joined Lady Holt and me for lunch. Lord Holt was still on the golf course, Zippy had gone into the village, and Serena had sent word she was working and would have a sandwich sent up. Lady Holt and I talked of books and mutual acquaintances in London. I continued to mull over my actions during lunch, and by the time dessert was served, I knew what I had to do—visit the police station in Hadsworth. My embarrassment was a small thing compared to a person's death.

With my course set, I felt lighter as the plates were cleared. "I do apologize for the disturbance this morning," Lady Holt said.

"There's no need to apologize."

"Nevertheless, it's not something one wants a guest to experience."

"No, but it couldn't be helped."

Lady Holt waited until the door closed behind the servant who was carrying our plates away. "And it would be disappointing if any hint of this were to get into the newspapers. I know no one in the household will mention it to them." She turned her long face to me and gave me a searching look I'd seen when she looked for mistakes in her manuscript.

I suppressed the flare of irritation I felt at her assumption she needed to warn me, but I kept my face impassive. "I have no interest in sharing the news with reporters."

"Good."

Once lunch was over, I went upstairs for my hat and gloves. I needed to telephone Mr. Hightower and let him know what had happened to Mayhew, but first, I wanted to go to the village and visit the solicitor's office on my way to the police station. I intended to gather all the information I could about Mayhew before I contacted Mr. Hightower. I hoped with the solicitor back in his office, he could either tell me when Mayhew's manuscript had been mailed, or—better yet— perhaps he still had it in his office.

I flexed my fingers inside my gloves, working them into place as I left my room. The murmur of voices floated down the hall, growing louder as I neared an open doorway, where two maids were making up a bed. My hat slipped, inching down over my eye. I pushed it back up. As I passed the open door, the maids' conversation paused for a few seconds. My hat slipped again, farther this time, and I stopped in front of a gilt-edged mirror on the other side of the open door to adjust it.

The snap of linen being shaken out cracked through the air like the report of a gun, then a voice floated out of the room. "A woman wearing men's clothes. Shocking, that's what it is."

So the word was out that Mayhew was a woman. I wasn't surprised the servants already had all the details. I twitched a flower on my hat back into place.

A different deeper voice, an alto, asked, "How can they be so sure it was Mayhew?"

"She was wearing Mayhew's clothes and had the mask. No one's seen Mayhew since last week, poor lad—er—girl. She must have been on her way to catch the train—she had a suitcase—but the station master and porters never saw her. No one in the village did. Well, except Miss Serena when she was golfing."

The deeper-voiced woman said, "The mistress will have nothing to worry about now when it comes to her son visiting East Bank Cottage."

I froze, elbows in the air as I adjusted the brim of my hat. Nothing good ever came of eavesdropping, but after Lady Holt had gone white as plaster at the news of Mayhew's death, I was too curious to walk away.

"What do you mean?"

"Her ladyship was upset with Mr. Edward. I heard them arguing a few weeks ago out in the garden. He'd returned from a walk, and she told him she knew he'd been to East Bank Cottage. She forbade him to go there again."

"No! Why?"

"It weren't natural, she said."

"Not natural? What does that mean?"

Fabric rustled. The maid with the deeper voice said, "You are an innocent, aren't you?"

"No, I'm not."

"You are if you don't know what her ladyship meant." Fabric snapped again. "She meant some men like other men instead of women."

A few beats of silence followed, and then the other maid said, "No." Her tone indicated she thought the other woman was joking.

"Yes. But now Lady Holt won't have to worry about it. Straighten that corner there, and then you better do the other room before . . ."

I moved away, the thick carpet muffling my footsteps. Perhaps Zippy hadn't been as unaffected by the news of Mayhew's death as he'd seemed?

CHAPTER EIGHT

esides the half-timbered pub, the Norman church, and the brick inn, Hadsworth's High Street consisted of a row of connected shops, each with its own stepped A-frame roof, which created a sawtooth pattern against the sky. I was curious to see if Zippy still had his careless air about him, but I didn't see him strolling down the road or across the green.

I made my way around the village green and passed a cenotaph topped with a Celtic cross. When I entered the police station, the constable looked up from his typewriter.

"I'd like to speak to Inspector Calder."

"He's at the golf course. Not playing," he added quickly. "He's asking questions about Mr.—Miss—er, about the death. He should be back soon if you'd like to wait."

The last thing I wanted to do was sit in the tiny room listening to the *rat-tat-a-tat* of the typewriter. "No, I'll stop back later." I closed the door of the police station behind me and set off around the cenotaph again. I went into the village shop and asked for directions to the solicitor's office.

The woman behind the counter whisked a speck of dust

off the cash register. "He's not in, and his secretary is gone as well. Closed up early on account of the tumble he took."

"Yes, I heard about that, but I thought he was back at work now."

"Only two hours a day from nine to eleven. He's already gone home."

"Do you know where—"

"And no visitors allowed there. His wife turns everyone away. Doctor's orders, you understand. I imagine he'll be back tomorrow at the same time."

"Thank you. I'll return then."

Since I couldn't speak to the solicitor, there was one other person who might be able to help me find Mayhew's manuscript. A small sign with the words *Doctor's Surgery* pointed to the other end of the village, away from the pub and the golf course entrance.

Dr. Finch's house was at the end of one of the short lanes that crossed the main road. Built of red brick, it was designed along similar lines to Blackburn Hall but quite a bit smaller. Dr. Finch's surgery, a separate building of the same red brick, sat to the side of the house.

Since I wanted to speak to Anna, I went to the house and rang the bell. A maid answered, and when I asked if Miss Finch was in, she asked me to wait a moment. The muted clack of typewriter keys and the ding of a bell drifted through the house. The rhythmic noise cut off, and the maid returned a few seconds later. "Miss Finch is in the garden. Please follow me."

I trailed the maid through a spacious drawing room and out into the garden, where Anna was seated at a small wooden table that was bare except for a typewriter and two stacks of paper, one blank and the other turned facedown with the imprint of dark letters faintly showing through. Anna pulled the sheet of paper out of the typewriter and placed it on a stack under a paperweight that was protecting the pages from being blown away. "Hello, Olive. I'm so glad you dropped by."

"I'm sorry to interrupt your work."

She waved a hand. "You're not interrupting. In fact, I was about to take a break." She asked the maid to bring tea, then gestured to a grouping of white wicker chairs under a chestnut tree. "It was too delightful of a day to stay indoors. I love the fresh-washed smell of the air after a storm."

"It was quite a storm last night. Did you have any damage?" I glanced around the garden with its towering trees.

"A little standing water at the bottom of the garden, but that always happens. It's a bit low lying down there."

"A tree came down in the river between Blackburn Hall and the golf course."

"Oh, that's such a shame." She tilted her head up and looked at the branches. "They look so steady and immovable, but it does happen occasionally when the ground gets saturated. They just can't stand up and topple right over like toothpicks."

I wasn't sure how I should approach the subject of Mayhew with her. I'd spent the time on my walk thinking about how I would speak to the solicitor, but I'd decided to visit Anna on the spur of the moment. "Have you heard any news from the village?"

"No, I've been out here in the garden typing all morning. I haven't gone anywhere. Why? Has something happened?" She leaned forward, her eyebrows raised and her face alight with interest.

"I'm afraid so, but it's rather tragic."

She straightened and pulled in her chin. "Tragic? Is Dad needed?"

"No, I'm afraid it's too late for that."

"Oh. Who?"

"Mayhew."

Her brow furrowed, and she glanced at the table with the typewriter. "But that's—"

The maid approached with a tray, and Anna waited until the maid had returned to the house. "What happened?"

As I described the scene at the river, Anna crossed one arm over her stomach, propped her elbow on it, and pressed her fingers to her mouth for a moment. When I stopped speaking, she was silent, her gaze fixed on the tea tray, which she hadn't touched. She moved her fingers from her mouth and said, "That's—so difficult to believe." She had fair translucent skin, but it had gone a shade lighter than usual, causing her freckles to stand out. "And they think he was there for a while?"

"Yes. Serena saw Mayhew when she was playing golf last week."

She lunged toward the tray. "Oh, the tea. I'm sorry. I'm being a terrible hostess." The cup rattled in the saucer as she handed it to me.

"Thank you." I stirred my tea while Anna poured hers. "So you haven't had any contact with Mayhew?"

"No, I only type what he's sent, then send it back, dropping it off at his cottage each time." She focused on her teacup as she replied. The answer seemed to be a mechanical response she'd spoken many times.

"And you haven't seen Mayhew at all lately?"

"No." She blinked and looked at me. "Never." She leaned back in her chair, whirring her spoon around her cup. "It's so strange . . ." She continued to stir her tea, her gaze focused across the garden.

"There's something else that's even more curious."

She stopped stirring. "What do you mean?"

"When Serena found the body, it was wet from the rain. The clothes were molded to the body, and . . . well, it was a woman's body."

She stopped stirring. "I'm not sure I understand. What are you saying?"

"Mr. Mayhew was actually a woman."

"A woman?" Her cup tilted, and tea splashed onto her skirt. "Oh—"

"Oh no. Did it burn you?"

"No, it's a thick material." She plonked her cup and saucer onto the tray, took a handkerchief from her pocket, and blotted the stain. "Are they sure?"

"Yes, it appears Mayhew was living in the cottage, dressing as a man, and wearing the tin mask to hide her identity."

Anna pressed the handkerchief to the fabric. The joints around her fingers turned white from the pressure. "But then that means—why would she do that?"

"I have no idea. I hoped you'd know."

"Me? I know the least of anyone, it appears. All those weeks of working with him—I mean, her. It's amazing. *I* never guessed." She flicked a glance at the surgery. "Never even suspected."

I tilted my head and looked at her through narrowed eyes. "But someone else did?"

Anna jumped a little bit and looked at me as if she'd forgotten I was there. "No. No, of course not." She blotted and brushed at the stain with renewed energy.

"You think your father knew? Did he treat Mayhew for something?"

Anna's hands stilled. She stuffed the handkerchief down the side of the chair and turned fully to me. "Dad came home one night . . . I don't know, a year or two ago. It was before I went to London. That's neither here nor there, but he behaved so strangely that night. Not like himself at all. He said Mr. Mayhew had pneumonia. I *knew* Dad wasn't telling me everything, but I couldn't get it out of him." She sighed. "He does that, closes up tight as a clam and never releases a bit of information. But I knew something bothered him. He never spoke about it, and I couldn't figure it out. It had to be about Mayhew." Her shoulders relaxed. "Oh, it's such a relief to have someone to talk to— someone my own age. You don't know what it's like to live here and be the only young person." Her gaze shifted to the middle distance as she looked out over the garden. "But to think Mayhew was actually a woman . . . unbelievable. I know R. W. May was a pen name. Who was she, really?"

"I don't know. I believe Police Inspector Calder is working on that now."

Anna made a huffing sound. "Well, we may have to wait awhile. Police Inspector Calder is a nice enough man but not exactly the most intelligent chap." We sat for a few moments in silence, then she poured herself another cup of tea and offered me one.

I shook my head and returned my teacup to the tray. "I'm afraid this is going to sound mercenary, but one of the reasons I wanted to talk to you today is about Mayhew's last book. I have to telephone Mr. Hightower and let him know what's happened with Mayhew, but before I do that, I wanted to check with you to see if you had a copy of the last manuscript."

"A copy of the manuscript?" She glanced over her shoulder at the table with the typewriter. "Why would you need that?"

"Because Hightower Books hasn't received Mayhew's manuscript for *Murder on the Ninth Green*."

"But I finished it weeks ago, and he sent it off."

"Mayhew had some sort of Machiavellian system. She would send it to Hightower Books through the local solicitor here, but with his accident . . ."

"Oh, that makes sense now. Mayhew did have me drop —" Her cheeks went pink. "Er . . . something off with the solicitor once." She hurried on, her words coming quickly.

"How terrible—about the manuscript, I mean. Hightower Books is probably beside themselves wondering what happened to it."

I leaned in. "That's actually why I was sent here—to find out what happened without causing a lot of fuss."

"Oh. Well, in that case . . ." She caught her necklace between her thumb and fingers and rubbed her thumb over the beads. "I never told Mr.—I mean, Miss—Mayhew, but I kept a carbon copy of the manuscripts I typed."

"Don't look so guilty. I think that's wonderful. Mr. Hightower will be very grateful, I'm sure."

Her thumb traced over the beads more quickly. "I thought Mayhew might want changes. If I had my own copy, it would be so much easier."

"You don't have to explain to me. Would you entrust your copy to me to give to Hightower Books?"

Her words came slowly as she said, "I guess I could do that."

"It would ensure the book is actually published. I don't know if the copy Mayhew sent to the solicitor will ever show up."

"Yes, you're right. I suppose if you promise to hand-carry it to Mr. Hightower, I could give it to you."

"I think that would be the best thing to do. We wouldn't want it to get lost in the post."

"That would be disastrous."

I'd said the line about it getting lost in the post as a bit of a joke and blinked at the intensity of her tone. She seemed rather passionate about the manuscript, considering she had only typed it. But I supposed she was invested in the book and wanted to see it in print.

She dumped her cup onto the tray with a clatter. "I'll get it for you now." She disappeared into the house and returned a few moments later carrying a flat box tied with string. She held it with two hands and hesitated a moment before she handed it to me. "There you go. That's *Murder on the Ninth Green*—the only copy I have."

"Thank you. I'll personally hand it to Mr. Hightower." I settled the box on my lap.

Footsteps sounded, and Dr. Finch came through the garden toward us. "What's this? No typing?"

"Hello, Dad. I'm taking a break to talk to Olive."

"Oh, hello, Miss Belgrave. I didn't see you there for a moment. The racket of the typewriter is usually constant. Silence is the exception rather than the rule around here." He sat down. "I believe I'll join you."

Anna poured him a cup of tea. "Have you heard the news about . . . Mayhew?"

"I've been in the surgery all morning, catching up on paperwork. No one's been in. What's happened?"

Anna looked at me. "You'd better tell him since you were there."

Dr. Finch looked at me over the rim of his cup with what I thought was polite interest. By the time I finished, he was taking sips of his tea in a rote manner, and his relaxed demeanor was gone, replaced with a stiff posture.

Anna touched his sleeve. "Dad, you knew, didn't you?"

Dr. Finch leaned forward and put his cup on the tray, breaking the contact of her hand on his arm. "I don't know what you mean, my dear."

"It's no use, Dad." Anna refilled his empty cup. "You behaved so oddly after Mayhew had pneumonia. You wouldn't say a word about what was bothering you, but this has to be what you discovered. I'm sure you had to . . . examine Mayhew. You would have been . . . um . . . aware of Mayhew's gender. You *had* to have known."

Dr. Finch waved off the brimming teacup Anna held out. "And now she's dead." He ran his fingers through his thinning reddish hair.

"Did Mayhew tell you why she was masquerading as a

man?" Anna hesitated. "Was she . . . did she . . . well, I've heard about people who do that sort of thing because they enjoy it. Was she that way?"

He stood. "If you'll excuse me, I need something stronger than tea." He went into the house.

I looked at Anna with raised eyebrows. "Will he come back?"

"Oh yes. It's been weighing on him. He wants to talk about it. I can tell. He just has to work up to it."

The deep rumble of Dr. Finch's voice floated out of the open window of the house, then he returned carrying a tumbler of amber liquid and a large envelope. He took his seat again and put the envelope on his knee, but he didn't speak for a few moments. "I've telephoned Colonel Shaw. He'll be here shortly. He was home and said he'd come straightaway."

"I'll ring for more tea."

"Better have the whiskey brought instead."

Anna gave him a doubtful look but called the maid, gave the instructions, and then turned to me. "Colonel Shaw is the Chief Constable. He lives up the lane and should be here any minute." Anna shifted her attention back to her father. "So you *do* know why Mayhew pretended to be a man?"

Dr. Finch nodded. "Yes, and I suppose you'd better stay and listen. Otherwise, rumors"—he arced his glass through the air—"like those things you mentioned, will get started. That would be unfair to her."

Although I was dying to hear what Dr. Finch had to say, I inched to the front of my chair. Good manners dictated it was time for me to leave. "I should go."

"No, you were there, and you're with Hightower Books," Dr. Finch said. "They should know as well. Heaven knows, it will impact them."

Anna turned sharply to him. "What's this about Hightower Books?"

Dr. Finch patted her hand. "And it will affect you too, my dear."

"Of course it will. All those . . . manuals . . ."

"But they weren't manuals, were they?" Dr. Finch said.

Anna stared at him a moment, then her gaze dropped. "I don't—um—know what you mean."

"You knew I was keeping a secret but thought I didn't know you were doing the same thing?" Dr. Finch gave a small smile. "I never did believe that claptrap about Mayhew writing technical manuals. You were typing manuscript pages —reams and reams of them. And then you had a sudden interest in crime fiction. You'd never read an R.W. May book —or any book of detective fiction—until you started typing up the 'manuals.' No, it wasn't hard to put two and two together when you borrowed all my books by R. W. May and then started muttering about fictional detectives and red herrings and clues. You thought I wasn't paying attention. Let this be a lesson to you, my dear. Fathers always keep an eye on their daughters—especially grown-up daughters. Ah, here's the colonel."

CHAPTER NINE

Colonel Shaw was a tall, skinny man somewhere in his late sixties or early seventies with a weather-beaten face, grayish hair, and a white toothbrush mustache. Introductions were made, chairs were shuffled, and drinks distributed. Shaw looked at me as if he'd like to shoo me away, but Dr. Finch said, "I believe Miss Belgrave should remain, Colonel. She works for Hightower Books, which, as you'll see, is related."

The colonel didn't look happy, but Dr. Finch's word must have carried a lot of weight because after a second's pause, Shaw nodded his assent and turned to Dr. Finch. "You said this is about Mayhew? You know about—" He cleared his throat and darted a glance at Anna and me.

"That Mayhew was a woman?" Dr. Finch said. "Yes." He gestured to Anna and me. "And they know as well. The whole village knows at this point, I'm sure."

"In that case . . ." Shaw leaned back in his chair and indicated that Dr. Finch had the floor.

Dr. Finch took a gulp of his whiskey, then held the glass with both hands and stared down into it. "Two years ago, Mayhew came down with pneumonia. She went for over a week before she sent for me. She was fatigued and had a high fever. We both ignored the obvious fact that she was a woman until after she began to recover. Once she began to feel better and didn't have a hacking cough, she wanted to explain. I told her there was no need. But she said she wanted to tell someone, that she'd feel better. In case anything happened to her, someone would know the truth."

Shaw paused, his glass halfway to his mouth. "You mean she worried someone would try to harm her?"

I leaned forward. Lady Holt had been so insistent that Mayhew's death had been an accident. Calder seemed willing to go along with it, but I supposed the likelihood of Mayhew being pushed was just as possible as the likelihood of her falling and being buried in a landslide at the riverbank.

Dr. Finch tilted his glass one way and then the other, watching the liquid slosh from side to side. "I'd say she wasn't in fear for her life at that moment. She was worried, though. Apparently, she had reason to be."

Anna patted Dr. Finch's shoulder. "There's nothing you could have done. I'm sure she swore you to secrecy."

"Yes, she did. But she did want her story told if anything happened to her." He tossed back the rest of the drink and set the glass down with a thump. "Have you heard of the pixies at Pikenwillow House?"

Anna said, "Yes, of course. It was a hoax that took in so many foolish people. What does that have to do with Mayhew?"

I straightened as Mr. Hightower's words echoed in my head. What had Mr. Hightower said about Mayhew's pen name?

Dr. Finch said, "Mayhew's pen name of R. W. May was a based on her given name, Ronnie May."

My thoughts traced through the names, making the connection. "Ronnie . . . it was short for Veronica, I bet." I'd been looking at the springy grass under my feet as I thought, but now I looked up. "Mayhew was Veronica May, wasn't she?"

"Yes."

Anna looked between me and her father. "R. W. Mayhew was Veronica May? *The* Veronica May who was in all the papers? Veronica May from Pikenwillow House?"

Dr. Finch nodded. "Yes, that Veronica May." He turned to Shaw. "You're familiar with the incident?"

The pixies at Pikenwillow House had caused a media sensation several years ago. It had begun when a young girl —Veronica May—and her friend took some photographs in the girl's back garden. The photos showed pixies playing among the flowers. Veronica's father sent them to several societies, including an organization interested in psychic phenomena.

The colonel frowned. "I don't remember much of anything about it except it was a pack of nonsense. It was debunked years later, I believe."

"Yes, that's exactly what happened." Dr. Finch opened the envelope that rested on his knee and removed a yellowed newspaper clipping. He handed it to Shaw. "After she recovered from pneumonia, Mayhew sent this to me. The two girls created the photographs as a joke. A prank. But her father saw the reaction to the photos and realized he could exploit them. Perhaps he was a believer in spiritualism and whatnot. Or maybe he was simply an opportunist. I think the latter is probably the correct description, but I've never met the man."

Dr. Finch picked up his glass, tilted it so that the dregs of the drink ran across the bottom, then set it back down. "Whatever the case, Mr. May capitalized on the interest in the photos. I read up on the situation after Mayhew sent the clipping. Before the photographs were debunked, Mr. May became a speaker, traveling to lecture organizations all around England and even on the continent. He gave tours of his home and charged people fees to come and stay in the cottage at the bottom of his garden, where they could possibly see pixies if the conditions were perfect, or they could participate in séances he ran in his home."

Shaw had screwed a monocle into one eye socket and skimmed the article, then passed the clipping to me. The headline read, *Pixie Photographs A Lie! Paper Cutouts Says Daughter.* I held the thin paper by the edges. "But the story fell apart when Veronica told the truth."

Dr. Finch pointed to the newspaper article. "She described exactly how it was done. Debunked the whole thing."

Anna leaned on the arm of the chair to read over my shoulder. "I don't remember the details."

I handed the article to Anna as Dr. Finch continued, "Mayhew told me she had reached a point where she couldn't continue to defraud people. She contacted a reporter and described how she faked the original photographs. She traced images of pixies from a children's book, added a couple of details of her own—hats and gloves —then used hat pins to prop up the cutouts among the flowers in the garden. She thought it was a great joke, but when her father latched onto it as a way to dupe people, she became more and more uncomfortable. Mr. May got ahold of a moving picture camera and made a film. Then he bought a projector and played the film of the supposed pixies."

Dr. Finch waved a hand toward the far side of their garden. "At night, he projected the pictures of dancing pixies onto various bits around the garden—a shed wall, strategically placed white rocks, and a fountain base. Of course the images only lasted a few seconds, but apparently it was enough to keep the legend going with those susceptible to believing that sort of thing. He was making hundreds of pounds from each séance. He charged for daytime tours of the garden and even more for the overnight visitors who got to see his private cinema show. Mayhew said she couldn't stand the deception anymore, and that's why she revealed the truth."

Dr. Finch took the newspaper clipping from Anna and replaced it in the envelope. "Veronica May had a vivid imagination and a talent for writing. While her father was making money hand over fist with the pixie legend, she threw herself into writing a book, a detective novel. Once she received an offer from Hightower Books, she made plans to tell the truth about the pixies to the newspapers and then disappear." Dr. Finch handed the envelope to Shaw. "You'd better keep this now."

Shaw nodded and tucked it into the side of his chair. "I gather she disappeared because she was afraid of her father?"

"Mayhew said her father would be furious when the article was published. She was frightened he'd harm her." Dr. Finch cleared his throat. "She said her father had hurt her before."

I couldn't imagine having a father like that. "How shocking." While my father was absentminded and often lost in his own world of research, books, and writing, he was kind and gentle. "And Mayhew's mother, was she part of the deception?"

"No. She died when Veronica was born." Dr. Finch reached for the whiskey decanter, poured himself another drink, then raised the decanter in Shaw's direction. Shaw shook his head, and Dr. Finch continued. "Of course, I tried to convince Mayhew to come out of hiding, but she would have none of it. She said she'd changed her appearance and taken several precautions so her father would never find her. She was serious when she told me if anything ever happened to her, the police should find out where her father was when she died. She feared he would track her down and . . . well, she was blunt about it. 'He'd do away with me if he could,' she'd said. She thought once she was gone, her father would release a 'newly discovered' letter or statement from her—forged, of course—in which she recanted her earlier statements about the pixies, so he could draw the psychic seekers back to Pikenwillow House."

Anna shook her head. "And so she wore a mask, masqueraded as a man, and lived a lonely life here in Hadsworth."

Dr. Finch sipped from his glass. "I asked her if she was lonely, and she said no, that she was a 'solitary soul,' as she called it. She said she liked living in the cottage, writing her books, and rambling about the countryside in the evening. She told me she was happy, and I believed her."

We were all silent for a few moments, and then Dr. Finch said, "Mayhew didn't think her father would try to release any new statement recanting her previous debunking of the pixie story unless he was absolutely sure she was dead. While she was alive, she could always counter any statement he made." He gestured to the envelope with his glass. "Along with the newspaper article, she also sent a sealed letter with the request that I give it to a specific newspaper reporter if she died unexpectedly. I'd give it to you, Colonel, but I made a promise to her. I intend to keep it."

"Quite." Shaw ran a finger over his narrow mustache. "But perhaps you could delay until we've confirmed the whereabouts of her father."

"That's reasonable."

Shaw looked at me. "And I would appreciate the same courtesy from Hightower Books. Please keep the information about Mayhew's true identity secret until the investigation is complete."

As Dr. Finch said, it was a reasonable request, and I agreed to it. Shaw stood and put the envelope under his arm. "I'll take care of this."

Dr. Finch braced his hands on his knees and pushed himself up. "I'll come down to give a formal statement."

Shaw consulted his pocket watch. "Time enough for that

later. I'd rather focus on finding Mr. May at the moment. Come down to the police station tomorrow morning."

Shaw waved off the offer to be escorted out of the house through the drawing room, saying he would leave by the path that ran between the house and the surgery.

I rose and held the manuscript box to my chest. Anna hadn't mentioned the manuscript, so I'd stayed silent, but I did need to tell the police officials about what I'd seen in Mayhew's cottage. After hearing what she'd been through, I was surer than ever that I'd made the right decision to confess about my snooping. I just hoped the police wouldn't want to keep the manuscript, because I was determined not to give it up. It wasn't related to Mr. May at all, and I'd fight to make sure I could send it to Hightower Books. "I should go as well. I must get back to Blackburn Hall." I turned to Dr. Finch. "Thank you for letting me hear what happened."

Dr. Finch said, "Hightower Books should know . . . eventually. You can give them the full story once Shaw—or whoever is in charge—clears you to do so. They'll have a bit of interest, I should imagine. Mayhew's death will make all the papers, I'm sure." He nodded to the box I held. "His last novel will be a sensation."

"I'm sure Hightower Books will want to get it out as soon as they can." They'd have to make the most of it, considering there wouldn't be any more books from R. W. May. I patted the box and said to Anna, "Thank you for giving it to me. I'll take good care of it."

She jumped a bit at my words. "Sorry. Woolgathering."

"Thank you for entrusting me with the book. I'll make sure it gets to the publisher."

"Good." She glanced at the typewriter then back to me, her eyebrows furrowed. "Yes. That's what Mayhew—or Veronica, I guess I could say now—would have wanted."

Anna moved back to the table with the typewriter as I walked down the same path Shaw had taken. I didn't hear the sound of the typewriter and glanced back before I turned in front of the house. Anna sat with her hands in her lap, staring at the typewriter.

Poor thing. Her biggest source of income was gone—a fact that paled in comparison to a death, but I knew exactly how it felt to have work dry up like a rain puddle that evaporates when the sun comes out after a storm. I made a mental note to speak to Mr. Hightower about Anna and sing her praises. She'd saved Mayhew's last book. Surely the publisher could send her a bonus . . . or perhaps find some work for her. I'd drop that idea into Mr. Hightower's ear.

Colonel Shaw was several steps ahead of me down the lane. I quickened my steps. "Colonel Shaw, may I have a word?"

"Certainly." He paused and waited for me to catch up on the quiet stretch of the lane before it reached High Street.

"I have a confession to make."

He wheeled and looked at me. "A confession?"

"Perhaps that was the wrong word to use in this situation. I have something to tell you. It's rather embarrassing. I stopped by the police station this morning to speak to Inspector Calder, but he was away. I think I should let you know now. Mr. Hightower sent me to Hadsworth to look for Mayhew and this manuscript." I tapped the box, then explained about Mayhew's arrangement with the solicitor and how the manuscript hadn't arrived. "So when Anna mentioned Mayhew lived in East Bank Cottage, I went there and had a look around myself."

"Nothing wrong with that." Shaw began to stroll again.

"Inside."

Shaw stopped and looked at me. "You broke into the cottage?"

"No, of course not. I found a key. It's above the window frame on the right-hand side of the front door. I looked around inside and several things stood out to me." I described the wilted flowers, the open book on the chair, the bread in the kitchen. "In short, it didn't look as if someone had prepared for a trip."

We reached the main road and turned onto it. "Perhaps you could accompany me to the police station now and make a statement?"

So I wasn't to be given the same courtesy Dr. Finch received of being asked to come in the next morning. I couldn't blame the colonel. He didn't know me at all. "Certainly." I followed him across the green to the little building that housed the police station.

CHAPTER TEN

$\mathcal{M}$y second visit to the police station took less than a quarter of an hour, and the whole thing was handled in a matter-of-fact way. I recounted my visit to the cottage, and Shaw had a constable type it up. Shaw handed the statement to me along with a pen. I read over it and signed my name. How silly I'd been to agonize over telling the police what I'd done. They obviously felt my snooping was a small matter, barely worth their time. If Shaw said he wanted to keep the manuscript as evidence, I was poised to point out that it was Anna's property, not Mayhew's, but Shaw didn't bring it up.

I stood, and Shaw picked up the statement from the desk. "I'll hand this off to the detective inspector from Scotland Yard when he arrives. He may have more questions for you."

The weight of worry descended onto my shoulders again. "Scotland Yard will be taking over the case?"

"Undoubtedly."

"I thought you were going to find out where Mr. May was when Mayhew died."

"That's beyond the scope of our abilities here in Hadsworth. Definitely something for the Yard."

"I see." Shaw had merely been going through the motions, collecting information from me, but he'd toss the case into someone else's lap soon—that's why he hadn't had any probing questions for me.

I trooped back across the green. I'd probably have to tell about snooping around East Bank Cottage again to the detective inspector from Scotland Yard. I wrinkled my nose. I should have kept quiet, but my conscience got the better of me. It was quite inconvenient to be a vicar's daughter at times.

I left the village and paced along the tall hedge that lined the road. I crossed the bridge and used a brisk pace to work through my worry. I shifted the cardboard box with Mayhew's manuscript to the crook of my other arm. Huffing along, I decided telling the story again would be embarrassing, but I'd get through it. Time enough to worry about that later. I had other things to focus on right now.

I didn't want to announce my return from the village, so I walked around to the back garden and entered Blackburn Hall through the open French doors into the drawing room. The dark paneled entry hall was silent and empty. I settled into the chair beside the telephone table and asked to be connected to Hightower Books in London. I admired the hefty board and batten paneling on the wall under the stairs as I listened to a series of clicks and long silences.

When I was finally connected, I said, "Mr. Hightower, this is Olive Belgrave. I have some good news as well as some distressing news."

"Better let me have the bad news straightaway."

"Very well. Mayhew's body was found this morning by the river."

"Good heavens. What happened?"

"At this point, no one's sure. Serena Shires, Lady Holt's sister, saw Mayhew on Wednesday morning, and he was found not far from there wearing the same clothes, so it must have happened sometime Wednesday morning."

"I knew something was wrong. I hate to be proven right, but I was sure Mayhew wouldn't miss his deadline. To think that he's been dead that long. Tragic. Just tragic." A long sigh came over the line.

"Yes, it is." I thought of East Bank Cottage with its reading glasses and sad wilted flowers. Mr. Hightower was the only person who'd shown even a trace of grief for Mayhew.

Mr. Hightower's voice brought me back to the present. "Did you say you have some good news?"

"Yes. Mayhew used a local woman as a typist, and she made carbon copies, which she kept, of the manuscript pages of *Murder on the Ninth Green*. I have it here with me. "

Mr. Hightower's voice perked up. "Excellent."

"I promised I'd hand it to you directly. I can leave now and be in London by this evening."

"No need. I'm sending Leland—Mr. Busby—down with a contract for Lady Holt to sign."

"Really?"

"Yes, I had a lengthy conversation with Lady Holt this afternoon. We've had some changes in next year's publishing calendar—an unexpected opening. Lady Holt's book will add a certain cachet to our roster of upcoming publications. So you don't have to hurry back. Give the manuscript to Leland."

I didn't want to break my promise to Anna. "It's too bad Mr. Busby has to make a special trip. It's not a problem for me to run up to town and drop the manuscript with you, then return with the contract for Lady Holt."

"I leave for Edinburgh shortly. It's no trouble at all. Leland planned to go to Hadsworth later this week anyway. He usually goes down to Kent on Friday to play golf. This will work out better. He'll be able to handle any issues Lady Holt has with the contract."

"I'm sure she'll have plenty of questions and requests."

"Been like that, has it?"

I glanced around the entry hall to make sure it was still empty. "Lady Holt is extremely thorough."

"Glad I'm sending Leland, then."

"I did promise to personally hand the manuscript to you. Anna—she's the typist—seemed a bit reluctant to give it up, and I assured her I'd give it to you directly."

"Let her know it went to my second-in-command. I trust Mr. Busby implicitly. Fine chap. Hightower Books can sort out a bonus or some other sign of our appreciation to . . . um . . . what was the name?"

"Anna Finch. I'm sure she'd appreciate that." If Mr. Hightower wanted Mr. Busby to have the manuscript first, I couldn't argue with him. It was his company, and he made the decisions. I'd just have to tell Anna it was what Mr. Hightower wanted. "Anna was also interested to know if there were any typist jobs available through Hightower Books. Just passing that along, so you know. She's good at what she does."

Or at least from what I'd heard when I visited her, it sounded as if she was a speedy typist. I plucked the string around the box, untied it, and lift the lid. A quick peek showed a pristine sheet of paper with the title centered over the name *R. W. May.* The pages fit snugly into the box, and I couldn't flip through them easily with one hand. I replaced the lid. I'd have a look at the manuscript before I handed it off to Leland to make sure it was all in order.

"I'll pass her name along to the appropriate person," Mr. Hightower said. "Well, Miss Belgrave, thank you for your work on this."

Mr. Hightower was wrapping up, so I said quickly, "There's one more thing you should be aware of in regard to Mayhew's death."

"What's that?"

"Mr. Mayhew was actually a woman." Colonel Shaw didn't want Mayhew's identity as Veronica May broadcast, so I kept that bit of information back, but the news that Mayhew was a woman was all over Blackburn Hall already, which meant the whole village would probably know within a few more hours, if they didn't already. The silence stretched. "Mr. Hightower? Are you still there?"

"A woman? What—? Are you sure?"

"I saw the body myself. It was definitely a woman dressed in men's clothing."

"Well, I'll be." He laughed suddenly. "No wonder Mayhew didn't want to come up to London and have dinner and meet everyone."

"And it explains the horrible picture too," I said. "She disguised herself so no one would recognize her."

"What an interesting twist. Mysterious author, living incognito." He cleared his throat. "Sorry, I tend to get a little carried away when it comes to business, which is not at all what should be the focus right now. Poor chap—or lady, I suppose I should say. Poor lady."

I didn't want Mr. Hightower to ask any more questions about Mayhew's real identity, so I moved the conversation back to the death. "Yes, apparently when she fell, a cascade of earth covered her, hiding her body until a storm came through this week. A waterlogged tree fell over, unearthing the body."

"Horrible. Just horrible." A sigh came over the line. "Of course this will mean the end of books from Mayhew. I suppose we'll have to make the best of it." He spoke under his breath, and I thought he was probably jotting notes as he talked. "Extra large print run for *Murder on the Ninth,* and reissue all the other titles in special editions. That'll hold us for a while, I suppose." His voice returned to its normal pitch. "Sorry. That's something to think about another time. Thank you for your information, Miss Belgrave. Hand off *Murder on the Ninth* to Leland, and then finish out your stay at Black-burn Hall."

As I rang off, Lady Holt came down the stairs. "Did you hear the news, Miss Belgrave? Mr. Hightower is sending his associate from Hightower Books down with a contract for the etiquette guide. I think a celebration is in order. Perhaps another little dinner party. I know it's not quite the done thing, considering what happened to . . . um . . . the occupant of East Bank Cottage, but Mr. Busby will be our guest. I must provide some entertainment for him. You'll stay on, won't you?"

"Yes, that would be lovely."

"Excellent. I'd like you to look over the last few chapters before Mr. Busby arrives. I think we can go over at least one more chapter before tea."

I flipped the last page of the etiquette guide over, putting it facedown on the stack of completed pages. "And we're done." My brain was full of information about introductions, invitations, and etiquette at meals, including the proper way to eat a banana if one was served at dinner—remove the skin, place it on the dessert plate, and cut it into small pieces with the blunt edge of the fork.

A wrinkle appeared between Lady Holt's eyebrows. "Perhaps I should include a chapter on lesser-known situations."

I tapped the pages to even the stack. "I don't think so. You've covered everything in great depth, and I'm sure Mr. Hightower will be pleased." Lady Holt didn't look convinced, so I said, "Perhaps let Mr. Busby look over it and then ask his opinion?"

"Yes, I suppose that's the best plan."

I scooted my chair back before Lady Holt could change her mind. The deep timbre of male voices sounded, then

Zippy entered the drawing room. "Hello, Mater. I've brought a few chaps for tea."

I blinked when Jasper Rimington strolled in behind Zippy's broad-shouldered form with Monty Park at his side. Monty and Jasper weren't exactly close friends, and I was surprised to see them together. Under Monty's thatch of dark hair, his face was set in what I'd have called a pout if he'd been a girl. He greeted everyone perfunctorily while Jasper lingered over Lady Holt's hand. Jasper turned to me, and I said, "What a surprise. You should have told me you were coming to Hadsworth."

"I didn't know it myself until this morning. Felt like a day on the links."

"I see. And you—all three—played together?"

"Yes," he said as we moved to the chairs grouped around the fireplace. "An enlightening experience. I find there's no better way to get to know someone than participating in a sport together."

Monty's pout deepened. "I believe you're misquoting Mark Twain. And he was speaking about travel, not golf."

Jasper smiled. "Was he? You're probably right about the quote—never was good at memorizing trivia, but I stand by the gist of my statement."

Lady Holt poured out the tea, and I accepted a cup. I'd already had afternoon tea with Anna, but social conventions had to be observed. I stirred my tea, my glance going back and forth between Jasper and Monty. Jasper looked as if he hadn't a care in the world, while Monty looked as if he'd like to hit something. Lady Holt asked, "How was golf today?"

Jasper lifted his teacup in a salute to Zippy. "Your son outdid us all, Lady Holt."

"That's what comes of living so near a course," Zippy said. "I'm able to play often."

I studied Zippy, thinking of the hints I'd overheard this morning that Zippy had been involved with Mayhew. Now that I knew Mayhew was a woman, the conversation took on a whole new meaning. But Lady Holt apparently hadn't known Mayhew was a woman. Lady Holt had been upset because she thought Zippy was visiting a man's cottage. But had Zippy known Mayhew was a woman? Perhaps they'd been in love and were meeting secretly?

Zippy lounged against the arm of the settee, his sandy hair windblown from the day on the course, sipping tea and eating sandwiches. He certainly didn't look like he'd just learned a secret love had died. Sunburned and relaxed, he looked like a man whose biggest concern was how soon he could get back on the golf course . . . so perhaps Zippy hadn't known Mayhew was a woman. I thought back, trying to remember if Zippy had singled out any girls during the season. I couldn't remember any. He'd always been sports-mad, not girl-mad. Had Zippy been . . . interested . . . in Mayhew?

Monty shifted in his chair. "I still say there must be something off with my three iron."

I selected a sandwich of cress and cucumber. "How is your golfing holiday, Monty? Are you enjoying it?"

"Disappointing. The greens at Lightway left a lot to be desired."

"I'm sorry to hear that," I said. "Have you played anywhere else?"

"Yes, Dowly, but the links were terribly overcrowded."

"Perhaps you shouldn't have gone on a Saturday." Jasper said.

"Says the man who only plays golf twice a year." Monty's tone was sharp.

"Yes," Jasper said in his easy manner. "I only play occasionally. Can't say I find the sport that compelling—chasing a small ball around and knocking it into a hole. Fatiguing, really."

Monty banged his teacup into the saucer. "Then the finer points of the game have completely eluded you."

"Must have," Jasper said in the same slightly bored tone, but I knew him well enough to recognize he was goading Monty. "Although I have to say, I did admire Zippy's long putt on the last hole."

Jasper and Zippy kept up a light patter of conversation. Monty ate sandwiches mechanically and didn't participate. I wondered if anyone would mention Mayhew, but Lady Holt kept a firm hand on the conversational reins, guiding us from golf to mutual friends. Watching her orchestrate the discussion, I wondered how she would react when she learned Scotland Yard was taking over the investigation into Mayhew's death. I was sure she'd try to manage whichever detective inspector arrived and ensure the whole incident went away. Indignation flared through me. It wasn't right to brush away someone's death—to act as if they had never existed.

The click of Jasper putting down his cup as he shifted forward in his seat brought me back to the conversation. He said, "I'd like to take a turn around your beautiful gardens, Lady Holt."

"By all means."

Jasper looked at me. "Care to accompany me?"

"I'd like that."

We strolled away from the house along the gravel path in silence. I drew in a deep breath of the flower-scented air, glad to be out of the stilted atmosphere of the drawing room. Low boxwood hedges on either side of the path enclosed swaths of flowers laid out with geometric precision. I asked, "What's wrong with Monty?"

Jasper turned down a path that forked off the main walkway. "What do you mean?"

"He seems out of sorts."

"Oh, that. He's sulking. Sees himself as some sort of

athletic paragon on the golf course, but he played badly today. Sliced on nearly every hole. Blames his clubs."

I shifted to the left so I was walking in the shade of one of the tall hedges. "Well, anyone can have a bad day."

"You mean he doesn't behave like that all the time?"

"No, he's usually charming and funny."

"Hmm . . . must only extend himself to do that for the ladies. He's never charming or funny when it's only us blokes."

I stopped to smell a pink tea rose in full bloom. "I didn't know you and Monty were well acquainted. Have you joined him on his golfing holiday?"

"No, I happened to meet him and Zippy as I arrived at the course this morning, and we agreed to play together."

"But somehow I feel that your arrival in Hadsworth isn't quite so accidental."

Jasper clasped his hands together behind his back. "Why do you say that?" His tone changed, losing a trace of his nonchalance.

"Because you're usually far too languid to indulge in athletic activities. At least recently. I do remember when you and Peter played cricket from sunrise to sunset at Parkview during your holidays. But golf doesn't fit with your laconic façade."

"Everyone needs a spot of exercise now and again. I also had a desire to see how your commission for Mr. Hightower was progressing." We paused beside a fountain of nymphs. "I heard about the discovery of Mayhew's body. Sad situation."

"Tragic. Have you heard the whole story—that Mayhew was a woman masquerading as a man?"

"That's the bit that gets told first, don't you know. It's the most salacious part."

I wanted to tell him about the background and the reason why Mayhew was hiding out and dressing as woman, but I couldn't. I'd promised Colonel Shaw I'd stay silent. "When you spoke to Mr. Hightower, how specific was he about the situation?"

"Mr. Hightower only gave me the barest details. No names, but when I heard the name Mayhew . . ." He shrugged. "I knew you were going to Blackburn Hall to look for a missing author. Hightower Books publishes the R. W. May novels. With the similarity in the surnames . . . I wondered if there was a connection. It seemed a logical conclusion."

The wind shifted, and the fine spray from the fountain prickled across my face. I stepped back. "The good news is Mayhew's last book will be published. I located a copy of it for Mr. Hightower."

I turned to retrace our steps back to the section planted with rosebushes in shades ranging from apricot to blood red. Jasper fell into step with me.

"Excellent. I'm sure Mr. Hightower was pleased. Does that mean you're returning to London?"

"I intend to stay on a few days."

"Why? You found out what happened with Mayhew and recovered the manuscript."

I fingered the velvety petals of a rose. "Because Mayhew is dead, and I'm interested in finding out exactly what happened."

"That's the police's patch, not yours."

"If we all took that attitude, the world would be a terrible place." I released the rose and paced down the path. "And Lady Holt is pressing for Mayhew's death to be declared an accident. She's so forceful. I wouldn't put it past her to go over the head of the person in charge. She's the sort who cultivates contacts and knows exactly who to call to make sure the investigators back off."

"I think you overestimate her power."

"Then you haven't been around Lady Holt long enough to fully understand her." I sighed, thinking of Mayhew's cottage

—homey and comfortable, it looked as if someone had stepped out for a moment and never came back. "There's more going on here than what you see on the surface—I'm sure of it."

I walked on, picking up my pace. "It's not right that Mayhew's death be hushed up because it might reflect badly on Blackburn Hall. I can't walk away. *Someone* has to care about Mayhew. Besides, you know me. I'm incredibly curious. I want to know the whole story."

"That worries me more than anything else."

"It's sweet of you to worry about me."

I was a few paces down the path when I realized Jasper had stopped walking. I turned back. The sun was glinting off his blond hair, and his hands were still clasped behind his back, but his face was different, tighter, as if he wanted to say something and was fighting to get the words out.

"What is it?" I asked.

He released his hands and quickly closed the distance between us. After a quick glance around the garden, he lowered his voice. "I *do* worry about you. You haven't stated it outright, but you suspect Mayhew was killed, which means someone around here is a murderer."

"That's what I want to find out."

"And that's why I'm worried."

Irritation simmered through me. "Stop treating me like a child. We're not climbing trees and wading in the river at Parkview. You don't have to protect me."

"I never said you were behaving like a child."

"No, but you want to hem me in. You'd hustle me back to London if you could, wouldn't you?"

"You rush in headlong without thinking. That could be . . . dangerous."

"So I'm impetuous and shortsighted?" More words bubbled up, but I pressed them down. "There's so much I want to say to you right now, but I'm keeping it inside. I don't want to regret it later—and that's hardly impetuous or short-sighted. Quite the opposite, in fact."

Jasper looked away and ran his fingers through his hair, causing the hair around his forehead to spring up. "*I* sent you to Hightower."

"And I didn't have to take the job, but I did. That's on me, not you."

We stared at each other for a moment. Somehow we'd squared off and now stood on opposite sides of the path. I breathed out a sigh and crossed to him. "Don't let's fight. You're the one person I always want on my side. It would be much easier to go back to London, but I wouldn't be able to forget Mayhew. If I can contribute in some small way to getting to the truth of Mayhew's death, I'm going to do it. You might as well accept that. Besides, I have to give the manuscript to Mr. Hightower's associate, who's coming down tomorrow. Lady Holt has asked me to stay on for a few days, and I've agreed. Truce?"

He gazed out over the garden, his eyes narrowed for a few seconds. "On one condition. If you're going to play Sherlock, I'm your Watson."

I reared my head back. "You'd be my Watson?"

"Well, I'd prefer Sherlock, of course, but that role seems to be taken."

"I see what you're doing, you know. It's an excuse to keep up with me."

"That blatant, am I?"

"Yes. But I wouldn't be opposed to having a partner," I said slowly. "Someone to bounce ideas off of."

"Well, then." He extended his arm.

I slipped my hand around his elbow, and we strolled on, our steps slow and tentative as if we weren't sure how to move forward on our new footing. We strolled in silence, and my thoughts returned to the quiet little cottage and

Mayhew's solitary existence. "So . . . um . . . partner, how well do you know Zippy?"

"As well as one can know a chap who's a few years younger than oneself. We've met occasionally, but I wouldn't say we're especially close."

We walked on to the next set of roses, which were crimson like blood. "Would you say he's one of the sort of fellows who . . . um . . . prefers men to women?"

Jasper halted. "Olive, you shock me. Young ladies are not supposed to know of such things, much less speak of them."

I laughed. "Jasper, I've had a classical education."

"So you have. I'm afraid to ask why you want to know."

"Just one of those odd things that tend to nag at me. I'd like it sorted away."

"One of the reasons that you're staying on?"

"You know me too well."

"I see." We began walking again. "Well, in that case, I would say no, Zippy is firmly in the camp of men who prefer women."

"You're sure?"

"Let's just say he's been known to be extremely friendly with at least two dancers from certain popular shows. And I won't be more specific than that. It wouldn't be fair to the ladies involved."

"I don't need names. Just his proclivities." We drifted toward the yew walk. "That's interesting. I wonder if his mother knows?"

"His proclivities for dancers? I should hope not. That's the sort of thing a chap keeps from his mother."

"I suppose so. That may be part of the problem."

CHAPTER ELEVEN

*D*inner was a quiet affair, with only Lord and Lady Holt and myself. After Jasper and I returned from our walk in the garden, Jasper and Monty departed to have dinner with a mutual friend in Sidlingham, a neighboring village. Zippy said his throat felt scratchy. Lady Holt declared it was the pollen—it always caused Zippy's allergies to act up.

"Nevertheless, better safe than sorry," Zippy said. "I'll excuse myself in case I am coming down with something." When Zippy bowed over my hand as he said goodnight in his best gallant manner, I'd noticed neither his eyes nor his nose were red. I hadn't heard him sniff once all day either, but I wasn't about to call him out. Perhaps he did feel bad . . . or perhaps it was his way of escaping his mother's managing personality for a few hours.

Lady Holt was almost giddy and shared all her plans for the publication of the manuscript during the four-course meal. Lord Holt contributed little more to the conversation than an occasional grunt or rumbling noise that I took to be agreement with Lady Holt's plans for a dinner party the following evening. Serena hadn't come down for dinner either, sending a message that she was at a critical point and couldn't stop working.

Before I went down to dinner, I'd explored the upper floors of Blackburn Hall and found Serena's workroom. I'd followed a loud whirring sound to a paneled door, which was open a few inches. I'd raised my hand to knock, but then the whirring sound cut off abruptly. A thud sounded. "Worthless piece of dross." The words trailed off into muttering with a definite angry overtone.

I decided it was not the ideal time to ask to see Serena's work.

After dinner, once coffee was wheeled in and placed on the table in the drawing room, where we could help ourselves, I made my excuses, saying that I had to compile a report for Mr. Hightower. Upstairs in my room, I wrote out a summary of the etiquette book for Mr. Hightower, describing what I felt were its strengths as well as a few places where it might be improved with some trimming of the content. I would let someone from Hightower Books bring up that subject with Lady Holt—I wasn't about to do it.

I set aside the report, then curled up in an armchair with the manuscript box on my lap. I removed the lid and flipped over the title page. The book was dedicated to "A. F." and the line underneath it read, *This wouldn't have been possible without you.* I turned to the first chapter and was immersed in the story after a few pages.

While the names were different, the setting of the book was clearly modeled on Hadsworth and Rosewood Hills Golf Course. This book featured Lady Eileen Dunwood and her chauffeur, Nick Fitzhugh, the detecting duo from the set of the Bright Young People who had made their appearance in the first book of the series. In *Murder on the Ninth Green*, Lady Eileen goes to the country for a golfing holiday. With Nick acting as her caddy, she's enjoying a round of golf, but then she finds a dead body on the ninth green, and they become embroiled in a murder mystery. I snuggled deeper in the chair, enjoying the story. Jasper was right—these stories were entertaining.

Chimes from the clock on the mantelpiece sounded, and I looked up. Two in the morning? Could it really be that late? Goodness, I'd been swept up in the story. Even though I wanted to find out why the course groundskeeper had disappeared, I marked my place. There was something about the book that teased at me—some interesting scrap of a thought that flitted through my mind while I was reading, but I was so engrossed in the story that I hadn't stopped to think about it, and I couldn't bring it back. Now that I'd stopped reading, my eyes felt heavy, and I yawned. The elusive thought or impression or whatever it was would probably come to me in the morning when I wasn't so exhausted. I replaced the manuscript in the drawer of the writing desk, crawled into bed, and switched off the light.

The curtains hadn't been pulled completely closed, and a gap of the night sky showed between the panels. I pushed back the covers and went to close the curtains. The sunlight would wake me in the morning, and I wanted to get as much sleep as possible since I'd read far past when I should have been in bed.

My room had a view of the back of the house, and I paused to admire the formal gardens before I swished the curtains closed. A sliver of the moon showed among a layer of clouds, whitewashing the garden in monochrome shades. Something flickered at the corner of my eye, and I shifted my attention from the gardens to the swath of blackness that bounded Blackburn Hall's grounds. A golden beam cut through the darkness for an instant, then was gone. Another brief flash, a bobbing yellow streak, lit up the path that ran beside the river from Blackburn Hall to East Bank Cottage, then it was dark. I gripped the fabric of the drapes in either hand and watched the path, letting my gaze skim back and forth along the dark section beside the river, but the light didn't flash again.

I closed the curtains and crawled into bed. Why would someone be on the path at two in the morning? It was a little late for a nighttime stroll. And why not use the torch all the time? It was certainly dark enough to need it on a cloudy night with only a slim slice of moon showing.

I turned on my side and curled up. I must have dropped into sleep right away because I awoke in that same position, instinctively knowing something had woken me. I reached for my wristwatch on the bedside table and titled it so I could see the radium-painted face. Three in the morning.

A floor board creaked in the corridor, then the faint sound of whistling penetrated the panels of my door. The whistling grew louder, then faded. I slid out of bed, padded to the door, and inched it open. A little way down the hallway, a door opened, and the light inside a room was switched on, throwing a bright bar across the hallway that highlighted Zippy's sandy hair and threw a monstrous shadow of his bulky frame across the hallway carpet. He stepped into his room whistling the last bars of *Ain't We Got Fun*. The door clicked closed, and the corridor went dark.

My night-owl behavior caught up with me the next morning. I was the last one to arrive in the breakfast room. I filled my plate then sat down across from Zippy. "How was your evening? Late night?"

"No. Turned in early, and I feel much more the thing today."

"I'm glad to hear it. Speaking of hearing, do you have a ghost?"

Zippy paused, spoon poised over the marmalade. "A ghost?"

"Does Blackburn Hall have one, I mean? Is it haunted?"

Zippy spread the marmalade. "No, nothing so romantic. Mother would never stand for it."

"That's odd. I thought I heard whistling last night."

Zippy focused on distributing the marmalade to the edge of his toast. "I've—ah—never heard of anything like that happening."

"I must have dreamt it."

Lady Holt sailed in. "Oh, you're finally down, Miss Belgrave." I opened my mouth to apologize, but Lady Holt went on, "We're all set for a small dinner party this evening in honor of Mr. Busby. We'll have Dr. Finch and Anna, the colonel and his wife, Victoria, as well as that nice young man Zippy brought yesterday, Mr. Rimington. I invited the other young man as well, Mr. Park, wasn't it? But he's leaving today."

"I won't be here." Zippy ate half of his toast in one bite. "I'm meeting a friend in Sidlingham."

Lady Holt frowned. "Why didn't you say so earlier? I could have arranged everything for tomorrow night. Who invited you for dinner?"

"Oh, it's not a dinner." Zippy popped the last of the toast into his mouth.

Lady Holt's forehead smoothed. "Oh, good. You can join us for dinner and slip out afterward." Lady Holt paused, repeated the names as she ticked them off on her fingers, then added, "And Don and Emily will be here as well."

Zippy saw my puzzled look. As he pushed back his chair, he said, "The solicitor and his wife."

"Oh, that reminds me." I laid my silverware across my plate and checked my wristwatch, then twisted in my chair. "Bower, could you have the Morris brought around?"

"I'll see to it."

"Off for a drive?" Zippy asked.

"Only to the village. I want to visit the solicitor during his shortened office hours. I tried yesterday but was too late." Taking the Morris would save me a bit of time, and I should make it before he closed his office. In case Lady Holt might want to sidetrack me, I added, "At Mr. Hightower's request."

Lady Holt said, "Don won't be in his office today. Emily promised to keep him home all day so he can rest for tonight."

"Oh." I was already striding across the room. I stopped. "Well, I suppose I can chat with him at dinner tonight." It wouldn't be ideal, but since I hadn't been able to run him to earth, I'd better take the opportunity this evening and speak with the solicitor then. I'd have to make sure Lady Holt wasn't nearby. It would be terrible manners to mix business with a social occasion.

A few minutes later, I nearly collided with Bower as I came out of the breakfast room. I hadn't realized he'd left the room earlier, but Bower had a tendency to drift along as silently as a ghost. "Pardon me, Miss Belgrave."

"It's my fault—" I broke off, noticing the man with light brown hair and a thin mustache trailing along behind Bower. "Inspector Longly. I wondered if it would be you."

"Miss Belgrave."

I remembered in the nick of time not to extend my right hand. Longly's right sleeve was empty and pinned against his jacket—a war injury. We shook hands left-handed, which felt awkward. It had to be difficult for him since the simple social interaction of shaking hands highlighted his injury. Longly said, "I read your name in the statements and wondered how long it would be before you popped up. I should have known you'd be front and center."

My sympathy melted away at the trace of weariness in his tone. "I'm only here by coincidence, Inspector."

Longly tilted his head side to side, disagreeing with my words. "More than that, I think. I'd say peripherally involved. I must remind you, Scotland Yard is always happy to hear any theories, Miss Belgrave. Just make sure they remain theories this time, shall we? No taking matters into your own hands."

I flushed. The cheek of the man, essentially telling me to mind my own business when he'd closed the case at Archly Manor only because I'd nudged things along. Before I could answer, Longly said to Bower, "Never mind about Miss Shires. If Miss Belgrave will give me a moment of her time, I'll speak to her first."

He'd phrased his sentence as a question, but that was only a formality. "Of course I have time to speak to you, Inspector Longly," I said tightly.

Bower said, "Very good. Lady Holt has said you may use the small sitting room." Bower escorted us into a room I hadn't been in before. It was on the west side of the house and shadowy in the morning. A busy old-fashioned wallpaper of birds and flowers covered the walls while mismatched furniture of different styles filled the room. Bower switched on several lamps.

Longly surveyed the room, which didn't contain a desk. His lips twitched to one side briefly, obviously not happy with Lady Holt. I was sure the choice of interview room was intentional—a subtle message to Longly that he wasn't welcome at Blackburn Hall. Longly picked up a Hepplewhite chair and moved it in front of the cold fireplace. He gestured for me to sit on the sofa. "Please have a seat," he said and sat in the chair.

As I sank into the sofa and crossed my arms over my chest, I considered asking Bower to have a fire lit. Even though it was summer, the dim room was chilly. But that would only prolong the time I spent with Longly, and I didn't want to do that. I'd rather shiver a bit and be out of here in a few moments.

Longly had positioned the chair so a side table was on his left. He placed his notebook and pen on the table and laid a folio across his lap. "Let's begin with what brings you to Blackburn Hall. You're working for Hightower Books now?"

I'd forgotten how thorough Longly was. His questions took me from my meeting with Mr. Hightower to the discovery of Mayhew's true identity. I squirmed a bit as I described entering Mayhew's cottage, but Longly seemed to take it in stride, noting down what I described but not asking any further questions about it. He was more interested in the discovery of Mayhew's body. By the time I described Serena's appearance on the path in front of me, my toes and fingers were cold.

I didn't keep anything back except Mr. Hightower's true reason for wanting to keep Mayhew's disappearance quiet. If Mr. Hightower wanted to share that his company was stretched a little thin, that was up to him. I shifted a little, burrowing back into the corner of the sofa in an effort to stay warm. "Have you been able to determine if Mayhew's death was an accident?"

"I can't comment on that. The results of the post mortem haven't been made public."

His cageyness made me think he was considering Mayhew's death suspicious. "Lady Holt won't be pleased."

He made eye contact without lifting his head, which was bent over his notebook. "Why do you say that?"

"Lady Holt wanted the Hadsworth police inspector to declare it an accident and forget the whole thing."

"Then I suppose Lady Holt will have to be unhappy."

A few seconds ticked by as Longly's pencil scratched over the paper. I pushed my hands down into the cushions, preparing to stand. "Would you like me to have Bower send in Serena?"

"Yes. If you remember anything else relevant, I'm putting up at The Crown in Hadsworth. One more thing, Miss Belgrave." He focused on his notes as he asked, "Your cousin, does she plan to join you here?"

"Violet? No, she's in France at the moment."

"No—I mean your other cousin, Gwen—er—Miss Stone."

Was that a flush creeping across Longly's cheekbones? Longly had seemed taken with Gwen at Archly Manor, but since Gwen hadn't mentioned him again, I'd assumed his brief interest had fizzled . . . but it seemed that wasn't the case. "Oh, *Gwen*. She's in France as well. Aunt Caroline thought a holiday would do them all good."

"Yes, I'm sure that's true."

"So, no, there are no plans for Gwen to visit Blackburn Hall," I said. "Next time I speak to her, I'll tell her you were asking after her."

"Don't do that." Longly ran a finger along one side of his collar. "I mean, no need. Don't go out of your way."

"All right. I won't mention it," I said.

Longly seemed both sad and relieved at the same time. I turned to the door, and Longly said, "One last thing."

I paused, my hand on the doorknob. "You already said that."

Longly cleared his throat. "Yes. Right. Well, this *is* my last question. Where did you put the envelopes?"

"Envelopes?"

"Come, Miss Belgrave," he said, his voice returning to its normal confident cadence. He tapped the folio. "You mentioned the envelopes in your statement to Colonel Shaw. You're here as a representative of Hightower Books. It would only make sense you'd gather up all of Mayhew's written material you could find so you could give it to Mr. Hightower. Although, I am surprised you'd be so sloppy as to mention it in your statement and think it would be overlooked."

"The envelopes in East Bank Cottage?"

"Yes. You stated that you saw them."

"I did. They were on the rug inside the front door. I left them there."

"I've just come from East Bank Cottage, and they're gone. I understand you'd want to retrieve them for Mr. Hightower, but breaking a window is going a little bit far, don't you think?"

Irritation shot through me. I didn't feel cold anymore. "I'd never break a window. I used the key on the window frame when I looked for Mayhew and replaced it when I left. That's in the statement too. If I wanted to get back into the cottage, why would I break a window? I'd use the key again."

"So—for the record—you don't have the envelopes?"

"No. Are they important?" I asked as my mind raced. Anna had said Mayhew had sent her a note when she left town. I couldn't remember her exact words, but I thought she'd said the note said to continue typing the next book. And Anna had been clacking away at the typewriter when I arrived at her house . . . that large stack of pages beside her typewriter. Surely it was too big to be notes from one of the meetings she occasionally typed for the WI?

She'd been jumpy when I told her Mayhew was dead. It would be disconcerting to learn a man you were working for had died several days earlier—and that the man was a woman. If Mayhew had sent her several chapters, and she'd been typing them up and dropping them off as she completed them, it would explain the pile of envelopes inside the cottage as well as her nervous reaction to the news Mayhew was dead.

Longly spoke, pulling me back to the present. "No idea."

"If you don't know if the envelopes are important, why accuse me of taking them?"

"To see your reaction. Don't worry. You passed with flying

colors, and I'm convinced you don't have them. They're a side issue, anyway."

"Then why are you concerned about them?"

"Loose ends, Miss Belgrave. I don't like them. In my experience, they can come back to haunt me."

CHAPTER TWELVE

*W*hen I left Longly, Bower intercepted me and said Lady Holt wanted to see me. I followed him to the morning room, where Lady Holt sat at a round table with stacks of papers spread in front of her across the polished wood surface.

"Oh, good. Miss Belgrave, I'd like your advice." Bower faded away as she indicated the chair beside her. "I've decided the etiquette guide is too short. It would benefit from the inclusion of at least three additional chapters. I'd like your opinion on which of these articles I've written would be the best to include."

"But your book is thorough as it is."

"It will be the definitive guide to proper behavior. I must explore every possible topic. What do you think of this one on etiquette for children?"

Lady Holt was not to be distracted. In her opinion, the book needed at least three more chapters, and she would find three more chapters to include. I sat down and took the article she held out.

She kept me busy as we discussed the positives and negatives of including various chapters. We took a short break for lunch, then returned to the task. It was after three o'clock before Lady Holt was pleased with the selection of new chapters, their content, and the arrangement of the chapters within the manuscript. I escaped after tea and went up to my room, saying I wanted to rest until dinner.

As I worked with Lady Holt, part of my mind had been on Longly's questions about the envelopes from Mayhew's cottage. It seemed to me that there were two likely candidates who'd taken the envelopes—Zippy and Anna. Why on earth Zippy would want them, I couldn't imagine. Could he have known Mayhew was writing crime fiction? It didn't seem likely, but I didn't know why he'd been around East Bank Cottage so much that Lady Holt had become aware of it.

And he'd been creeping about last night on the path that ran from the cottage to Blackburn Hall. I hadn't seen more than Zippy's back as he entered his room last night, and he could have been carrying the envelopes. Anna seemed a much more likely candidate to have taken the envelopes, and I would have liked to ask her about it, but it was too close to dinner for me to go into the village.

I did have some time before I needed to dress for dinner. I learned from Bower that Zippy was still on the golf course. I checked the time as I went back upstairs. Zippy was cutting it fine. Lady Holt wouldn't be happy if he was late for dinner.

I paused at the door to my room. The house was in its predinner lull and extremely quiet. No servants hurried along the hallways, Zippy and Lord Holt were out, and Serena and Lady Holt were occupied in other parts of the house. If I took a quick peek in Zippy's room, would I see the envelopes? I wrestled with my conscience for a few seconds, then let my curiosity override the sensible voice in my head.

I padded down the hall to Zippy's room. The door handle turned easily, and I stepped inside. Closing the door quietly, I stood with my back to it, my hand still gripping the handle as if I wasn't totally committed if I didn't let go. No stack of discarded envelopes sat in the open on the writing desk or in a chair. Blast. It was the height of bad manners—not to mention impropriety—to be in Zippy's room, but since I'd come this far, I might as well finish the job.

I released the door handle and scurried around the room, checking under the bed and—after a deep breath to steady my nerves—in the wardrobe and the bureau drawers. The writing desk contained only blank paper, a few pencils, and a couple of programs from London plays. I dragged a chair over to the wardrobe, stood on my tiptoes, and patted around the top, but there was nothing there either, not even a speck of dust. I had to admire the housekeeping standard Lady Holt set, and I carefully replaced the chair so its legs rested exactly in the grooves it had left in the rug. I went back to the door and checked the hall. It was empty, so I dashed to my room and closed the door, my heart thudding.

I blew out a long breath. I wasn't sure if that had been a waste of time or not. With a whole house at his disposal, Zippy could have put the envelopes anywhere. His room was probably the least likely place for them, but I now knew they weren't there. I still had time before I needed to dress for dinner, but I didn't want to go back downstairs in case Lady Holt drafted me to work on the manuscript again.

The thought of Lady Holt's manuscript brought to mind Mayhew's last book. I hadn't finished it yet, and I only had a short time to finish reading it before Mr. Busby arrived. I'd have to hand it off to him then, and I really did want to know "whodunit."

I felt edgy with nervous energy and wasn't sure I could settle down and read, but within a few moments, I was engrossed in the story. I didn't move until I read the words *The End*. The book concluded with a satisfying wrap-up that included an explanation of the crime, the apprehension of the guilty party, and a hint Lady Eileen might have more than friendly feelings for her chauffeur.

But a stack—a thick stack—of manuscript pages remained after the page with *The End* typed at the bottom. Perhaps the book had a lengthy epilogue? I didn't remember an epilogue in Mayhew's other book, but I supposed he didn't have to do the same thing in each one.

The next section wasn't an epilogue. It was headed with the title *Chapter Thirty,* but I'd just read Chapter Thirty. I recognized the opening lines. It was the same chapter, but scribbles and annotations in two different sets of handwriting covered the page. One was looped and curving. The other was more angular, and the letters were written closer together. Anna must have accidentally included a section of an earlier draft with the final manuscript.

I skimmed over the handwritten notes. It was a fascinating look at how the chapter had been written. Who had Mayhew worked with to bring the chapter from its rough early form to its final polished prose? Mr. Hightower couldn't be the editor. He was anxious to get the manuscript and read it.

As I skimmed the handwritten notes, a pattern emerged after a few pages. The person who wrote with the more angular scrawl that was harder to read tended to write in complete sentences and ask questions. At one point, a note said *Is it too soon to reveal the pipe was a red herring?*

The person who wrote with the curving handwriting in large loops answered the questions with short sentences or phrases, such as *This is good,* or *blue eyes, not brown.*

I flipped to the final page of the draft. Under the last line of the typed text, the person who wrote with the angular scribble had penned a short note.

The next book is coming along. I have Lady Eileen going on a journey to the South of France to spend time on a friend's yacht where someone will be pushed overboard (of course!). What do you think? Will Hightower like that idea? I've written the first three chapters.

The answering note was written in the looping handwriting.

Well done, Anna. Hightower will be pleased with this one. It's come together really well. Just type up a clean version, and I'll send it off. As far as the next book, a mystery set on a yacht sounds perfect. I'm sure Hightower will like it. I'll mention it in my next letter to him.

I dropped the pages into my lap and pressed my fingers to my temples. Anna was so much more than a typist. She was Mayhew's ghostwriter.

CHAPTER THIRTEEN

The dull boom of the dressing gong pulsed through the air, and I jumped up from the chair, scattering manuscript pages across the carpet. I'd been so involved in the story and then in reading through the handwritten notes in the draft that I hadn't realized how much time had passed. I gathered up the manuscript pages and returned them to the box, but I kept the draft pages separate.

Mr. Busby had probably arrived while I was reading the manuscript. It was too late to deliver it to him before dinner, and it wouldn't be appropriate to hand it off to him in the drawing room. I'd have to give it to him either after dinner or tomorrow.

I rubbed my forehead. What should I do with the draft pages with the handwriting? Should I return them to Anna . . . or give them to Longly? If Mayhew's death was suspicious, did being Mayhew's ghostwriter give Anna a motive to want her dead?

A tap sounded on the door and the maid, Janet, entered to help me dress for dinner. I shoved the draft pages in the drawer of the writing desk under the manuscript box and turned to tell Janet which dress I wanted to wear that evening.

I was glad I hadn't worn my best dress yet. It made the choice of what to wear simple, and I could mull over what I'd learned about Anna and Mayhew while I went through the motions of preparing for dinner. Janet wasn't one to chatter, and her reticence let me think while I changed. The royal-blue silk gown, another of Gwen's hand-me-downs, whispered over my shoulders and settled around my legs with a ripple. The beads that fringed the zigzag hem quivered as I moved.

I was confident now that my guess about Anna taking the envelopes was spot-on. I'd maneuver her away from everyone else and have a chat tonight. Janet handed me Mum's rope of pearls. I draped them around my neck, smoothed my gloves over my elbows, and went down to dinner.

I entered the drawing room, and Jasper came across to me, a drink in his hand. "You look smashing."

"Thank you. You look as dapper as always." I didn't recognize the drink, which was a pale yellow. "What's this?"

"A concoction of Zippy's. He calls it the *Three O'Clock in the Morning*."

"He should know all about that."

Jasper frowned. "Meaning?"

"Zippy wasn't feeling well and missed dinner last night, but I saw him return to his room—fully dressed—at three in the morning." If I was right and Anna had taken the envelopes from the cottage, then where was Zippy returning from at that hour?

Jasper sipped his drink. "And what were you doing awake at that hour?"

"I wasn't awake. Zippy's whistling woke me. I had been reading but not that late." I tilted my glass. "This is actually quite good—sweet with a kick of citrus."

"So you're enjoying the lurid detective fiction I gave you?"

"I haven't gotten to the book you gave me yet. But I am enjoying the genre."

"I'm intrigued. Were you perusing Mayhew's last manuscript?"

"I really shouldn't say."

"So you *were*. How is Lady Eileen? And has that Nick chap worked up the courage to jump the social barriers and propose?"

"You'll have to read it yourself. What do you think about Mayhew's books?"

"I enjoy them. Always a good mystery. The first books were a little serious for my taste, but they've lightened up considerably as the series has progressed. I prefer a touch of humor with my murder."

His words resonated. I jabbed my glass at him. "That's it."

Jasper stepped back. "Glad you agree, connoisseur that you are."

I gave him my most disapproving look, the one I used with young men who tried to misbehave with me in taxis. "No need to jump like that. I have better manners than to slosh my drink onto your evening clothes. You reminded me of something." Jasper had described what bothered me about the difference between Mayhew's first book and the latest manuscript—the tone.

Murder on the Ninth Green was madcap and fun, while the first book had a more somber mood. I knew from the hand-written notes on the draft pages that Anna had written *Murder on the Ninth Green*. It definitely had a lighter tone. Jasper had noticed the more recent books had a similar tone. Did that mean Anna had been ghostwriting for Mayhew for several books?

I scanned the room for Anna, but she and Dr. Finch hadn't arrived yet. I wanted to speak to her before I told Jasper what I'd learned about Anna writing Mayhew's books.

Lady Holt joined us. "Olive, let me introduce you to our

guests." Jasper saluted me with his glass and moved off to talk with Zippy as I followed Lady Holt. She stopped beside Colonel Shaw. A plump woman with a feathered clip in her faded brown hair stood at his elbow, fanning her face. Her dress was pale pink, the same shade as her flushed cheeks. She closed the fan as Lady Holt began the introduction. "Colonel and Mrs. Shaw, this is Olive Belgrave, one of our guests from Hightower Books."

"How do you do?" I said to Mrs. Shaw and waited a beat for Colonel Shaw to mention I'd met him earlier, but he only smiled and said, "Pleasure." I was relieved I didn't have to explain to Lady Holt why I'd been chatting with the Chief Constable.

Mrs. Shaw opened her fan. "What do you do for the publishing company, Miss Belgrave?"

"Yes, what is it that you do?" The second question came from a deeper voice at my shoulder.

Lady Holt and I both stepped back, and Leland Busby entered our circle. I'd seen him across Mr. Hightower's office, but now that I was closer, I realized he wasn't as young as I'd thought. His dark hair, which fell across his forehead, had a few threads of gray at the temples, and a couple of wrinkles radiated from the corners of his eyes. He removed a cigarette from his lips. A smile played at the corner of his mouth as his gaze swept around the circle. He was only a few inches taller than me and had a spare build, which reminded me of a jockey. He angled his arm to one side, and the cigarette smoke curled up over his back as he lowered his voice. "Miss Belgrave is such a new employee that even *I* haven't met her."

Lady Holt's eyebrows shot up. "Surely that's not true."

He drew on the cigarette. "Yes, it is, my lady," Mr. Busby said and looked to me as if to say *talk your way out of this one.* He exhaled, and I stepped back.

Irritation simmered inside me, but I smiled at Mr. Busby. If he thought I'd slink off after a few challenging words, he was mistaken. "So nice to meet you, Mr. Busby." I used what my cousin Gwen would call the "lady of the manor" voice.

Clearly, Mr. Busby wasn't pleased Mr. Hightower had hired me and sent me to Blackburn Hall. Whether Mr. Busby was irritated because the decision had been made without his input or whether he thought he should have been the one to visit Blackburn Hall, I had no idea, but I wasn't about to stoop to his childish behavior.

I shifted my attention to Lady Holt. "Mr. Hightower brought me on at Hightower Books specifically to work with you, Lady Holt. He felt the situation needed a special touch, not"—I glanced at Mr. Busby—"the normal run-of-the-mill handling."

Lady Holt nodded and looked satisfied. "Very appropriate to send a lady to speak with me."

Mr. Busby excused himself to refresh his drink, leaving a puff of smoke hanging in the air. As he turned away, he murmured under his breath so that only I could hear, "Round one to you."

Beside me, Mrs. Shaw swished her fan back and forth so quickly it blurred, dispersing the smoke. Wisps of her hair fluttered around her pink face.

"Are you all right?" I asked.

Mrs. Shaw shook her head, drew in a labored breath, and patted Colonel Shaw on the arm. "Rodney, my—cigarettes." Her words came out in a wheeze.

"Oh dear," Lady Holt said. "Victoria, are you having one of your spells again?"

Mrs. Shaw nodded and whipped the fan faster.

"Asthma?" I asked.

"Yes." Colonel Shaw patted his pockets. "I don't have your cigarettes," he said to his wife. "Must have left the case in my other jacket."

Lady Holt said, "I'll send someone for them. Your house

isn't far. It won't take long, Victoria. Dr. Finch should be here any moment. Do you need to sit down?"

"Asthma cigarettes?" I thought of the box Essie had pushed on me. Had I taken them out of my handbag? No, I didn't think so. And I'd brought that bag with me to Blackburn Hall. "I think I have some. Upstairs in my room."

Colonel Shaw, who had taken Mrs. Shaw's arm, supported her to a chair. "We'll have something for you in a moment, dear."

Lady Holt motioned that I should speak to Bower, who nodded to a footman. I said to the footman, "In my handbag. I left it on the bureau in my room." I turned back to Mrs. Shaw. "A friend gave them to me. I have asthma too."

Mrs. Shaw fought to pull in another breath of air. "Not if —you—need them."

"Oh, no. I don't. I mean, I still do have attacks occasionally, but I don't use cigarettes. My friend didn't realize, and she insisted I take them."

Colonel Shaw, who had been checking his pockets, stopped his frantic patting and digging. "Wait. Here's one." He drew out a single cigarette from his breast pocket. He handed it to Mrs. Shaw. "It must have fallen out of the case and my man overlooked it," he said to me.

Jasper had crossed the room to us, and he flicked open a lighter for Mrs. Shaw. She drew on the cigarette, pulling the fumes into her lungs, waited a moment, then expelled the smoke, her shoulders relaxing. She drew in a strangled breath. "That's . . . better."

"She'll be fine now," Colonel Shaw announced.

"It's so embarrassing," Mrs. Shaw said between puffs on the cigarette. "I'm sorry to spoil your lovely evening, Maria."

"Nonsense," Lady Holt said. "Nothing is spoiled. The evening hasn't even started. Just rest there until you feel more the thing."

The footman returned with the cardboard box of asthma

cigarettes and handed them to me. I offered them to Mrs. Shaw, but she waved them off. "Thank you, but I'm fine now. I find one cigarette takes care of it." Her breathing was much easier, and she didn't look so flushed.

I put the package on the lace-edged runner that covered the table behind the sofa. "I'll leave them here for you in case you change your mind."

"That's thoughtful. Thank you."

"We'll leave you to rest a moment, Victoria," Lady Holt said and drew me away. "I believe you've met everyone except our solicitor. He and his wife arrived during Mrs. Shaw's episode." Lady Holt guided me toward an older man with a beefy physique, grizzled hair, and a waxy skin tone. A woman stood slightly behind his shoulder. She was at least two decades younger and had raven black hair and light green eyes. She glanced at the man's face several times as Lady Holt and I crossed the room to join them.

Lady Holt said, "Don and Emily, let me introduce you to Miss Olive Belgrave. Miss Belgrave, this is Mr. Donald Pearce and his wife, Emily. We were delighted when they moved to Hadsworth recently . . ."

Lady Holt's voice droned on, but the only thing I heard was the name Donald Pearce. It echoed around in my head. *Donald Pearce.* Could it be the same Donald Pearce? How many solicitors named Donald Pearce could there be?

A rush of cold numbness and then hot fury came over me, just as it had a year ago.

Lady Holt's voice faded completely, and I was back in Father's study, still reeling from the shock of learning Father had married his nurse, when I realized something else was wrong too. Father had been evasive when I'd talked about returning to the university in America to continue my education, but when I'd mentioned I'd looked into the cost of purchasing passage back to America, I'd caught the significant look Sonia gave Father.

Like a little boy called to the headmaster's office, he'd led me to his study and closed the door. The shelves of books went from floor to ceiling, the gold-tooled spines shining even in the dull twilight. I perched on the arm of the chair by the fire, where I'd spent many an afternoon reading while Father worked at his desk.

He sat heavily in the chair behind his desk, then removed his spectacles and rubbed his eyes. "I'm sorry, Olive. There's no easy way to say this, so I'll come right out with it. I followed some bad advice. I can see that now, but at the time it seemed completely safe. Pearce assured me everyone who'd invested had received double, sometimes triple, their money. But that's not what happened." He carefully arranged the arms of his spectacles.

"What are you saying—that you're done in?" I glanced at the bookshelves and hoped he didn't have to sell any of his rare books. It would break his heart.

"No, thank goodness. I didn't put in the principal from my inheritance. That would have been . . . awful. No, it's not as bad as all that, but it's—I'm afraid your trust is gone. Completely wiped out."

CHAPTER FOURTEEN

*L*ady Holt's voice brought me back to the drawing room. ". . . glad you've recovered from your spill, Don. Oh, excuse me. I must have a word with Serena . . ."

I reached out to steady myself, pressing my free hand against the back of a chair. "Mr. Pearce, formerly of Mercer, Blackthorne, and Thompkins?" I asked.

The width of Pearce's smile decreased several degrees. Beside him, a hiss sounded as his wife sucked in a sharp breath. Pearce asked, "Have we met?"

"No, but not for want of trying on my part. You're acquainted with my father, Cecil Belgrave." My tone was even, but my chest rose and fell, and my heart pounded. "In fact, you gave him some ghastly financial advice."

Mrs. Pearce's hands fluttered up to her hair and then to her pearl choker. Mr. Pearce's smile became fixed. "I suppose you're referring to the Hartman incident. Unfortunate business, that. Lost quite a bit of money in it myself, so your family has my sympathies. Most regrettable."

Pearce looked over my shoulder. "Emily's parched. We must get a cocktail. Pleasure to meet you." He moved away, his wife trailing after him. He looked back at her, and his steps checked. When she came even with him, he put his hand at the small of her back and propelled her forward with a little push.

Jasper appeared in front of me. "You look as if you could use a fresh drink." He removed my cocktail glass from my hand and replaced it with another.

The cool of the glass pressed against my hot palm. "That man is a charlatan. I can't believe he's moving about in society as if nothing happened. He convinced Father to invest all of my trust in some shady operation."

"Ah, so that's why you look like the illustration out of one of my schoolbooks, *Avenging Fury*, plate number five."

I gulped the new cocktail. It had a sour edge to it, and I winced. Across the room, Pearce said something to Dr. Finch and everyone in their group laughed.

"Careful, you'll scorch the furniture if you continue to glower at him," Jasper said.

"I looked for him—Pearce, I mean," I said. "After Father told me the trust was gone. I wanted to speak to Mr. Pearce, but he'd suddenly retired. I know he left his firm in disgrace. No one said as much outright, but I heard rumors Pearce got a kickback for every investment he procured for Hartman's laughable 'investment.' Nothing was ever proven, but the fact he disappeared from town and hid himself away in a small rural village speaks for itself."

Jasper touched the back of my hand, where I still gripped the chair. "I'm sorry, old thing."

I'd been staring at the back of Pearce's head as I spoke, but now I looked at Jasper. The sympathy of his gaze quenched some of the fury radiating through me. I turned my hand under his and gave his fingers a quick squeeze, then removed my hand and squared my shoulders. "If Pearce thinks I'll drop it, he's sadly mistaken."

"What will you do?"

"I'd like to wring his neck." I tilted my drink up, finishing it off. "But that would be unladylike."

"In the extreme. I'm sure Lady Holt has a chapter on it in her etiquette guide." He glanced at the empty glass in my hand. "Would you like another? I'll bring you one more, but then I'm cutting you off."

"Yes, I could use one more. I think it's going to be a long evening. I must plot my revenge on Mr. Pearce. It's unbelievable he's gotten away scot-free."

Jasper took my glass. "Until now. I'm sure you'll see he gets his comeuppance."

As Jasper departed with my glass, Anna left her father's side and joined me. "Good evening, Miss Belgrave. I'm so glad you're here." She glanced around the room and then looked back at me. "I have something I must ask you."

I stared at her, my mind so filled with the encounter with Pearce that it had blanked everything else out. What was it I'd wanted to talk to her about? Oh, yes. The manuscript draft pages. I wrenched my thoughts away from Pearce and focused on Anna. "I wanted to speak to you too."

Jasper arrived, said, "Excuse me, ladies," and deposited my fresh drink. "I can see you're having a good gossip, so I won't intrude."

Anna watched Jasper as he moved across the room. Mrs. Shaw said something to him, and he sat down near her. Anna turned back to me. "It's about my dad." She drew me a few paces away to a pair of chairs in a far corner of the room. "The postmortem on Mayhew is back."

"I didn't realize your father was doing it."

Anna shook her head. "He didn't, but the police surgeon is a friend. He stopped by to visit Dad this afternoon." Her gaze went to Dr. Finch, who stood across the room. "They were in the garden, and I was in the drawing room. With the windows open, their voices carried. Once I heard . . . well, I couldn't leave when I realized what they were talking about." She fiddled with the beaded clip holding back her auburn hair. "And then the detective inspector arrived—oh, it's all so complicated. I don't know what to do. I heard about what happened at Archly Manor, how you proved your relative wasn't involved in that—er—incident." Her cold fingers clamped on my wrist. "I need you to do the same for Dad. If this gets out—if there are rumors—it will devastate him. His reputation—" She let go of my wrist and pressed her fingers to her lips for a moment as she fought to control her emotions. "A doctor's reputation is everything. You must see that. He didn't kill Mayhew. I *know* he didn't."

I choked on my drink. "Inspector Longly accused him of killing Mayhew?"

"No, nothing so straightforward. It was all hints and questions and subtle accusations." Her gaze darted around the room. "Please don't mention this to anyone."

"I won't, I promise."

"It's just so distressing. Dad's putting up a good front tonight, but he's been walking around shell-shocked since Inspector Longly left."

Longly must have some new information that had led him to question Dr. Finch in that way. "What were the findings of the postmortem?"

"Inconclusive. There was a blow to the head, but the police surgeon couldn't say definitively when it happened. It could have occurred before Mayhew fell or during the fall. The riverbed is rocky. But since they can't rule out foul play, it makes the death suspicious. You see that, don't you?"

"Yes, Inspector Longly will have to continue to investigate. But what does it have to do with your father?"

"They found a handwritten will in Mayhew's cottage. Dad is the only beneficiary."

"Oh my."

"I knew you'd understand." Her gaze whipped to Dr. Finch again, then back to me as she lowered her voice even more. "But no matter what Inspector Longly hinted at, even if Dad had known he was the beneficiary—which he didn't— he'd never do *anything* to hurt anyone. It goes against everything he stands for—his whole nature."

"Did your father know about the will?"

"No." Her short hair brushed against her cheeks as she shook her head. "I'm sure he didn't. Dad was so shocked, he couldn't speak for a few moments."

"I wonder why Mayhew made your father her beneficiary."

"Longly read part of the will to Dad. Mayhew was grateful Dad had kept his—I mean, *her*—true identity secret."

"The will was handwritten, you said?" I gazed across the room. Mr. and Mrs. Pearce were chatting with Lord and Lady Holt. "Why didn't Mayhew have Mr. Pearce draw up the will?"

Anna shifted so that her back was to the room. "Between you and me, I don't think Mr. Pearce is actually that . . . trustworthy. Maybe Mayhew didn't have complete faith in Mr. Pearce. There've been a few rumors about Mr. Pearce—that he left town in disgrace and *had* to come here. I hate to speak ill of someone without any basis, but that's what the whispers about him have been."

"You don't have to apologize to me. I have the same feeling about him."

"You do?"

"Yes, but I'll tell you about that later." So Mayhew had trusted Pearce to send off her manuscripts to Hightower Books but not to make a will.

"But you see where this leaves Dad, don't you?" Anna gulped her cocktail. "It's all a terrible muddle. How do you prove a negative? There's no way to show Dad *didn't* know about the will."

"Then I suppose the best thing for your father to do is prove he wasn't around when Mayhew died. Did the postmortem give a time of death?"

"Nothing very specific—between five and seven days ago."

"But we know that Serena saw Mayhew on . . . let's see . . . she said it was Wednesday morning. She saw her on the path, only a short distance away from where her body was found." And the servants had said Mayhew hadn't been seen in the village. "Mayhew must have died shortly after Serena saw her. That timing fits with the time of death estimate. I bet Longly will focus his attention on Wednesday morning. I think your father should document where he was that morning."

"I suppose that's the best course. And it should be possible . . . I think." She stared into her empty glass for a moment, her gaze unfocused. "Yes, he had to go out to Birchwick Farm, and I drove him. Mrs. Birchwick went into labor. We were gone all morning. It's a good distance away." Anna's head jerked up. "I'm sorry. I've been terribly rude. What was it you wanted to talk to me about?"

I'd debated whether or not I should mention the extra manuscript pages. Anna's role as a ghostwriter was obviously a secret. Even Mr. Hightower didn't know about it because surely he'd have gone in search of Anna if he'd known she existed. But now with the news about the postmortem being inconclusive and Dr. Finch being a beneficiary to Mayhew's will, I couldn't gloss over Anna's ghostwriting. I didn't see how I could ease into the topic, so I went for the straightforward approach. "How long have you been ghostwriting books for Mayhew?"

Anna was reaching to set down her glass. It clattered onto

the table. "What?" She steadied the rocking glass. "I—don't know—what you mean."

"Anna, you gave me several pages of a draft manuscript along with the finished manuscript. The draft was marked up with notes between you and Mayhew. Your notes even discussed the next book. The one about Lady Eileen going to visit her friend on the yacht."

Her pale skin went lighter, causing her freckles to stand out. Anna leaned onto the arm of her chair. "I can't believe I was so stupid." She fisted one hand together in her lap. "But I was in such a rush."

I sat down beside her. "You were Mayhew's ghostwriter." I said it as a statement, not a question.

Anna nodded, then glanced around, seeming to remember we were in a room full of people.

"No one's listening," I said. "Was *Murder on the Ninth Green* the first book you wrote for her?"

She drew in a deep breath and relaxed her hand. "The second."

"Oh my. How did it happen?"

"I did begin as a typist for him. I suppose he'd heard—I mean 'she.' I've thought of Mayhew as a man for so long, it's hard to switch my brain over to the other pronoun." She shifted so that she was facing me. "I suppose Mayhew had heard somehow that I did typing. One day about . . . let's see, it would have been about two years ago, I received a note from—um—*her* asking if I would type her completed manuscript. I said of course I would. I was happy to have the work. She sent me the handwritten chapters, and I typed them up. At first, she sent a chapter every few days, but then the interval between the chapters got longer and longer. Finally, she sent a note saying she was stuck, and she'd send some material when she had something."

Anna touched the clip in her hair, her fingers tracing nervously over the beads on it. "I had an idea that might work. I'd been typing up the story. I knew the characters and the scene where Mayhew was stuck. I sent her a note with a suggestion. She liked it and used it. She sent me the next chapter."

Anna locked her fingers together in a tight clasp in her lap. "After that, we sent notes back and forth discussing what would happen. Then she hit another rough patch with the story. She said in one of her notes that I should give it a try. I didn't know if she was serious or not, but I decided I'd do it. I typed up the scene and sent it off to her. Mayhew sent it back and said it was wonderful. From that point, my input gradually grew until I was writing the stories, and she was editing them. Mayhew was quite sick of Lady Eileen."

"After only a few books?"

Anna shrugged. "I don't know why. I think Mayhew wanted to write another story that wasn't a mystery, but Hightower Books wasn't interested in that." The tension in Anna's shoulders eased, and she leaned back against the cushion. "Oh, you don't know how good it feels to speak about this. Keeping it all inside has been horrid." Her face fell. "Of course, it only makes a complicated situation even worse. If Longly knew . . ."

"Then both you and your father would have a motive to want Mayhew gone."

Her gaze flew up to my face. "What do you mean?"

"You're the only person in Hadsworth who knew Mayhew was actually the author R.W. May. What if you killed her, so you could continue writing the series?"

"But how could I continue the series?" Her eyes widened, and she shook her head. "I don't have contacts at Hightower Books."

"With the system Mayhew had set up of sending the manuscripts through Pearce, you wouldn't need to know anyone at Hightower Books. What's to keep you from writing the books, then sending them through Pearce? No one at

Hightower Books would know the manuscripts weren't actually coming from Mayhew."

Anna drew away from me as if I had a contagious disease. "But that's absurd. But that's—I'd never—" She swallowed, then drew in an unsteady breath. "I didn't even know Mayhew was dead."

She was so agitated, I patted her hand. "I'm just saying what Inspector Longly will think, you know." I kept my voice matter-of-fact as I said, "You did know about Mayhew sending the manuscripts to Hightower Books, didn't you?" I went on in the same soothing tone. "When we talked at dinner last time, you said you'd dropped something at the solicitor for Mayhew, but then hesitated when you were about to mention what it was that you had given to Mr. Pearce. It was a manuscript, wasn't it?"

Anna's cheeks went rosy. "This is why I'm terrible at cards. I can't bluff at all. Yes, Mayhew had me take the previous manuscript. We were down to the deadline. She wrote me a note, asking me to type up the last chapter, then bundle up the whole thing and drop it off with Mr. Pearce. Mayhew's note said Pearce would see it got to Hightower Books. I thought it was a bit strange, but Mayhew was an odd fish, so I didn't dwell on it too much." Her words sped up, and she leaned forward. "I didn't have anything to do with Mayhew's death."

"Of course you didn't," I said, but in reality, I had no idea whether or not that was true. I could see why Longly had spoken to Dr. Finch. Much of Mayhew's life intersected with the doctor and his daughter. But one couldn't come out and say something like that to an acquaintance. Fortunately, I'd had years of practice in schooling my expression so it didn't show my true feelings. More often than not, I'd used the skill to mask boredom when some old codger droned on at dinner about hunting or long-ago military exploits. I'd rarely used it to keep questions about murder from showing in my face.

Anna looked so anxious, I shifted the conversation. "What did the note Mayhew sent you say, exactly?"

At my conversational tone, Anna eased back into a more normal posture but still kept her distance from me as if she wasn't sure she trusted me. "Which note?"

"The one saying Mayhew was leaving Hadsworth."

"It said she was leaving and to carry on with the next book until she returned."

"Was it handwritten?"

"No, typed."

"Was that normal? Did Mayhew type her notes to you?"

"No. They were usually handwritten at the end of the manuscript drafts." She swallowed. "Oh, I see. You're saying it's more evidence that could be used to show Mayhew was murdered. A typed note instead of a handwritten note. That's good, isn't it? It shows someone else made it look as if Mayhew would be coming back."

Bower announced dinner, interrupting us. "It could be," I said as Anna and I stood. "Let's talk after dinner. Do you still have the note?"

"I suppose so. I usually put everything in the folio. I have one for each book. It should be there. I'll look when I get home."

We moved toward the drawing room door, but before we merged with the other dinner guests, Anna said, "No one else knows—about what I really did for Mayhew. You can't tell anyone else. Not now. It would make things even worse." She'd kept her voice low, but panic edged her words.

"No, I won't," I said, promising myself I would find some way to check if she and her father really were at Birchwick Farm last Wednesday morning. Perhaps one of the servants here knew of it. I could ask Janet or Bower how far away the farm was and about the birth of the baby—well, I could ask Janet. I couldn't picture Bower chatting about the birth of a baby. But a new infant would surely be circulating as village news.

If Dr. Finch and Anna weren't at the farm—well, lies voided a promise to keep a secret, especially since Mayhew's death might be due to foul play. But I couldn't give away Anna and her father, not after experiencing first-hand the awfulness of having people suspect you and your loved ones of murder.

As we went in to dinner, I wondered how many type-writers there were in Hadsworth and who had access to them.

CHAPTER FIFTEEN

J wasn't aware of what was served for dinner that evening. My mind was too full of the encounter with Pearce and the fact that Anna was Mayhew's ghostwriter. Thankfully, I was seated next to Lord Holt, who provided a running monologue of his most recent golf games. I only had to murmur an occasional "I see," or "How interesting." When we turned, Jasper was on my other side, and he seemed to sense that I couldn't handle anything more than light conversation. He kept a surface discussion rolling about our acquaintances in London and his time on the golf course.

I spent most of the evening watching Pearce, who was seated at the other end of the table beside Lady Holt. Pearce, relaxed and smiling, told several stories that caused Lady Holt to laugh. Across the table from him, his wife maintained a quiet conversation with Mr. Busby, and then later with Colonel Shaw, but her gaze continually darted back to her husband.

When Lady Holt rose and led the ladies into the drawing room, I found myself beside Mrs. Shaw, who struck up a conversation about travel. I wanted to speak to Anna, but Mrs. Shaw launched into a complicated story about her and the colonel's time in India, their bungalow, and its resident ghost. "She liked to rearrange the table service," Mrs. Shaw said, "which was a bit difficult when one had guests, but one couldn't blame the poor woman. Her husband *had* stabbed her with a dinner knife. It would rather make one want to throw the silver on the floor."

Dr. Finch came into the room and made his excuses to Lady Holt. "I've had a telephone call and must leave."

Anna, who had been talking with Serena, moved to his side. "I'll come with you."

Lady Holt said, "There's no need for you to leave as well, Anna. We can have the chauffeur bring the motor around and run you home later."

"I'd better go with Dad."

"No, stay," said Dr. Finch. "Enjoy yourself."

Anna arranged her shawl more securely around her shoulders. "You left your glasses at home on the table by the door. You know you're better off with me driving. Your distance vision is terrible at night."

Dr. Finch didn't argue. Within a few moments, his motor had been called for, and he and Anna departed. After they left, a servant entered and placed a coffee pot on a table at the back of the room, where cups, cream, and sugar were arranged.

"Oh, here's the coffee." Mrs. Shaw scooted forward on the sofa cushion. "I believe I'll have some."

"Let me." I stood. "How do you take it?"

"So kind of you. A dash of cream."

I crossed the room, then paused at the edge of the table behind Mrs. Pearce. She poured herself half a cup of coffee, added a heavy dollop of cream, then ducked her head as she stepped out of my way.

Dr. Finch's departure must have led the men to cut short their time alone in the dining room because they appeared in the drawing room as I poured coffee for Mrs. Shaw and me.

Pearce stepped up to the table as I set down the coffee pot and added cream to Mrs. Shaw's cup.

Pearce picked up the coffee pot. "It was a lovely dinner tonight, wasn't it?"

Anger set my heart racing and my hands trembling. The teaspoon jangled against the china saucer. "Don't think you can smooth over what happened and pretend to be a genial country solicitor."

Pearce moved smoothly, reaching to replace the coffee. "I can see you have an animosity toward me, Miss Belgrave, but I assure you, I did nothing wrong. You'd be better off channeling your anger into something else. The incident was investigated, and I was found to be blameless."

"On the contrary, you were investigated, but there wasn't sufficient *evidence* to prove your guilt. That's why you were allowed to leave London and take up your law practice in this quaint village."

Pearce picked up his coffee and gave me what appeared to be a pleasant smile, but it didn't stretch to his gray eyes, which were the color of sheet metal. "Don't make trouble. You'll regret it, I promise you."

He ambled away. I turned and caught Mrs. Pearce's worried gaze fixed on him from across the room. Once Pearce took a seat beside Mr. Busby, Mrs. Pearce's attention skipped back to me. She studied me, a wrinkle between her eyebrows. Emily Pearce must be one of those sensitive souls who were attuned to atmosphere and could pick up the smallest vibrations of displeasure. I took a second to compose my face into careful social blankness, then I picked up the two cups of coffee.

I returned to the sofa and handed Mrs. Shaw her coffee. "I've heard in India, everyone retreated to the mountains in the summer."

Mrs. Shaw sipped her coffee. "Perfect. Thank you. Yes, anyone who could escape to the mountains did so in the summer. It was lovely and cool, and there was the most beautiful lake . . ."

Mrs. Shaw was happy to chat about India, recounting her memories, which allowed me time to calm down. Even though I'd put on my outward social veneer, my heart pounded and my hands quivered, causing my cup to clink in the saucer. How dare Pearce tell me to forget everything? He'd turned my world upside down. I couldn't just forget it, but now was not the right moment to dwell on that.

I forced my thoughts away from Pearce. Lady Holt suggested bridge, and despite my best attempts to avoid it, I found myself at a table with Mr. and Mrs. Pearce. Lady Holt was determined that we should play cards. Zippy attempted to make his excuses and fade out the door, but Lady Holt said, "Nonsense. You have time for bridge. Your friend will wait," and steered him to her table.

Mrs. Shaw said she'd sit out because the numbers were uneven, and Lord Holt quickly motioned for Mr. Busby to have a seat at the card table with Lady Holt. "Guests must have priority," Lord Holt said and retreated to the drinks cabinet.

At least I was partnered with Jasper. Pearce pointed out several mistakes to Mrs. Pearce, who murmured, "Yes, of course, I should have done that," in the same tones one would use to ask for the butter to be passed down the table. Jasper wasn't a competitive sort, but he was a good player and we won most of the tricks.

While I was shuffling the cards, Mr. Pearce shoved back his chair. "More coffee, my dear?" he asked Mrs. Pearce.

She didn't look up from the score sheet. "Um—yes, thank you," she said in a distracted way.

Pearce stalked away, carrying Mrs. Pearce's cup. His own coffee cup was half-full, and he left it on the table. I thought he probably wanted to walk off his frustration with his partner. He returned, set down Mrs. Pearce's half-full cup of buff-colored coffee with a thump, then jerked his chair into place.

Near the end of the next hand, the pace of play slowed. It was Pearce's turn. I'd been concentrating on the cards, and I looked up to see what was taking Pearce so long. His face was flushed as he studied his cards, blinking several times. He pulled at his collar, then turned to a servant who was clearing the coffee. "Bring me a glass of water."

The servant departed, and Pearce turned back to the table. "Warm tonight."

The temperature of the room seemed fine to me, but I had my back to the open French doors, and a cool breeze wafted across the nape of my neck. When the water arrived, Pearce drank it in a few gulps. Play continued for a few minutes, then Pearce slapped his hand onto the table. Mrs. Pearce, Jasper, and I started at the sudden violent movement. "Got it," Mr. Pearce said.

He jerked his hand away, but there was nothing underneath it. We all sat in stunned silence. "There's another one." Pearce smacked his hand down again, then he pointed across the table to Jasper. "It's by your arm, man. Quick, get it."

Jasper put his cards on the table facedown. "What do you see?" His voice was a calm counterpoint to Pearce's strident tone.

"Bugs . . ." Pearce pulled his collar again. His ruddy complexion was now bright red, and his chest rose and fell as if he'd been sprinting.

Mrs. Pearce put a hand on his arm. "Don—"

He threw her hand off, his gaze darting around the table. "Hurry, get them! Don't you see? They're all over the table!" He stood, and his chair toppled. Stepping back, he tripped over the chair leg. He grabbed for the table and caught the edge as he fell.

The table jumped. Cards slid. Cups fell and splintered, and Pearce collapsed among the china shards.

CHAPTER SIXTEEN

*F*or a second or two, the room was completely silent except for the ticking of the clock on the mantelpiece and the whisper of the wind gusting through the trees outside the open doors. Across the table from me, Mrs. Pearce sat frozen in her chair, the fingers of both hands pressed over her mouth, her gaze fixed on her husband on the floor. At the table beside us, Lady Holt's expression conveyed disbelief as she surveyed the scattered cards and Pearce's prone form. Lady Holt seemed to be at a loss. The collapse of a guest isn't a topic covered in etiquette manuals.

Serena was the first to move. She left the other table and knelt beside Pearce.

Mrs. Pearce leaned forward and gripped the edge of our table. "Is it his heart? He has a weak heart." Emily Pearce's light green eyes looked enormous as her gaze darted from her husband's form on the floor to Serena.

Lord Holt, who'd taken a seat across the room, turned and rested his arm along the back of his chair. "Old boy had too much to drink, did he?"

"No, that's not it." Serena felt for a pulse, pulled open one of Mr. Pearce's eyelids, then sat back on her heels.

Lady Holt put her cards down on the table and turned to Zippy. "Send for Dr. Finch."

Zippy stood but hesitated as Serena spoke.

"No, I'm afraid . . ." Serena shot a glance at Mrs. Pearce, who had gone as pale as the china cups we'd been drinking from. I shifted my chair back and stood, which gave me a better view of Pearce.

I sat down abruptly. He was dead—I knew it from a glance. Pearce's jaw hung loose, and his form had the lifeless quality of a carcass that an insect leaves behind when it sheds its skin. Mrs. Pearce, her skin paper-white, asked, "He's gone, isn't he?"

Serena stood. "Yes. I'm afraid so, Emily."

Mrs. Shaw put down the magazine she'd been looking through and came across the room. She removed her shawl and dropped it around Mrs. Pearce's shoulders. The shawl draped down on each side of her, the fringe pooling on the scattered playing cards on the table. "Oh dear. Perhaps some brandy for Emily might be in order?" The shawl began to slip, and Mrs. Shaw readjusted it so that it wouldn't slide.

Lady Holt blinked. After a second, she said, "Yes, of course." She motioned for a servant to see to it.

Serena moved to Colonel Shaw, who was still seated. She bent and spoke a few words in his ear. The colonel's face didn't change, but his posture stiffened, and his gaze leaped from Pearce's body to our table, then to something on the floor.

I tilted my head so I could see under the table. Colonel Shaw's attention was fixed on Pearce's shattered cup. The dregs of coffee had spattered across the rug, leaving dark spots . . . along with something else. I moved the toe of my shoe lightly across a brown stain by my foot, dragging away a small piece of what looked to be a leaf from the liquid soaking into the rug.

A servant moved forward to right the fallen chair, but

Colonel Shaw held out a hand. "Best leave it for now." Colonel Shaw pushed back his chair. "Lord Holt, I think we should all move into the library. We need to lock this room." He turned to our table. "Except for Miss Belgrave and Mr. Rimington. I'd like to speak to both of you."

My legs felt spongy as Jasper and I walked down the hall to the small sitting room where Colonel Shaw said he'd meet us. I'd never seen someone die. I'd seen a dead body before, but it was shocking to think that only moments before he collapsed, Mr. Pearce had been playing cards beside me. Jasper offered his arm, and I took it, glad for the solid feel of it under my hand. "Did you see anything?" I asked.

Jasper shook his head as he opened the door and let me precede him into the cold room. "No, but I'm not sure there was much to see."

The room was dark, and I made my way through the maze of furniture to a table and switched on a lamp. "There was something—bits of leaves, maybe—in his coffee."

"Then you saw more than me."

"Some of it splashed under the table and landed by my foot."

"Hmm . . . something that produces hallucinations." Jasper rang for a servant and instructed him to make up the fire and bring tea. I waited, arms crossed, until the servant finished, then I took a seat near the crackling fire. "I'll pass on the tea." A tremor raced up my spine as I thought of Pearce's wide-eyed gaze skittering around. "He was convinced bugs were crawling across the table."

As the servant moved to the door, Jasper said to him, "Never mind about the tea. Bring brandy instead."

I watched the flames for a few moments, then the door clicked again and the servant returned.

"Here, drink this." Jasper handed me a tumbler. I sipped and sputtered, but the drink warmed me from the inside out. Jasper had a matching glass. He sat down on the sofa and took a drink.

I cradled the tumbler in my hands. "You don't look rattled at all. In fact, you look like one of those adverts for the new shirts with the collars attached—a coolly debonair chap in evening clothes."

"Oh, I'm rattled all right. I'm just good at hiding it."

I took another drink, a smaller sip. "Two deaths so close together . . . surely they're related."

"Mayhew and Pearce? Possibly. Did they know each other?"

"Yes. Pearce was Mayhew's solicitor."

"That's hardly a reason—"

"There's more." I took another gulp of the brandy, grimaced, then sat forward on the cushion. "I didn't tell you before because I knew you'd fuss, but I had a quick look around Mayhew's cottage." I told Jasper about the state of East Bank Cottage and the inconclusive post mortem.

"I suppose I should frown and scold, but—"

"Skip that," I said. "There's more important things to concentrate on now."

"I agree." He gazed at the fire. "Since the link between Mayhew and Pearce is a business relationship, I suppose the question is, who would want to kill a solicitor and his client?"

The side of my leg near the fire felt too warm, and I shifted away from the flames. Both Anna and Dr. Finch had a reason to want Mayhew and Pearce out of the way. But they were both supposedly at Birchwick Farm. Since I'd promised Anna I would keep quiet about what she'd told me tonight, I didn't say anything about Dr. Finch or Anna to Jasper.

Jasper settled deeper into his chair. "It sounds as if his coffee was tampered with, so I suppose the main question is, who poured Pearce's coffee?"

"He did."

"You saw Pearce pour his cup of coffee himself?"

"Yes, I was right beside him."

"Anyone else come around?"

I stared down into the tumbler. "I don't think so, no." I'd been so focused on Pearce's taunts about channeling my anger away from him that I hadn't noticed much going on around me, but I didn't think Pearce would have made those comments if there was a chance of anyone overhearing them.

"Did you notice who he was around after he got his coffee?"

"No. I took Mrs. Shaw her cup and sat with her. A few minutes later, Lady Holt suggested bridge, and Pearce brought his cup to our table."

"And in the commotion of setting up the tables and taking our places, anyone might have dropped something into his coffee."

"But surely he'd have noticed those bits of leaves in his coffee," I said.

"Not if they were saturated and had sunk to the bottom of the cup," Jasper said. "His coffee was right by my elbow, and I didn't notice anything floating in it. Someone must have made sure the leaves were well-steeped before adding them to Pearce's cup."

"But how could someone do that?"

"Probably in their own cup," Jasper said. "That would be the easiest way. Then when we were setting up for bridge, the person only had to tip the contents of their cup into Pearce's and make sure it settled before Pearce noticed."

"And of everyone at dinner tonight, the three of us had the best opportunity to add something to his coffee—you, me, and Emily Pearce." I felt queasy. "Which is why the colonel wants to speak with us."

"I'm sure you're right. He'll give Mrs. Pearce some time to recover before he speaks to her."

"What impression did you get of Mrs. Pearce?" I asked.

"She seems timid."

"Yes, not the sort to poison her husband—and in company too."

Jasper tapped the edge of his tumbler as he watched the fire. "Although that trick she played early in the game—it was quite bold."

The door opened, and Inspector Longly entered with a constable. He nodded to us both. "Good evening. Colonel Shaw has asked that I interview you." His words were clipped and his manner was formal. "Mr. Rimington, if you'd wait in the next room . . ." Longly held the door open with his left hand.

Jasper stood. "Of course, Inspector." Jasper turned so only I could see his face and gave me a warm smile, then he ambled out the door with his tumbler.

I set my glass down on the side table. I didn't want anything to cloud my thinking. If Colonel Shaw had already turned to Longly, then Pearce's death was definitely being treated as a crime. The constable took a seat to one side of the room, and Longly sat down where Jasper had been. "Miss Belgrave, if you could describe what happened this evening . . ." he said as he arranged his notepad on his knee and took out a pencil.

"We were playing bridge—"

He circled the pencil in the air. "No, go back to the beginning of the evening. What time did you arrive in the drawing room, and who else was there?"

Longly took me back through the evening, reconstructing my movements around the room. When I described pouring coffee for Mrs. Shaw and myself, Longly asked, "Mr. Pearce joined you at the table?"

"Yes, that's right."

"Did anyone else approach the table?"

"No, I don't think so."

"What did you do?"

"I poured two cups of coffee."

"And that was all?" Longly asked.

"Yes."

"You didn't add anything to the cups?"

"Only cream for Mrs. Shaw. I take my coffee black."

"And no one else approached the table during this time except for Mr. Pearce?"

"As I said, I don't think so."

He took a piece of paper from his pocket. It was a sketch of the drawing room. "Show me how you walked to the table where the coffee was laid out."

I was relieved he didn't ask about what Pearce and I had talked about. I traced the route from the chairs where Mrs. Shaw and I had sat, through the room, and around the sofa to the table with the coffee.

Longly folded the paper and put it away, then he worked a glove onto his hand. He reached into the bag the constable handed to him and pulled out my box of asthma cigarettes. "Is this the box of asthma cigarettes you had the servant retrieve from your room?"

"Yes." My stomach roiled. I didn't know exactly where Longly was going with his questions, but my gut told me it wasn't good.

"How many cigarettes were in it?"

"I don't know. Perhaps half a dozen. I don't smoke them."

"You didn't check?"

"No. As I told you, I don't smoke them. I only kept them because it was easier than trying to give them back to Essie— Essie Matthews. If you knew Essie, you'd understand. She doesn't take no for an answer."

"Where did you leave them in the drawing room?"

"On the table behind the sofa." My heartbeat fluttered. I'd just traced my finger along the paper, showing my route through the drawing room, which had taken me near the sofa table.

"Did you move them later?" Longly asked.

"No. In fact, I forgot all about them."

Longly replaced the box of cigarettes in the bag, put it aside, and then took off the glove. "Were you acquainted with Mr. Pearce?"

"No. I did know who he was, but I've never met him before." I leaned forward. "You think the asthma cigarettes were used to poison Mr. Pearce? Was that what was in his coffee?"

Longly's eyes narrowed. "You noticed something about Mr. Pearce's coffee?"

"Only after it spilled. There was something on the rug with the coffee. It looked like bits of leaves or grass."

Longly made a note. "Did you speak to Mr. Pearce?"

"Of course," I said, noting Longly hadn't answered my question about the substance in the coffee. "We all chatted throughout the evening."

"But your conversation with Mr. Pearce was tense. What was that about?"

"I can assure you that had nothing to do with Mr. Pearce's death."

"What did you argue about?"

Someone must have overheard either my conversation with Pearce before dinner or his comments to me as he poured his coffee. For a moment, I debated glossing over my connection to Pearce, but I quickly decided it would be much better to tell Longly myself what had happened. That way, it wouldn't look as if I were trying to hide something. I asked, "Do you know anything about Mr. Pearce other than his position in the community here? No? Mr. Pearce was involved in recruiting investors for Hartman Consolidated. Have you heard of it?"

"The scam that masqueraded as an investment? Yes, I'm familiar with it."

"Mr. Pearce convinced many people to invest in it, I've learned. My father was one of them, and he invested a significant amount of money—well, the entire amount of my trust fund. It was all lost. Mr. Pearce says or—said—he lost money as well, but I didn't believe him."

"No?"

"No. I think Pearce was in on it, receiving money for every single 'investment' he recruited for Hartman. I've heard plenty of rumors to that effect. When the whole thing came crashing down, he was investigated, but there wasn't enough evidence to charge him."

"You know quite a bit about this."

"If your means of financial independence were suddenly taken away from you, you'd look into it too, I think."

"I'm sure I would. How far did your inquiries go?"

"I researched everything I could find in the newspapers, and then I went to the office of Mercer, Blackthorne, and Thompkins. I wanted to speak to Mr. Pearce myself, but he no longer worked there, and no one would give me his current address."

"So when you saw him here, this was the first time you'd met him?"

"That's right."

"And you're very angry." Longly set down the pencil he'd been rotating. "It would be understandable if you wanted revenge."

"I was angry and upset, but I didn't do anything to hurt him. In fact, I was going to contact you and let you know about his background."

"I see." Longly said, but his tone sounded doubtful.

CHAPTER SEVENTEEN

"*A*nd then he wanted to inspect the trays of dirty cups and glasses from the drawing room," Janet said as she put away my shoes.

I tied the belt of my dressing gown and reached for my hairbrush. When Janet had arrived to help me change, I'd asked her if Inspector Longly had been below stairs, and she was relating what one of the kitchen maids, Bess, had told her. "And did he seem interested in anything he found?" I asked.

Janet lifted her shoulders. "There was nothing to find. All the cups and glasses from the drawing room were already washed up, weren't they?" Janet closed the doors of the wardrobe. "Then he looked in the rubbish," she said, her tone indicating it was an outlandish act. "Took out a little scrap of paper and put it in another bag, even though the paper was soaking wet."

"How big was it?" I asked. "The paper, I mean. Did the scullery maid see it?"

"Yes, the inspector showed it to her, and she said it was shoved down in the dregs of one of the dirty coffee cups on the tray. Some people do that, stub out their cigarette in their coffee cup."

"Yes, I know," I said. "So it was a cigarette paper?"

"That's what Bess said it looked like. She saw it when she brought the tray of dirty cups from the drawing room to the scullery."

I dismissed Janet and climbed into bed, my thoughts spinning.

Later that night, I rolled over and tucked the pillow under my cheek. I'd been awake for hours. The house had settled into silence, but each time I closed my eyes, I saw Pearce, his hand slamming down, and his frantic gaze. I drew the blanket over my shoulder. If only Father hadn't invested my trust fund in Hartman Consolidated.

Questions rotated through my mind, and worry gnawed at me as I circled through Longly's questions. Why had I used words like *revenge* and *comeuppance* when I talked to Jasper about Pearce? I squirmed into a new position under the sheets. Had someone overheard me? Surely Longly knew I only wanted the truth about Pearce to come out. But the way Longly had looked at me with his cool gaze worried me. I'd thought of telling him what Jasper and I had worked out— how someone could add steeped leaves to the coffee so that it wouldn't be noticeable--but I didn't want to give Longly a reason to suspect me more than he already did.

I shifted again, wondering about Longly's questions about the cigarettes. Even though Longly hadn't stated it outright, it seemed the asthma cigarettes had something to do with Pearce's death. Longly's interest in the discarded cigarette in the kitchen rubbish indicated he thought the cigarette was important.

Had someone eased a cigarette out of the discarded

package in the drawing room and used it to harm Pearce? Was that what Longly thought had happened? If it was, then he'd have the package analyzed for fingerprints, I was sure. And my fingerprints would be on the package. Perhaps he'd find another set? My heart lifted at the thought, then sank. All the ladies had on gloves. Then my spirits dropped again as I remembered the lace-edged runner on the sofa table. If it was a man who'd taken a cigarette, he could use the fabric to cover his thumb as he edged the box open and tilted it so a cigarette slid out.

No, I couldn't count on the possibility of another set of fingerprints on the box taking Longly's attention away from me. If someone had been clever enough to use the cigarettes to kill Pearce, I doubted they'd conveniently left their finger-prints on the cigarette box, especially since it seemed they'd been sharp enough to soak the cigarette paper in a coffee cup and destroy any fingerprints on it.

But asthma cigarettes were common. Plenty of people used them. One could buy them at any chemist. How could they be used to hurt Pearce?

I squished the pillow, readjusting it under my ear. Mrs. Pearce had said her husband had a weak heart. I'd seen the bits of leaves in the dregs of his coffee, so I knew something was in it, but was that what killed him? Or was it a combina-tion of the two things—the asthma cigarettes and his weak heart—that had caused his death? A post mortem would be done, but it would take a while. The results might not be made public for days and days.

I forced myself to close my eyes and breathe in a steady rhythm. The faint tick of the clock marked the seconds. After a few minutes, I threw back the covers, shoved my feet into my slippers, and reached for my dressing gown. I had no way to figure out if Pearce's health had any impact on his death, but I might be able to answer my questions. Blackburn Hall had a large, well-stocked library. I could at least read up on asthma cigarettes. I'd feel better if I did something instead of worrying.

I closed the door to my room and padded silently down the thick hallway carpet, staying to the middle of the rug to make sure I didn't bump into the furniture. Once I reached the staircase, the moonlight filtering through the tall windows over the landing provided enough light so I could see my way. I crossed the entry hall on the tips of my toes so my slippers didn't slap against the parquet. Then I closed the library door, turned on a few lamps, and went to examine the bookshelves.

After hunting through the books, I found a shelf dedicated to medical topics. I skimmed over titles about tropical diseases, equine health, and a thick anatomy book. About halfway along the shelf, I found a general medical tome. As I pried it out, a smaller book fell to the floor.

I picked up the thin book bound in tan leather. I'd seen it on Lady Holt's writing desk. It didn't have a title on the spine, and the front was also blank. I flipped to the first page. Spidery handwriting proclaimed, *Lady Holt's Herbal*. The date underneath it was from the seventeen hundreds, so it must have been handed down from generation to generation, from one Lady Holt to another.

I took both books to the library table. I set aside the leather-bound herbal and focused on the medical book first. I found asthma cigarettes listed in the index, then went to the section describing them. I skimmed until I found a list of ingredients. My eyebrows went up. They didn't contain tobacco, but were a mix of herbs from the nightshade family. My knowledge of plants was sketchy, but even I knew nightshade could be deadly. The most common ingredients in asthma cigarettes were belladonna and *datura stramonium*, also known as thorn apple. The plants contained atropine, which dilated the airways in the lungs and made breathing easier when it was inhaled. But when too much was inhaled, a person could die. My heart thumped. Longly had asked so many questions about the cigarettes. I took a deep breath and flipped to another section, looking for more information.

The pages fell open at the entry for *datura stramonium* where a folded sheet of paper had been left in the book. I opened the paper. The heading read, *A Comparison on Deterioration Rates of Types of Fabric* by Serena Shires. The whole thing had been handwritten in a hurried cursive. I skimmed over the description of how cotton, linen, wool, and silk broke down when buried. Parts were lined through and some words changed or deleted. It must have been a draft of the article Serena had mentioned to Calder. But why was it in the medical book . . . at an entry about *datura stramonium*? Odd to find it there.

I'd think about that later. I set it aside and focused on *datura stramonium* and the atropine it contained. Besides dilating the airways, atropine acted on the body in other ways. It dilated pupils, increased the heart rate, and often caused dry mouth, thirst, elevated body temperature, confusion, hallucinations, drowsiness, and even coma.

Earlier that evening I'd been focused on my playing cards and hadn't noticed what Pearce's eyes had looked like, but he'd asked for water and pulled at his collar as if he were overheated. Serena had lifted one of his eyelids. I could ask her what she noticed. Pearce had been confused, and the whole thing with the bugs—that had definitely been a hallucination. I couldn't suppress a shiver, remembering the intensity of his gaze and his urgent tone as he commanded Jasper to flatten the bugs on the table.

I shook off the memory and returned to the first entry to finish reading about asthma cigarettes. I read on, fascinated and slightly amazed that such a dangerous plant was used to treat asthma. While *datura stramonium* was the most common ingredient, the potency of asthma cigarettes varied. Different chemists had their own recipes and the different brands of cigarettes also had their own individualized compositions.

Essie had said the asthma cigarettes she gave me were a new brand that would be released soon, which meant I couldn't run down to the chemist in the village and pick up another box to see what the brand contained. And it probably wasn't a good idea to do that anyway. It would look suspicious to Longly since I'd told him that I didn't use asthma cigarettes. A summary at the bottom of the article stated cases of accidental overdose were known, but benefits outweighed the risk for most patients.

I fingered the piece of paper about Serena's research. Was it just a stray bit of paper someone had picked up and used to mark a place in a book? But why was it at the entry about *datura stramonium*? Had Serena placed it there? I put the paper aside and closed the book, wondering if Serena had consulted the medical book recently. It seemed I had two reasons to speak to her later.

I picked up the herbal and flipped through it, but there were no extra bits of paper or pages inserted as bookmarks. The leather-bound volume was filled with home remedies, including poultices for coughs and salves for burns as well as recipes for lotions and perfumes.

I went back through the book more slowly. The variety of handwriting showed different women had listed their own recipes and added notes to older entries. I paused and re-read one of the entries, a remedy for sleeplessness that listed crushed thorn apple leaves. Thorn apple was listed as one of the common names for *datura stramonium* in the medical book. I stared at the last line of the recipe. *Careful dosage is essential*, noted the cramped, old-fashioned handwriting. *Too much causes heart palpitations.*

I closed the herbal and stacked it on the larger book. Had Serena consulted the medical books . . . or the herbal? The books were shelved next to each other. It was possible she'd looked at both. But why would she want to harm Pearce? She had no connection with him that I could see. They hadn't spoken to each other much that evening, and I hadn't picked up on any undercurrents between them. I'd ask Jasper if he'd noticed anything. Despite his relaxed demeanor, he was incredibly observant.

I ran my finger along the edge of the herbal, which had been on Lady Holt's desk when I first arrived at Blackburn Hall. Did Lady Holt know thorn apple was a common ingredient in asthma cigarettes?

I pushed back the chair and stood. The thoughts were too absurd, too fantastic. Could I really be considering Lady Holt —the authority on manners and proper behavior—as someone who'd poison her dinner guest? I replaced the books on the shelf, picked up the paper about decomposition, switched off the lamps, and climbed the stairs through the silvery moonlight. My thoughts were full of what I'd read, and I was halfway down the darkened corridor upstairs when I heard the groan of a floorboard and the swish of fabric. I snapped out of my reverie and stood motionless.

I didn't want to be discovered in a darkened hallway. Certain people might take my presence here as an invitation. If I turned and went backward, the moonlight on the staircase would highlight me. I couldn't go forward because the sounds were coming from that direction, and all the doors around me were closed. I couldn't slip into a room—that could cause worse problems.

I darted to the side, hands outstretched. My fingertips touched the cool glass of a display cabinet. I squished in beside it. The swooshing sound grew louder, and a tall broad-shouldered form with the lithe movement of a young person walked by. The pace was brisk, and the person's steps didn't check.

Once the figure passed me, I let myself breathe again as I watched them disappear down the stairs. When I'd left my room earlier, the little clock on the mantelpiece had shown it was nearly one o'clock in the morning. Who would be creeping around at that hour? The ridiculousness of the question hit me. *I* was creeping around at an absurd hour. What was to prevent someone else from doing the same?

I stepped back onto the thick rug and crept down its center to the staircase. Moonlight fell on Zippy as he turned at the landing and trotted down the last flight of stairs to the entry hall. I waited until his head, which was visible through the balustrades, disappeared below the level of the floor, then I tiptoed to the top of the stairs but stayed in the shadows near the wall, away from the moonlight.

I expected the confident tap of Zippy's slippers on the parquet to continue across the entry, but he only took a few steps. A few notes of a whistled melody floated up, then a metallic click sounded. The murmur of his voice drifted up to me, but I couldn't distinguish the words. I moved down to the landing and leaned over the rail, then drew back. Zippy was seated on the chair beside the telephone table. I was directly over him, looking at the top of his head as he pressed the earpiece to his ear.

The call must have connected because he moved the mouthpiece closer. "It's me. I know—I'm sorry. I couldn't get away. No, no. It's not like that. I wanted to come. But Pearce had a fit—a seizure of some kind—and died. Yes, frightfully shocking. Had to stay. Questioned by the police, and the whole bit. Impossible to stroll out . . . yes, tomorrow. I'll see you then."

I scampered back up the stairs and down the hall to my room. I closed my door and leaned against it, waiting for my heartbeat to slow. As my breathing returned to normal, I heard the faint strains of whistling. It grew louder, continued past my door, then faded. Faintly, I heard a door open and close, then the hall was silent.

CHAPTER EIGHTEEN

*T*he next morning, I put on a light layer of powder and a dash of lipstick, and decided that was the best I could do to distract from the dark circles under my eyes. Between trying to figure out who Zippy was telephoning, wondering if it had anything to do with either of the deaths, and trying to work out who could have known about the dangerous ingredients in asthma cigarettes, I hadn't slept much.

In the darkness last night, I'd been more focused on the asthma cigarettes, but in clear daylight, it struck me that figuring out how Pearce had been murdered was the least of my concerns. I should be more worried about Inspector Longly's questions about my connection to Pearce and my opportunity to add something into his coffee. I expected Inspector Longly to arrive shortly to continue our conversation from the night before. I put down my comb and tried to slough off the uneasy, fidgety sensation that hung over me like a cloud. I was sure that by now the inspector would have looked into Pearce's background—and mine as well—and he'd have more pointed questions today.

I shoved those thoughts away and turned from the glass. I

went to the desk. Instead of focusing on worry and speculation, I had actual work to do. I removed the box with the manuscript of *Murder on the Ninth Green* that Anna had given to me. I hesitated over the pages of the original draft manuscript, the ones with the handwritten notes between Mayhew and Anna.

I curved the pages back and forth as I debated what to do with them. The perfectly straightforward thing to do would be to give them to Longly and let him sort it out, but I'd promised Anna I'd keep her secret—and I would, too, as long as she was telling the truth. I replaced them in the desk and lingered at the dressing table until Janet entered to remove the tray with the hot chocolate she'd brought earlier.

"Janet, did you grow up here in Hadsworth?"

Janet paused on her way to the door, the tray in her hands. "Yes, miss."

"Good. Perhaps you can help me. Is Birchwick Farm nearby?"

"Yes, miss. It's north of Sidlingham."

"Oh, you know it?" I put down the hairbrush and pivoted on the stool so I faced her.

"My aunt and uncle live there."

"I see. Miss Finch mentioned Birchwick Farm. She and Dr. Finch went there last week so her father could deliver a baby . . ."

Janet nodded. "That's right. Little Henry was a week old two days ago." Her normal reserve fell away as she grinned widely. "He's ever so sweet. Just coos and sleeps. Not at all like my aunt's first baby. Colicky, that one was."

"So it would have been Wednesday," I said more to myself than her as I calculated the days in my head.

But Janet heard me and said, "He was born on the stroke of noon. Isn't that interesting? And after five hours of labor too."

"I suppose Miss Finch helped her father?"

"Oh no. Miss Finch is the squeamish sort. She entertained my aunt's eldest and sat with my uncle. My mother went out to help Dr. Finch."

"I see."

"My uncle doesn't handle that sort of thing well. He said he'd have gone out of his mind if Miss Finch hadn't been there. She may not be good at nursing, but he said Miss Finch makes a good cup of tea." Janet's expression suddenly closed down as if she was worried she'd said too much. "If that's all, miss?"

"Yes, thank you."

Janet closed the door behind her, and I swiveled on the stool, turning back to the dressing table, where the manuscript box with *Murder on the Ninth Green* rested. At least now I could keep Anna's secret without my conscience pricking at me. I picked up the manuscript box along with Serena's paper about decomposition that I'd removed from the medical book. After I'd raced back to my room last night, I'd placed it under a perfume bottle. I folded Serena's paper and slipped it into my pocket. Hopefully, I'd be able to ask Serena about it today.

As I came down the stairs, Mr. Busby trotted up the lower flight, pushing his fall of dark hair off his forehead. He met me on the landing. "Miss Belgrave. Just the person I was looking for." He raised his eyebrows and dipped his head at the box in my arm. "May's manuscript, I believe."

I handed the box to him. "I was bringing it to you. With everything that happened yesterday, I didn't have a chance to give it to you."

"Yes, quite." A maid was crossing the entryway, and Mr. Busby snapped his fingers at her. "You there. Yes, you. Come up here."

The maid tucked the feather duster to her side and climbed the stairs to the landing. Mr. Busby handed her the box. "See this is put in my room."

She swallowed and glanced up the next flight of stairs then back to Mr. Busby. "Begging your pardon, sir, but which room?"

"You don't know which room your guests are in?"

"Sorry, sir. I've been out ill."

"I am Mr. Busby. I'm in the Hepplewhite room."

"Yes, sir. I'll take it there directly." The maid bobbed a curtsy and scurried up the next flight of stairs.

I watched her go, then turned back to Mr. Busby. "That's the only copy of the manuscript."

"You think I should keep it under lock and key?" His tone conveyed he thought I was a silly woman. "I know how to do my job, Miss Belgrave—unlike an upstart like you. I know you think you work for Hightower Books, but I assure you that this little excursion for Mr. Hightower will be your last for the publishing house."

A movement behind my shoulder caught his eye. He shifted to the side, his face transforming into a wide smile. "Good morning, Lady Holt." He brushed by me, climbed the stairs, and extended his arm.

I'd have loved to tell Mr. Busby I had no desire to go on working at Hightower Books as long as he was employed there, but I only said good morning to Lady Holt, then went downstairs ahead of her and Mr. Busby.

Bower met me at the bottom of the stairs. "A telephone message for you, Miss Belgrave, from Miss Finch. She's engaged this morning but invites you to visit her at home at three o'clock. She said it was in regard to a note you discussed."

Anna must have found the typed note she received from Mayhew. I thanked Bower for the message and went into the breakfast room, intending to eat quickly and leave as soon as possible. I didn't want to be around Mr. Busby any longer than I had to be.

Since Anna wasn't available until later, I went in search of Serena after breakfast. I tapped on the door of her workroom, and it opened at my touch. I stepped inside, but the room was empty.

Tall uncurtained windows lined one side of the long, narrow room, and two chandeliers hung from plaster ceiling medallions. The chandeliers were the only ornate fixtures in the room. No carpets or soft furnishings here. Several trestle tables stood on the bare hardwood floors. Cabinets had been fitted across the room's shorter walls, and bookcases lined the longer wall opposite the windows.

It was such an interesting space that I couldn't leave without a quick look around. Pens were scattered across the work surface of one of the tables along with bits of fabric and pots of ink. Another table held a Bunsen burner, glass test tubes, and flutes along with metal tongs and thick gloves. Wooden boxes mounded with dirt were enclosed in a miniature glass house on another table. I drifted close enough to read the labels affixed to the boxes—*velvet, tweed, canvas, chintz, leather,* and *felt.* A sheet of paper filled with meticulous notes rested in front of each box, describing the state of the material over time. *Mold spores present. Right edge fraying. Extensive staining.* The handwriting was similar to the messy cursive I'd seen on the paper tucked into the medical book last night.

Another table was strewn with the parts of a disassembled vacuum, while the glass-fronted cabinets at the far end of the room held various bottles and jars filled with specimens preserved in liquid. I recognized an octopus, an eel, several types of fish, and a few things that looked suspiciously human—like eyeballs and fingers—but surely Serena wouldn't have human specimens in her workroom . . . would she?

I moved to the door but stopped and returned to look at the books. Several medical texts lined the shelves. If Serena wanted to look up *datura stramonium*, she had plenty of opportunities to do it here. Why would she look for a book in Blackburn Hall's library and leave one of her papers in it? It was another question I couldn't answer.

I left the workroom and paced around the rest of Blackburn Hall, but I couldn't find Serena. I discovered her golf clubs were still in the closet under the stairs, so I didn't think she was on the course. As I backed out of the closet, Bower's voice sounded at my shoulder. "May I help you find some sporting equipment, Miss Belgrave?"

"No, I'm actually looking for Serena. I see her clubs are here."

"Miss Shires has gone to the village. I believe she intends to return before lunch. Would you like me to tell her you wish to speak to her?"

"Yes, thank you."

"Very good."

"Has Mr. Rimington stopped by today?" Since Bower kept tabs on everyone, I might as well use his knowledge.

"He and Mr. Brown breakfasted early and departed for the golf course."

It took me a second to remember Mr. Brown was Zippy. "Thank you. I believe I'll walk in the garden until lunch." I intended to go out the French doors in the drawing room to the garden, but as soon as I reached them, I halted.

Mr. Busby was seated at a round table on the terrace, smoking a cigarette and reading the manuscript I'd given him that morning. The box sat on his lap, and he'd propped a stack of pages on top of it. I didn't want to encounter him again, so I went back through the drawing room to the morning room, intending to leave the house through those doors because they opened to the gardens on the east side of the house.

Lady Holt was arranging flowers in the morning room. "Pardon me," I said. "Sorry to disturb you."

"It's quite all right. In fact, I'd appreciate your opinion on this arrangement." She turned a vase with irises so I could see it from every side. "Will it interfere with dinner guests seeing each other across the table?"

"I don't think that will be a problem at all." The vase alone reached nearly to my elbow, and the flowers Lady Holt had arranged in it were strong-stemmed purple irises. The few bits of trailing ivy that softened the arrangement didn't hang over the edge.

"Good," Lady Holt said. "I do hate droopy flowers blocking my view."

Lady Holt picked up an iris from a basket on the table. Since Serena wasn't here, this seemed to be an ideal time to ask Lady Holt about the herbal. I asked, "Would you like some help?"

"Yes, if you could hand me those clippers—thank you." Lady Holt turned to a second vase of irises and snipped a few leaves.

I couldn't ask Lady Holt about the herbal directly. I gathered the leaves as she cut them, brushing them into a pile. "I noticed the herbal on your desk when we were working on the etiquette book. I wonder if Mr. Busby would be interested in publishing something along those lines?"

Lady Holt paused, her clippers held in midair. "I hadn't thought of that."

"It might be interesting to compile a list of recipes and remedies for publication. I suppose your herbal goes back many generations."

"It does." She rested the handles of the clippers against her chin. "It would have to be edited. Some of the information is outdated, but it does have some interesting and useful recipes."

"You still use it?"

"Oh yes. In fact, I consulted it a few days ago to confirm my recipe for hand cream contained a full tablespoon of honey." She gave a little shake of her head. "Henderson—my maid—insisted it was only a teaspoon. But I *knew* it was a full tablespoon."

"You should mention the idea to Mr. Busby and see if he's interested."

Lady Holt adjusted the position of one of the irises. "I will. It's an excellent suggestion." She twisted the vase around and added flowers to the other side. "These are for dinner tonight. You're staying on?"

"Yes, if it's not inconvenient. With Mr. Pearce's death . . ." Yesterday I hadn't seen how I could extend my stay at Blackburn Hall any longer. Once Mr. Busby was on the scene, there wasn't any need for me to cosset Lady Holt, but I doubted Longly would want me to race off to London immediately after a suspicious death. Longly had an issue with me leaving a country house when an investigation was underway.

Lady Holt swiped the clippers through the air with an impatient motion. "Such an upset. Of course you must stay until that dreadful inspector stops his pestering questions and the—er—inquest is held." She stabbed a few more flowers into place. "And the cheek of the inspector to think someone would do *that*"—she waved her clippers back and forth again, and I assumed she didn't want to actually say the word *murder* —"during one of my evenings, *and* during a bridge game as well. So rude."

I thought murder went far beyond rudeness, but I was her guest and kept that thought to myself. Instead, I asked, "Do you have any idea what Inspector Longly thinks happened?"

She sheared off a sagging leaf. "No idea. He wouldn't tell me or Lord Holt anything. Very disrespectful. The least he could do is keep us informed." Another leaf hit the table. "The silly man seemed to think one of the guests intentionally poisoned Mr. Pearce. I told him that was impossible. No one disliked Mr. Pearce."

"Mr. Pearce had a good reputation in the village?"

"Of course." She said it as if anyone who associated with Blackburn Hall had a sterling reputation by default. She inserted some ivy into the arrangement. "And poor Emily."

I picked up the last of the stray leaves and added them to the pile. "How is she?"

"Devastated. Such a sweet woman. So devoted to her husband. I don't know why that inspector treated her so roughly."

"Inspector Longly upset Mrs. Pearce?"

"Had her in tears. I intervened, of course. She's a delicate woman. Nervy, you know. Mr. Longly said he was only asking routine questions, but he must take into account a person's disposition. Emily is delicate. He shouldn't take the same line with her as he would with a hardened criminal." Lady Holt stepped back to view the second flower arrangement, then twitched a few stems. "I'm sure Inspector Longly will find it was all an accident."

Accidents seemed to be Lady Holt's default answer for anything she didn't like that happened at Blackburn Hall. I didn't try to argue with her. She twisted the vase to examine it from all sides. Her tone said the subject was closed, so I cast around for a new topic of conversation and thought of Zippy's telephone calls and nighttime rambles. "Will Zippy's friend join us for dinner tomorrow?"

"Whom do you mean?" Her tone was as sharp as her clippers.

"Oh, doesn't Zippy have a friend here in Hadsworth? Someone he's especially close to? Didn't he mention—?"

"No. He does not." Lady Holt's lips pressed together.

CHAPTER NINETEEN

he door to the morning room opened, and Serena walked in. She'd obviously just returned because she still wore a hat and gloves, and carried a small metal handbag of silver mesh. "Hello, Maria," she said to Lady Holt.

"Serena," Lady Holt said in a frosty tone.

I glanced between the two women, sensing tension in the air. Lady Holt focused on the flower arrangements. Serena ignored Lady Holt. "Hello, Olive. Bower said you were looking for me."

"Yes, I'd like to chat with you for a moment, if it's convenient."

Lady Holt put the clippers on the table. "I'll leave you then."

"There's no need," Serena said to Lady Holt then turned to me. "Why don't you come up to my workroom, Olive?"

As we climbed the stairs, Serena said, "I must apologize for Maria. She's not happy with me."

"I think it's me she's upset with."

The metal of Serena's bag clicked as her arm swung. "You? Why would she be upset with you?"

"I asked about Zippy's friends here in the village, and Lady Holt wasn't pleased. I heard Zippy was—um—close to someone in Hadsworth . . ."

"Well, good news for me," Serena said. "That should distract Maria from being upset with me for a while. Zippy does have a special friend nearby, but it's not someone Maria approves of. None of the families are up to her standards—at least, that's what she believes, which is absurd. Anna, for one, would be good for Zippy, but his interests are engaged in another quarter entirely, shall we say."

"Currently engaged?"

"Oh yes. No doubt about it."

So Lady Holt said Zippy didn't have a "close friend" in Hadsworth, but Serena said he did. I thought Serena's assessment was probably the more honest of the two.

Serena pushed open the door to her workroom and waved me inside. "All the better for me. I'll let Zippy take the attention off me today."

"Why would your sister be upset with you today?"

Serena tossed her handbag on one of the tables, and it landed with a clink. "Maria's irritated with me because I attended the inquest into Mayhew's death." Serena tugged at the fingertips of her gloves. "According to Maria, we should completely ignore events such as the inquest because that makes it as if they didn't exist—at least in her world." Serena dropped her gloves on top of her handbag and pulled a bench out from under one of the trestle tables. "Have a seat, won't you?"

"I had no idea the inquest was today." It explained why Inspector Longly hadn't arrived at Blackburn Hall this morning.

"Maria's done her best to keep it quiet."

I slipped between the table and the bench. "Who was at the inquest?"

"The police surgeon, Colonel Shaw, Inspector Calder, and

Inspector Longly, and most of the village, it seems." Serena moved to the back of the room and took a teapot from a cabinet. "Care for a cup of tea?"

"Yes, that would be lovely."

She filled the teapot with water from a spigot at a small sink I hadn't noticed before. She plunked the teapot down on the Bunsen burner, opened another cupboard, and removed two thick mugs.

"I'm surprised they didn't want me at the inquest as well," I said. "After all, I was with you when you discovered Mayhew's body."

She shrugged. "Apparently, they only needed my testimony."

"Did they reach a verdict?"

Serena closed the cabinet door. "Accidental death."

"Really?" I was shocked. Hadn't they taken into account the state of Mayhew's cottage?

Serena put out sugar, spoons, and a tin of crackers. "At least Maria will be happy," she said, then cringed. "That sounds terrible. I only mean Maria will be glad the inquest is over, and the verdict was accidental death."

I lined up the spoons in a row. "Why is Lady Holt so set on Mayhew's death being declared accidental?"

Serena crossed her arms and leaned her hip against the table as she waited for the water to boil. "Because Maria doesn't want even a hint of scandal attached to Blackburn Hall. It doesn't fit with"—Serena waved her hand in a motion that encompassed the grounds and Blackburn Hall—"the image she wants to portray. I'm sure it will only get worse with the publication of her etiquette book." Serena sighed. "Maria will have endless reporters down and expect proper behavior from all of us—and she'll be more irked with me than usual." She tilted her head toward the table with the boxes of dirt and then glanced at the cabinet with the specimens. "I'm not exactly conventional. Maria finds me a trial."

Air steamed out of the teapot with a whistle, and Serena switched off the Bunsen burner. "The only other interesting tidbit of information that came out was Mayhew's father died six months ago. Just a quick mention. I didn't understand why that was entered into evidence, but apparently it was important."

I stopped shifting the spoons around. "Oh." If Mayhew's father had been dead for months, then he couldn't have had anything to do with Mayhew's death.

Serena carried the teapot over. "You know why it's important?"

"Mayhew was afraid of him," I said, thinking that was general enough that it would satisfy Serena's curiosity but not so specific that it broke the promise I'd made to Colonel Shaw about keeping Mayhew's past a secret. It sounded as if they'd decided to skip over Mayhew's connection to May and the infamous Pikenwillow pixies. I was sure if the pixie connection had been mentioned, it would have been the first thing Serena talked about. I sensed Lady Holt's influence in the inquest's outcome. I'd bet Colonel Shaw and the investigators had kept it out of the public proceedings to keep Lady Holt happy. If word got out that Mayhew was actually Veronica May, who was associated with the Pikenwillow pixies, every gossip sheet in London would send down a reporter.

Serena paused, the teapot poised over the mugs. "I see." She poured the steaming liquid, handed me a mug, and sat down opposite me, putting the teapot on a felt potholder.

"Did anything else interesting come out at the inquest?" I asked.

"No. It was all quite cut-and-dried."

So in addition to skipping over Mayhew's real identity, the investigators were also keeping Mayhew's vocation as a novelist quiet. A tactic to make sure reporters didn't descend on Hadsworth and Blackburn Hall? I cradled the mug in my hands. "Did Pearce's death come up today at the inquest?"

"No." Serena stirred her tea. "I expected his name would be mentioned, but no one said a word about him."

I had been about to take a sip of tea, but I pulled the cup away from my mouth. "How odd. I'd thought two deaths so close together in such a small village must be connected."

"But Mayhew's death was an accident. The situation around Pearce is completely different."

I wasn't convinced Mayhew's death was an accident, but unless I wanted to broadcast the fact that I'd been snooping around the cottage, I couldn't argue my point.

Serena sipped her tea, then said, "Enough about that. You didn't want to talk to me about the inquest. Did you want to chat about golf?"

"Golf?"

"Our tee time is tomorrow morning, remember? If you're feeling nervous, don't. I'll show you a few simple swings to get you started, and then it's always best to dive right in. Don't think too much—that's what can ruin your game."

With everything else that had happened, I'd completely forgotten I'd agreed to play golf with Serena. "I'm sure it will be an enjoyable time." I was interested to give golf a try, but it wasn't what I wanted to focus on right now. The tea was too hot, and I put down my mug. "Actually, I wanted to talk to you about something completely different—asthma cigarettes. After what happened last night, I read up on them. I had no idea they contain such dangerous ingredients, like belladonna and *datura stramonium*."

Serena's brows puckered. "Really? I didn't know that either. I don't have asthma and neither does anyone else in the family."

"I thought you might have researched them for some . . . scientific reason." I glanced around the workroom from the boxes of dirt to the table with the Bunsen burner.

"No. I'm focused on studying decomposition right now— well, I have a few side projects like the pen that doesn't have

185

to be refilled and the improvements to the vacuum, but those are more for a break from my real work. Palate cleansers, if you will."

"Then I wonder how this got to be in a medical book in the library." I took the paper out of my pocket. "It was marking the page with an entry about *datura stramonium*. It's yours, isn't it? I thought you might be looking for it."

Serena took the paper, her forehead wrinkling. She scanned the page, then her face smoothed. "Oh yes. I did look up a recipe for diffusible creosoted fluid, which must be on the same page. The entries are alphabetical." She said it as if that answered my question. "I don't need this." She lifted the paper. "This is an old draft—scrap paper. I must have grabbed it to mark my spot in the book."

"I'm not sure I understand. Diffusible . . . ?"

"Diffusible creosoted fluid. It's a preservative." She nodded toward the specimens in the glass-fronted cabinets. "I knocked over one of the jars. It cracked and some of the solution seeped out. I had to look up the proper recipe for the solution to refill it. I don't use the specimens, but they could be useful to someone else for scientific study."

It was a perfectly logical explanation, and Serena didn't look at all worried. Perhaps finding Serena's paper in the medical book near the entry about *datura stramonium* was a coincidence.

Serena dropped her handwritten notes on the table. "I wonder if Mrs. Shaw knows what's in her cigarettes? Perhaps I should mention it to her."

"I think that's a good idea. They're quite dangerous. One of the signs of an overdose is dilated pupils. You looked in Pearce's eyes. Were they dilated?"

She nodded. "They were huge. I've never seen anything like it. It was actually very interesting—scientifically speaking, you know." Serena gave a little shake of her head and reached for her tea. "And that's what gets me in trouble."

"I'm sorry?"

She took a long sip, then said, "Inspector Longly and Colonel Shaw had a few questions for me after the inquest."

"About Mayhew?"

"No, Pearce. Take my advice and don't pick up a hobby that involves anything related to death. Apparently, it makes you a suspect."

"What?"

"According to Colonel Shaw, I'm a rather strange woman with a fascination with death." She lifted her mug toward the boxes of dirt and the specimen jars.

"Your specimens make you a suspect?"

"The colonel is old-fashioned. He thinks a woman should marry and have children. I make him uncomfortable with my scientific studies and my interest in decay. And the specimens, of course. Those make him *extremely* uncomfortable. Not an appropriate thing for a woman to own, you know. The funny thing is, those aren't even mine." She lifted her mug in the direction of the cabinet with the specimens. "They belonged to Great Uncle Jonas. This was his workroom. He was one of those Victorians with the mania for classification. He spent his life collecting and preserving specimens."

"How does Colonel Shaw even know about the specimens?"

"Everyone in the village knows about them. Most people find them . . . distasteful. And Colonel and Mrs. Shaw live across the street from the church, so there's that too."

"What does the church have to do with it?"

"I like graveyards. I go there when I need to think. I find graveyards very peaceful. I like to stroll and read the dates on the tombstones. Helps me clear my head." She sipped her tea then set down the mug. "Thankfully, owning specimens and walking graveyards doesn't provide a foundation strong enough for them to arrest me and charge me with Pearce's death."

For a moment, I toyed with the idea that Serena's scientific mind combined with her interest in death had prompted her to put the *datura stramonium* in Pearce's cup of coffee. Could she have done it to watch someone die firsthand? It seemed an absurd theory. I pushed it from my mind. While her scientific interest might not be considered ladylike, I didn't think she was mentally unbalanced. And she didn't seem unduly worried. In fact, her head was tilted to one side as she fingered the square felt potholder the teapot rested on. "I wonder . . . I haven't tried felt . . ." she murmured, her gaze fixed on the table with the pens.

"Well, I should let you get to work." I stood. "Thank you for the tea."

"Of course." She said it automatically. "I think I have some leftover felt. If not, then Mrs. Jones will have some . . ." She was talking to herself. She moved to the cabinets and began opening doors and scanning the contents. While she was occupied, I picked up the paper I'd found in the medical book. She'd tossed it down casually on a messy stack of papers. I doubted she'd miss it. Serena didn't even seem to be aware I was still in the workroom as I moved to the door. She was pulling drawers open and rummaging through them. She was in a state I'd seen often with my father—preoccupied with her own thoughts and only dimly aware of what was going on around her.

I paused at the door. Serena was so focused, perhaps I could ask one more thing and she'd answer without thinking. "Do you ever consult Lady Holt's herbal?"

She pushed a drawer closed and opened the one under it. "No," she said without looking up. "I'm never sick, and I'm not interested in beauty lotions and potions."

CHAPTER TWENTY

$\mathcal{A}$fter lunch, I motored away from Blackburn Hall to visit Anna. As I left the Hall's grounds and turned in the direction of the village, I spotted a familiar blond figure walking toward me. I stepped on the brake as I came even with Jasper, who raised his fedora. "Good morning. Where are you off to?"

I swallowed. "To visit Anna."

"Capital. I'll come along." Jasper settled his hat on his head and climbed in and closed the door. "What's the delay? You were speeding along like a fireman on the way to put out a blaze."

"Yes—um, well . . . Anna won't be expecting both of us." I hadn't told anyone Anna was Mayhew's ghostwriter, and I wasn't about to start now, which put me in an awkward position.

"Oh." Jasper narrowed his eyes. "So this is more than a social call?"

"Perhaps." I'd thought eventually Anna would have to tell Longly about her ghostwriting secret, but if Mayhew's death wasn't being investigated, she didn't have to reveal the truth to anyone else.

"Intriguing," Jasper said. "You know I love a good mystery."

"As do I, but this isn't my mystery to reveal."

"Ah, I see. Been keeping secrets from your faithful assistant, have you?"

"I was sworn to secrecy," I countered.

"Hmm. Well, a chap has to respect that, I suppose. It wouldn't be cricket to talk out of turn." He adjusted his lapels and settled himself against the seat. "Of course, since you suspect we have a murderer among us, I should accompany you. It would be ungentlemanly not to."

I wasn't getting rid of him, that much was clear. Jasper could be quite stubborn. I let off the brake. "Then you may have to take a turn around the garden at some point."

"As long as I can keep you in sight, I don't mind a garden stroll. Beautiful things, gardens. I always enjoy looking at lovely things," he said. I could feel his gaze on me, but I kept my attention on the upcoming curve in the lane. I swooped the motor along the arc of the road.

Jasper gripped the top of the door with one hand. "Are you a good driver, by the way?"

"Excellent. I can drive on both sides of the road, you know. When I was going to university in America, one of my friends had a little Raceabout and let me drive it often."

"As long as you stay on the appropriate side of the road *now*, that's all I care about."

I straightened the wheel as we came out of the curve, and I downshifted as we bumped over the small bridge.

Jasper released his grip on the door. "I have news."

"If it's about the inquest, I already heard about it firsthand from Serena. I had an interesting chat with her this morning."

Jasper shook his head. "I should have realized. You know Mayhew's death was ruled an accident?"

"Yes."

"You don't agree?"

I glanced away from the road to focus on Jasper for a moment. "How did you—?"

"Your tone of complete disbelief is hard to miss."

"I suppose I should be more guarded." I shook my head. "I just don't believe two deaths in Hadsworth so close together aren't related somehow." I sighed. "I haven't heard one hint of how they could be linked—other than Mayhew and Pearce's business connection." I told him what I'd learned about asthma cigarettes, Zippy's late night telephone call, and my chats with Lady Holt and Serena.

"Goodness, how diligent of you."

"Being questioned by an inspector from Scotland Yard tends to give one an incredible motivation to sort things out, particularly in a way that shows I didn't have anything to do with Pearce's death. But things are getting more confusing, not less so."

A gust of wind hit us as we came out from behind a hedgerow, and Jasper reached up to hold his hat. "At least the question about whether or not Mayhew's father might be involved was answered."

"Answered very definitely." I shifted, leaning out to get a view around a lorry that we were closing on quickly. The other lane was clear, so I whipped around the lumbering vehicle. "The inquest also explained why I haven't seen Longly this morning. I was sure he'd show up first thing." My hands tightened on the steering wheel as a nervous feeling swept over me. "Obviously, he was busy with the inquest, but I'm sure it won't be long before he turns his attention back to Pearce's death." I slowed down as we traveled through the village.

Jasper scratched his cheek. "Possibly. When the verdict was read, he didn't look pleased."

I turned onto the lane that led to Dr. Finch's house and surgery. "He didn't?"

"No, more like he'd gotten a whiff of cream that had gone off."

"That's interesting." I rolled to a stop in front of Dr. Finch's residence. "I wonder if he'll keep investigating Mayhew's death? The case is officially closed now, I suppose."

"I imagine he'll have to turn his attention to Pearce." Jasper took a piece of paper from his pocket and unfolded it, then pressed it to his chest as he turned to me. "But you still think foul play was involved in Mayhew's death?"

I frowned at my reflection in the windshield. "Yes. I really do. There are too many things that feel off."

Jasper gave a decisive nod. "I suspected you wouldn't drop your interest in Mayhew's death." He presented the paper to me with a flourish. It was a list of names written in his careful block printing. Jasper pointed to the left column. "Guests staying at the pub on Tuesday, Wednesday, and Thursday." He moved his finger to the top of the right column. "And a list of players on the golf course those same days."

"Jasper, this is wonderful. How did you get it?"

"The pub was easy. The owner doesn't bother to put away the guest ledger. I waited until everyone was busy, then jotted down the names. It's only three, as you can see, so it didn't take that long. They have four rooms, but only three of them were taken during the time we're interested in. Getting the information from the golf course was more difficult. The starter wouldn't talk to me, but his daughter works in the clubhouse."

"Starter?"

"The person who runs the tee sheet, gets everyone off on time."

"You mean there's a record of everyone who played and the time they teed off?" I asked.

"Exactly."

"And this person who manages the tee sheet has an attractive daughter, with whom you flirted."

"You say that as if it's a foregone conclusion," Jasper said.

"Isn't it?"

"While she's attractive, she wasn't interested in any kind of dalliance. The only thing that convinced her to part with this list of names was some cold hard cash. Rather humbling, dash it."

"Shocking."

"Happens more than I care to admit."

"Somehow I doubt that." We both turned serious as we bent over the paper. While the pub's list was short, the list of golfers was much longer.

Jasper said, "The pub's overnight clientele are golfers. They'd be on the course as much as they could during their holiday. They were probably on the course every day."

I compared the two lists. "It looks like each one of the people staying at the pub was on the golf course Wednesday morning." I turned and faced Jasper. "You've played the course. Would someone have been able to check in for a tee time, leave the course, and get around to the place where Mayhew died—all without someone noticing?"

Jasper's eyebrows crinkled. "It would be difficult. Since the river separates the course from the grounds of Blackburn Hall, someone would have to backtrack all the way down to the village, cross the bridge, and then enter the grounds of Blackburn Hall. It would be a long trek. That's not to say that someone couldn't have done it. But players are usually grouped in pairs or foursomes, so the partners would have to agree to keep someone's departure quiet."

"And then there would be the bother of the golf bag," I said. "It would look odd if someone toted a golf bag through the grounds of Blackburn Hall. Or they'd have to stow it

193

somewhere, then pick it back up again before they rejoined their group on the golf course."

"Or have someone from your group carry your bag for you," Jasper said.

I leaned back against the seat. "Not to mention, how would someone know exactly what time Mayhew would be on the path from the cottage? Several people mentioned how reclusive Mayhew was. It sounds as if she was more of a homebody, not the type of person to take a morning walk at the same time every day." I handed the paper back to Jasper. "It seems the golfers are a long shot as possible candidates for being involved in Mayhew's death."

He refolded the paper and came around to open my door. "It's not as helpful as I'd hoped."

We walked to the front door, and I pushed the bell. "No, but it's a good idea to check who was in the area."

The maid led us into the sitting room. A few moments later, Anna came in from the doors that opened into the garden. "Hello, Olive." Her auburn hair was scraped back with combs into a style that emphasized the dark smudges shadowing her eyes. Her eyebrows flared slightly as she noticed Jasper. ". . . and Jasper, lovely to see you again. How is everyone at Blackburn Hall after . . . the events of last night?"

"Everything is quite the same at Blackburn Hall, actually," I said.

Anna grimaced. "Yes, of course. What was I thinking? Lady Holt would make sure life carried on as if a man hadn't been murdered. But it's dreadful, no matter how much Lady Holt tries to brush over it." She indicated a seating arrangement near an empty fireplace. "Won't you have a seat? I'd invite you out to the garden, but Dad sent the wicker chairs off for a fresh coat of white paint."

"No worries." I sat down on a squashy Chesterfield sofa.

Jasper took the other end of the sofa, and Anna perched on the edge of a club chair near me.

I looked through the doors into the garden. "Working outside again?"

"Yes, but not making much progress, I'm afraid. I can't keep my mind on my work with everything that's happened. Last night, when Dad finished his house call, we came back here. I didn't know anything of Mr. Pearce's death until Colonel Shaw stopped in this morning with the news. The colonel said it was obvious straightaway last night it was a crime scene and so he called the police surgeon and Inspector Longly." She fiddled with one of her combs. "I suppose Longly will stay on to investigate Mr. Pearce's death now as well. Do you know about the inquest verdict, that Mayhew's death has been declared an accident?" I thought the news would have relieved her worries about her father and herself being suspects, but her shoulders hunched forward with tension.

"But that's good news . . . isn't it?"

"Yes, except I—" Her gaze darted to Jasper.

Jasper put his hands on his knees. "I believe that's my cue to exit to the garden. You ladies would clearly like to chat alone."

Anna flushed. "No, it's not that—" Anna looked to me, her face the picture of indecision.

"You can speak about it in front of Jasper if you'd like." I leaned forward and said in a low voice, "I haven't told him anything, but he's absolutely trustworthy. In fact, Mr. Hightower tried to enlist Jasper to come down and look for Mayhew."

Jasper said, "I wasn't able to take on his commission at the time, but now I'm assisting Olive—her 'boy Friday,' you might say. But if you'd rather speak to Olive alone . . ."

Anna's cheeks went a deeper pink. "No. It's—fine, I

suppose. If Olive vouches for you, and Mr. Hightower trusts you . . ."

"I do vouch for him." I flashed him a smile. "I've known him for years and years, and he's never betrayed a secret."

"Well, in that case . . ." Anna smoothed her palms over the skirt of her printed cotton dress. "I found the note from Mayhew." She took a piece of paper from her pocket and handed it to me. I hesitated a moment before I took it, and she said, "I'm sure if there were any other fingerprints on it, I've completely blurred them by now."

Jasper raised an eyebrow. "Fingerprints?"

The paper, a full-size sheet, had been folded into thirds. I opened the page. "Anna received a note from Mayhew shortly after she died."

Jasper nodded. "Ah, I see." He looked at Anna. "You're wondering if it was actually from Mayhew."

"I am now." Anna said. "Ever since Olive asked me about it. It hadn't occurred to me until then that someone else might have sent it. Even though it was typed—Mayhew usually handwrote notes—I didn't think about it," Anna shrugged. "I supposed Mayhew just dashed it off in a hurry and stuffed it in an envelope."

Jasper scooted over to the sofa cushion beside me and looked over my shoulder as I read. Last Wednesday's date headed the page. I read it aloud. "I'm off for a holiday. Carry on with the next book. I'll be in touch. Mayhew." Even the last line, the name, was typed.

"You didn't save the envelope?" I asked.

"No, and I can't remember exactly when it arrived either." Anna clasped her hands together. "I didn't realize it would be important."

"Of course not," I said. "Was it typed on Mayhew's type-writer? Can you tell?"

Anna nodded. "Yes, it was." She pointed to the last line of the note. "See the y, how it's slightly raised? That's how all

Mayhew's typed pages looked. It's on all the drafts, well—on all the old drafts, the ones Mayhew used to send me before I began writing them—" Her gaze jumped from me to Jasper, then back to me. "Oh, I mean—" Jasper didn't say anything, but his eyebrows flew up in a silent question.

Anna hesitated a moment, then said in a rush, "I helped Mayhew with her manuscripts."

Jasper ironed out his expression to its usual blandness, except for his hooded eyes, which were alight with interest. "Working out the clues and whatnots?" he said, giving Anna an out, an opportunity to gloss over her slip of the tongue, but I was sure he'd worked out the implications of what she'd said.

"That's how it started," Anna said. She waved a hand. "But it became quite a bit more than that. I was her ghost."

Jasper glanced from Anna to me. "As in, a ghostwriter?"

Anna nodded as I handed the typed note back to her.

"Oh." Jasper ran a hand over his mouth. "I see. Yes, that does change things."

I gestured to Anna's pocket, where she'd tucked the letter. "You haven't had any other letters—typed or otherwise?"

"No. This is all. I've been working on the next book, just as Mayhew instructed. I expected to hear more within a few days."

"Why? Was that the usual time between your—um —communications?"

"I suppose so. I've never thought about it until now, but we did have some interaction about once a week. Either I dropped off a new chapter or Mayhew left notes for me, thoughts on what I'd already written."

"And that's why you broke into East Bank Cottage—to get the chapters you'd dropped through the slot in the door," I said.

Anna's eye widened. "How do you know about that?"

"I saw them." It was time to admit my little indiscretion to another person. I took a breath. "I took a quick look around East Bank Cottage. It was before we knew about Mayhew's death. I was trying to figure out if Mayhew had left Hadsworth. I saw the envelopes by the door when I went inside. I didn't disturb them, but when Mayhew's body was found, I had to confess my snooping to the police, and I mentioned the envelopes in my statement. Later, Inspector Longly went to East Bank Cottage, and they were gone. He accused me of taking them."

Anna's hand went to the pocket where she'd placed the note. "What did you say?"

"I set him straight. I didn't take them."

Anna jumped up and walked to the open door to the garden. Jasper stood as well, but she waved him back to his seat. "Please, have a seat. I'm too nervous to stay still." Jasper perched on the arm of a chair as Anna said to me, "But you worked it out, that I took the envelopes."

"Once I knew you were ghostwriting the books, you seemed to be the most likely candidate." Although Zippy's nighttime jaunts were still suspicious, I couldn't imagine why he'd break a window to get some envelopes from a deserted cottage.

Anna fingered the flat collar of her dress nervously. "And he's coming here."

"Who?" I asked.

"Inspector Longly." Anna moved around the edge of the room. "If I'd known Mayhew's death would be ruled an accident, I wouldn't have said anything." Her grip tightened on the edge of her collar, stretching the fabric. She paced back to the chair. "I couldn't sleep last night. I tossed and turned all night, thinking about the typed note and those envelopes."

She released her grip on her collar and dropped back into her chair with a sigh. "I wish I hadn't broken that window! I was so worried about losing those chapters. I didn't have a carbon copy of them. I only make copies of the final draft.

After such a horrible night last night, I decided to confess everything to the inspector." She looked toward the door. "He was out, but I left a message for him this morning. He telephoned later, and I told him about taking the envelopes. He said he'd come by today. If only I'd kept quiet a little longer, it would have all gone away."

"I don't know about that," I said. "Longly seems to be a stickler for details. He might have followed up on the envelopes anyway, despite the death being declared an accident."

Anna jerked toward me. "Could he reopen the case?"

"I don't know. I have no idea what the procedure is, but you should just tell him exactly what happened. You said you and your father were with a patient the morning Mayhew was killed—"

Jasper stood up and moved to the open door. "I believe I caught a glimpse of a Gadlington sparrow." He glanced between Anna and me. "You've never heard of it? Extremely rare. Unusual to see one at this time of year too. May I?" He gestured at the garden.

"Of course," Anna said.

I frowned at his well-tailored jacket as he stepped outside. Jasper had weak eyes. His poor vision was the reason he had spent the war at a desk, working for the Foreign Office instead of on the front lines.

Anna shifted over to sit beside me on the sofa. "Do you really think the inspector will believe me when I tell him I took the envelopes, but that was all I did? That he won't take it any further?"

"I don't know what Longly will do. I don't know if he'll want to reopen the case or if he's even able to do that. He's a thorough sort of chap, though. He'll probably check to make sure you were at the farm with a patient."

"And they'll tell him we were there." She fell back against the sofa. "Yes, you're right. It will be fine."

Jasper came back in the room. "False alarm. It was only a chaffinch."

Anna said, "I had better gather up the envelopes before Inspector Longly arrives."

I stood. "And we should be going."

CHAPTER TWENTY-ONE

*O*nce Jasper and I were on our way back to the village, I slowed the motor and pointed into the woods. "Isn't that a Gadlington sparrow?"

"I'm afraid not."

"I thought not. It doesn't exist, does it?"

"No." Jasper shifted in the seat. "Do you think Anna realized it was all a ruse?"

I shook my head. "She was so wrapped up in her own thoughts, she didn't even notice. You went outside to check the typewriter?"

Jasper grinned and took a piece of paper out of his pocket.

I pulled the Morris to the side of the road. "You are good at this."

"I aim to please." He'd typed Mayhew's name on the first line, then a string of letters underneath. The letter y in Mayhew's name was perfectly aligned, and it was the same in the line of random characters.

I gave the paper back to him. "So we know that Anna didn't type the notes herself."

"Or at least she didn't type it on her typewriter."

"You catch on to this assistant thing quickly," I said,

wondering how difficult it would be to get another look at the typewriter in East Bank Cottage. Another unauthorized visit probably wasn't a good idea, not with Longly already suspicious of me.

The sound of a motor coming up the lane broke the quiet of the forest. The motor halted as it drew even with us. Inspector Longly raised his hat as he leaned across his constable, who was driving. "Hello, Miss Belgrave, Mr. Rimington. Out for a drive?"

"Visiting a friend."

His gaze ran over the Morris. "I didn't realize you had a motor here, Miss Belgrave. You're not intending to run up to London, are you?"

"No, I don't have any plans of the sort."

"Good. I want to speak with you later. Will I find you at Blackburn Hall?"

"I'm on my way there now."

"Excellent." He replaced his hat and nodded for the constable to drive on.

"He sounded pleasant enough, but I don't like that he wants to talk to you again. Do you think it's about Pearce?" Jasper asked.

My hands felt shaky. I gripped the steering wheel tighter as I put in the clutch and let the motor roll forward. "Probably. I just hope he's not coming to arrest me."

When we arrived at the pub, Jasper stepped out of the Morris and closed the door, but didn't let go of it. "I should go with you to Blackburn Hall in case Longly gives you any trouble."

"You don't have an invitation to dinner at Blackburn Hall, and I couldn't foist an unexpected guest on Lady Holt." His posture was casual as he leaned against the door, but his hooded gaze was intense.

"If anything . . . distressing happens, I'll telephone you immediately." I was surprised at the warmth that edged through me as I made the statement. I savored my independence, but it was good to know Jasper was concerned.

Then Jasper ruined it. "Just don't do anything rash," he said as he tapped the door. He ambled into the pub.

Irritation zipped through me. I put the motor in gear and put Jasper's namby-pamby warnings out of my mind. I was well able to take care of myself. Besides, I had plans for the evening, and I needed to concentrate on them—as long as I could manage to not be arrested.

I'd missed tea and went up to my room to change for dinner, expecting Longly to arrive at any moment. To distract myself, I thought about the typewritten note Anna had received. Even though Anna said the note had been typed on Mayhew's typewriter, I wished I could double check that. The off-line y should make it easy to identify the machine that had been used to type the notes, which could help narrow down the suspects. But the question was, how many typewriters were there in Hadsworth? Besides Anna's, the police station had one, and Anna had mentioned the WI typed their minutes on their typewriter. And Dr. Finch, did he have one in his surgery?

It was rather a long list. Instead of trying to run down all the typewriters in the village, it would be much simpler to check Mayhew's typewriter first, but that might prove difficult. I'd have to get into the cottage again—was the key still hidden over the window?—and the typewriter might not even be there. Longly might have carted it away with Mayhew's possessions for the investigation.

I sighed and turned away from the window and saw the stack of Mayhew's books on the bedside table. The typed letter that had been in the first book! Had I brought it with me? I snatched up the books and fanned the pages. I'd used the letter as a bookmark when I'd read the first book. Had I moved it—?

A folded sheet fell out of *The Mystery of Newberry Close*. No, I'd returned it to where I'd found it, between the cover and end pages of the first book. I twitched the page open and scanned the list of titles. The letter *y* was sprinkled through the list and across some of the lines. In every instance, it rode higher than the other letters. I checked the date again. Three years ago, which was before Anna had become Mayhew's typist. So someone had used Mayhew's typewriter to write the note to Anna.

∾

When dinner was announced and Longly still hadn't appeared, I began to hope that he wouldn't show up at all that evening. Perhaps he'd been unavoidably detained.

Despite the fact that the table was full at dinner, it was a subdued evening. Even Mr. Busby seemed withdrawn and preoccupied, and only managed to insert one barb aimed at me. Conversation was a disjointed affair, alternating between Lord Holt's description of his round of golf and Lady Holt's plans for dinner the next night.

"I visited Emily today," Lady Holt said. "The poor thing. She's so distraught. I convinced her she should come tomorrow night for dinner. Just a quiet little gathering, ourselves, that nice Mr. Rimington—he has beautiful manners —and the colonel and Mrs. Shaw, I think. Emily is the sort who will mull over everything until she makes herself sick. She needs to take her mind off things, and no one will begrudge her a quiet evening with us. It will do her good."

I wouldn't have thought a widow dining with friends a few nights after her husband's murder would be something Lady Holt would endorse. Not good manners, as my new stepmother, Sonia, would say, but it seemed Lady Holt felt a liberality when applying etiquette rules to herself and her friends. Somehow I didn't think she'd extend that same grace to others, but she was set on her idea for another dinner party. "We might as well make the best of—ah—an unpleasant situation." She smiled in my direction. "Since you and Mr. Busby must remain until the inq— until *later,* we shall have a small gathering to take our minds off recent events."

"I'm sure dinner will be lovely," I said.

Mr. Busby ignored me and spoke to Lady Holt. "And I look forward to furthering my acquaintance with Mrs. Pearce. She seems a delightful lady. I'll do my best to distract her."

Lady Holt turned to Zippy. "And you'll join us as well. Don't make other plans."

It was a command, not a request. Zippy's lips flattened, a pale imitation of his mother's frequently displeased face, but he said, "Of course, Mother."

Lady Holt looked to Serena, who hadn't said a word all evening. "You'll be there as well, I trust."

Serena looked up from her plate. "What?"

"Serena! You haven't heard a word I've said, have you?"

"No. I have an idea that may work for the quiet vacuum. It just needs a few adjustments and then—"

"Pay attention, Serena. We're discussing dinner tomorrow night with Emily as our guest. I expect you to be here and be *attentive.*"

That surprised her out of her preoccupied state. "Emily's dining out? So soon?"

"It will be good for her and help her take her mind off things."

Serena raised her eyebrows. "Then we'd better not have coffee in the drawing room after dinner."

"Of course not," Lady Holt said. "I plan to have it on the terrace. It should be pleasant outdoors." The conversation turned to the weather, and that carried us through until the ladies withdrew. It was an abbreviated evening. Lady Holt didn't suggest cards, and we all retreated to our rooms fairly early.

I dismissed Janet when she came to help me change, telling her I could manage by myself. Instead of putting on my dressing gown when I removed my dress, I pulled on my jodhpurs. I shrugged into my cardigan and put the torch—which I had yet to return to the closet under the stairs—in my pocket along with a half crown, my means of making sure I could get back into Blackburn Hall. And Jasper said I didn't think ahead!

I settled down in the chair to wait, listening for the click of Zippy's door or his whistling. If he was going out tonight, I was following him. I wanted to see for myself exactly where he was going and what he was doing. I had so much nervous energy, I hopped up from the chair and paced around the room.

Longly's promise—threat?—to visit Blackburn Hall to speak to me loomed over me. Even though Longly hadn't arrived that night, I knew it was only a temporary reprieve.

I circled my room, my thoughts running along a familiar track. I couldn't think how I could find out anything else about Pearce's death. The postmortem was probably scheduled, if not underway, and I couldn't think of a way to talk to Emily Pearce before Lady Holt's dinner. I'd have to wait until then and see if I could discover something during casual conversation. My time now was better spent focusing on Mayhew. If I could sort out some of the questions around her death, I was sure it would reveal who'd killed Pearce as well because I couldn't shake my feeling that the deaths were linked.

I couldn't think of anything that connected Zippy to both Pearce and Mayhew, but Zippy's furtive phone call and nighttime strolls bothered me. It was odd. Like Longly and his aversion to loose ends, things that were a bit off bothered me. And keeping an eye on Zippy was something I could do.

I wasn't good at waiting. Patience wasn't one of my strengths.

I couldn't imagine I would get sleepy, but after an hour, my eyelids began to feel heavy. I pulled back the drapes and opened a window, letting in the muggy night air. I breathed deeply then went back to pacing.

I was on my seventh circuit of the room—I was counting to keep myself alert—when I heard a whisper of sound, a tune whistled quietly. I went to the door, crouched down, and put my eye to the keyhole. As the notes grew louder, I recognized *Shimmy with Me*. Zippy strode by, his arms swinging loosely. He wore a tweed jacket and a trilby, so he definitely wasn't about to retire for the night.

The whistling faded, and I inched the door open. I patted my pocket, even though I knew the torch was still in there. It had been banging against my hip as I walked around the room. A wave of nervousness hit me. I drew in a calming breath, closed my door, and followed him, staying far enough back that he couldn't see me as he went down the stairs and crossed to Blackburn Hall's main door. He opened it and stepped outside in a smooth, practiced movement. The lofty room almost absorbed the dull thud of the door closing.

I scampered down the stairs and crossed the hall in the opposite direction, heading for the back of the house. I hoped I wouldn't lose Zippy, but I couldn't risk being locked out if he returned before I did. The library was deserted, and I crept carefully through the darkened room to the closed drapes. I twitched back one fabric panel, opened the French door, and fished the half crown out of my pocket. I held it against the strike plate as I closed the door, a movement that required finesse, which was hard to do because my hands trembled with adrenaline. I released the door handle and breathed a sigh of relief when the coin stayed in place and didn't ping onto the stone terrace.

The terrace was dark and deserted, but I felt exposed even

in the weak moonlight. I moved to the wall at the corner of the house and waited, listening. Had I guessed wrong? Was Zippy not coming around to the back of the house? Had he gone out through the front gates? The air was heavy and still, and the only sounds were the faint burble of the river and the rustle of something in the undergrowth—the kitchen cat, I hoped.

I couldn't follow Zippy if I lost him after he cleared the front door. Curse Jasper and his inane warnings. I shouldn't have worried about being cautious or what Jasper would think. I should have followed Zippy out the front door, key or no key—

A snatch of a whistled note floated through the air. After a pause, I heard it again, louder this time. A few seconds later, Zippy's tweedy form appeared in a gap between the trees, highlighted for a moment in the faint silvery moonlight. He was on the path that ran along the river to East Bank Cottage.

I stole through the garden, staying on the grass that edged the gravel paths so I didn't make any noise. The path beside the river was hard-packed earth, and when I reached it, I could walk along it quietly. I stayed back so if Zippy looked over his shoulder, he wouldn't be able to see me. He didn't use a torch, and I didn't need mine either as long as he stayed to the path, weaving back and forth in a serpentine pattern. He whistled at full volume now, but his timing was a little off. I wondered how many drinks he'd had after dinner. It didn't appear any of them had been coffee.

I dropped back a bit farther as he neared the point where the tree had toppled into the river. I had to go into the belt of trees that lined the path at that point because the path still hadn't been repaired. I didn't want to make any noise as I walked through the undergrowth, and I was picking my way through the deeper darkness under the branches when a hand covered my mouth and an arm came around me, pinning me against a solid chest.

CHAPTER TWENTY-TWO

J twisted my head away from the hand and whispered, "Jasper, what are you doing?" The tall pines blocked some of the moonlight, but I could still see the faint shape of a fedora.

"I could ask you the same thing." His grip loosened.

"I'm following Zippy."

"I'm doing the same," he said. "Well, technically, I was waiting here to see if *you* were following Zippy. I was sure you would be. How did you know it was me?"

"Your citrus and cinnamon aftershave. Very distinctive." I stepped back. I felt bereft and a little cold for a second, despite the warmth of the summer night. I started walking. "Let's go."

"Seems a shame. I quite enjoyed that."

"Don't tease." I pointed a finger at him. "And don't you dare tell me to go back to Blackburn Hall."

"Never crossed my mind. I'm here as your assistant." We left the closeness of the trees and walked along, our words barely above a whisper. "Of course, it would be easier to assist you if you let me in on the schedule. Is this another secret you can't share?"

SARA ROSETT

"Shh." I put a hand on Jasper's arm, and he halted beside me. Zippy had stopped. I breathed, "That lane goes to East Bank Cottage."

A flare of light blazed through the darkness as Zippy focused a torch on his wristwatch. He doused the light and continued on along the main path, his steps meandering back and forth. We followed along behind him silently for a long distance, the only sound the hoot of an owl and the rush of the river. A cloud drifted over the moon, and the clusters of trees along each side of the path lost any sense of depth, becoming flat black outlines like enormous stage decorations. We trooped on in Zippy's wake. After a while, the clouds shifted, and the details of the landscape became a little more defined as we followed Zippy into a small village, its shops and cottages whitewashed in the moonlight. "Where is this?" I asked.

"Sidlingham. Monty and I came here a few days ago to have dinner with a friend."

"I didn't realize it was so close to Blackburn Hall." A sign in the window of the pub announced, *Rooms to Let.* "Someone could have walked from here to Hadsworth easily. You checked the guests at the pub in Hadsworth and the golfers, but I didn't think to check the surrounding villages. I wonder if this pub had anyone staying here last week."

"Good question," Jasper said. "I didn't think of it either."

Zippy made his way in an undulating line to the door of the pub. A golden glow and the murmur of conversation spilled outside. He closed the door behind him, and the little village was quiet again.

Jasper motioned me in front of him toward the door. "Shall we?"

"I'm not exactly dressed for it."

"I noticed that. Did you expect Zippy to go for a midnight ride?"

I slapped Jasper's arm with the back of my hand. "I didn't

know what Zippy was going to do. If I was going to be tromping around the countryside in the middle of the night, I wanted to be prepared for anything—like climbing over walls or perhaps trudging across muddy fields. I didn't expect a meandering stroll along a deserted lane and a visit to a pub."

"Rather mundane, isn't it? But then again, Zippy's not the most avant-garde of individuals."

I set off for the pub. "Maybe no one will notice how I'm dressed."

It was a fairly busy night at the pub. A few people looked up when we entered, but it didn't seem anyone was particularly interested in my clothing. We sat down at a table on the opposite side of the room from Zippy. He was so absorbed in speaking to the woman who brought his beer, he didn't notice us. The woman's thick brunette hair was cut in a bob that fell over one eye as she tilted her head to listen to Zippy. Her red lips parted, and she threw her head back as she laughed. Zippy watched her like I imagined a man lost in the desert would eye a mirage of palm trees.

"Well, I guess that explains what Zippy's been up to," Jasper said.

"Yes. It looks like Zippy finally has another interest besides golf."

Jasper said, "Would you like something to drink?"

"I'll have a ginger beer."

Jasper went to order our drinks, and I kept an eye on Zippy. Surely he was meeting someone else here? But even after Jasper returned and we lingered at the table over our drinks, no one else approached Zippy's table. It was clear from the way Zippy's gaze followed the barmaid that he was only interested in her.

I put my glass down. "I find it hard to believe Zippy's been sneaking around to meet a girl."

"You'd be surprised what men will do to meet a girl."

"Why wouldn't he meet with her openly?"

"You're the one who told me what a stickler Lady Holt is. Do you think she'd welcome her son's association with a barmaid?" Jasper cut his gaze to the woman who was picking up empty glasses and wiping tabletops. She kept looking at Zippy from under her lashes and going out of her way to make sure she passed Zippy's table at every opportunity.

"I'm sure Lady Holt would be horrified. But why all the creeping about at night?"

"Who knows? Men do tend to behave in inexplicable ways when a woman is involved."

I pushed my chair back. "Let's go ask him."

Behind my shoulder, Jasper said, "I don't think he's interested in chatting with us tonight."

"We'll only take a moment of his time." I wove through the tables and gripped the back of one of the chairs at Zippy's table. "Zippy, how are you? Mind if we join you for a moment?"

Zippy stared at my face for a long moment, then blinked slowly. "Er—Olive?"

I pulled out the chair. "Yes, it's me. And Jasper is here as well."

As we were seated, Jasper said under his breath. "This should be entertaining."

I shot him a look. I hoped it conveyed if he didn't have anything helpful to say to keep his comments to himself. It must have been evocative. Jasper waved a hand, indicating I had the floor, then asked me if I wanted another drink.

"No. I'm at my limit." Jasper didn't ask Zippy the same question. Zippy looked like he was about five drinks past his limit. His hands were wrapped around his half-full pint as if someone might try to take it away from him.

Jasper went to the bar, and I turned to Zippy. Considering his state, a direct approach phrased in simple words was probably best. "Zippy, why did you sneak out of Blackburn Hall tonight?"

He leaned forward as if he were about to reveal state secrets and spoke in a whisper, but he still managed to douse me with alcoholic fumes. "The *mater* doesn't approve." He leaned back and shook his head in an exaggerated way. "Not at all. She forbade me."

"She doesn't approve of your friendship with . . ." I let my gaze travel across the room to the brunette barmaid.

Zippy's face softened. "Lucy." The word came out on a sigh.

"Have you been seeing Lucy long?"

Zippy didn't reply. He continued to gaze at Lucy. I resisted the urge to snap my fingers in front of his face. "Zippy!"

"Hm? What?"

"Have you been seeing Lucy for a long time?"

"Ages! At least two months."

"Then why don't you come here during the day?"

"Can't. Too dangerous."

Jasper returned to the table and caught the last statement from Zippy as he took a seat. Jasper sipped his pint and leaned in. "Too dangerous in what way?"

"Mrs. Fenimore." Zippy's tone had a finality to it that indicated the name should explain everything. I exchanged a look with Jasper, but he lifted one shoulder.

I asked, "Who's Mrs. Fenimore, Zippy?"

Zippy took a slow drink, then set his pint down with great concentration. He was weaving slightly from side to side even seated in his chair, and I supposed the table might seem to be rolling like a ship deck to him. "Mrs. Fenimore lives dir—direct—" He swallowed. "Across the street." He nodded at the pub's door, then attempted to put his elbow on the table but missed the edge and listed toward me.

Jasper caught Zippy's shoulder and straightened him. "She lives across the lane from the pub?"

Jasper nodded with the solemnness of a judge pronouncing a sentence. "Yes. Nothing to do all day but watch the street. She's the *mater's* bridge partner. Never misses a game. If she saw me or my motor . . ."

I looked at Jasper, and he commented, "Zippy has a Bugatti. Red. Distinctive."

"Oh, I see," I said.

Zippy said, "If Mrs. Fenimore saw me, she'd be off to Blackburn Hall like *that*." He illustrated with a quick movement of his hand that nearly caught me in the throat.

I leaned back until he returned to his slumped posture. "So you're sneaking around to prevent Lady Holt from learning about Lucy."

He attempted to draw himself up, but his spine was nowhere near the ruler-straight line his mother maintained. "It isn't that," Zippy said. "I like my privacy." He spoke slowly, enunciating each syllable, and grinned a bit when he got the last word out without stumbling over it.

I sighed and said to Jasper, "Well, I suppose this is like your list of guests at the pub—good to know, if only for elimination purposes."

"Speaking of lists." Jasper handed me a piece of paper torn from a notebook across Zippy's line of vision, but Zippy's gaze didn't flinch. He seemed to have forgotten us. He'd propped an elbow on the table and rested his chin in his palm. His adoring gaze was fixed on Lucy again.

The paper contained another list of names—Mr. Timothy Hornby, Mr. and Mrs. Leslie Wellsby, Mr. Benjamin Leighland, Mr. and Miss Collingworth, and Mr. Rupert Jones. "What's this?" I put out a hand to stop the slow slide of Zippy's elbow in my direction.

"I took a quick peek at the guest ledger when I ordered our drinks," Jasper said. "It was unattended, so I copied the names down. The length of their stays varied, but all those names overlapped on either Tuesday or Wednesday of last week. I checked that list against the list of golfers. No matches. It doesn't get us any further along either."

I sighed and tucked the list away in my pocket. "Well, at least we've been thorough." I frowned at Zippy. I might as well be thorough with Zippy as well. Despite being rather drunk, he'd been forthcoming. I should find out all I could from him. Maybe I could wring some tiny detail from him that would help sort everything out. "Zippy, did you ever go to East Bank Cottage?"

He pulled his gaze away from Lucy and squinted at me. "Why would I do that?"

"To meet Mayhew? To chat? Or anything else . . . ?"

"Never saw Mayhew . . . like a ghost. People said someone lived in East Bank Cottage, but you never saw Mayhew."

"So you never saw Mayhew, not even when you were on your way to visit Lucy here at night?"

"Nope."

"But your mother thought you were visiting the cottage."

"I let her think that. Easier that way, don't you know?" Zippy's mouth curved into a smile. He looked like a little boy who had managed to sneak several treats from the cook without his mother knowing. "If she thought I was going to East Bank Cottage, I didn't have to worry about her finding out about this." He waved his pint around, indicating the pub.

"But Lady Holt was upset with you when she thought you were visiting East Bank Cottage."

"Yes."

"She thought that there was perhaps some . . . connection . . . between you and Mayhew."

Zippy frowned. "Connection?"

"An—ah—romantic connection?"

Zippy shook his head. "No. I'm not that sort." His gaze drifted to Lucy.

"But if Lady Holt *thought* there was a connection, what would she have done?" I asked.

"Ended it," Zippy said without missing a beat.

"Really? I can't picture Lady Holt doing something like that." She'd told Calder she'd never met Mayhew—not that she couldn't have lied, but it was difficult to picture the extremely proper Lady Holt doing something as primeval as bashing someone on the head or pushing someone off the edge of the path near the river.

"Not her," Zippy said. "She'd have someone warn Mayhew off."

"That's all she'd have done? A stern talking to? Not . . . something more?"

My hint went directly over his head. His gaze was focused on his nearly empty pint, and he giggled. "She couldn't find the cottage on her own. No. She'd send someone else."

"Who?" Jasper asked.

Zippy drained his pint and set it down with a clatter. "Bower. He'd do anything for her."

"Anything?" I asked.

"Yes. He's been with us for years and years. He was with the *mater's* family before she married father. He's one of those old-school retainers—loyal. The kind who don't seem to exist much anymore. He takes care of everything for her—all the problems."

CHAPTER TWENTY-THREE

"*D*o you think we should have left him there?" I asked Jasper as we walked back along the path from Sidlingham through the dark fields toward Blackburn Hall.

"Zippy will be fine. And short of bodily removing him, I don't think we could have convinced him to leave with us."

"But will he be able to get back to Blackburn Hall on his own?"

"I had a word with the owner of the pub. If the lovely Lucy leaves Zippy high and dry, I told the owner of the pub to put Zippy up for the night and I'd cover the cost."

"That's philanthropic of you."

"I'd hate to see him tumble into the river on his way home."

We'd walked through the fields away from Sidlingham, and now the path was near the river. We could hear the dull roar of moving water even though we couldn't see it yet. At the mention of the river, we both fell silent and paced along.

"No matter what Zippy says about his mother and Bower," Jasper said, "I have a hard time picturing either Lady Holt or Bower doing away with Mayhew."

"I do too." I shoved my hands deeper into the pockets of my cardigan, stretching the fabric as I shrugged. "But I learned at Archly Manor appearances can be deceiving."

Jasper dipped his head. "Quite."

"I'll just have to see if I can sort out where Bower and Lady Holt were on Wednesday morning."

"Don't you mean *we?* I thought this was a partnership. You seem to be forgetting that point—quite a lot, actually."

His tone was light, but that was Jasper's way. He didn't confront. He dodged to the side and came at the issue obliquely, usually with a diffusing humor or casual demeanor. The fact that he'd brought it up showed he wasn't going to dismiss it.

"I should've let you know I was going to follow Zippy tonight, but I thought you would try to talk me out of it."

"And miss all the fun? I'd never do that. Tooling around the countryside in deepest darkness is one of my favorite things to do."

We could see the river as we came to the portion of the path that had collapsed. The clouds had drifted away, and moonlight glittered on the rippling water. Our steps slowed, and we watched the water as it swirled around the massive trunk of the tree that still lay in the middle of the river. After a moment, Jasper asked, "You're sure Mayhew hadn't prepared to leave?"

"It didn't feel that way. By all accounts in the village, Mayhew didn't travel. And if Mayhew left the cottage on her own, where was she going?"

"Perhaps to visit Mr. Hightower?"

I shook my head. "No, Mr. Hightower said Mayhew had an aversion to London and refused to meet with him."

"Maybe Mayhew got word of his father's —I mean, her— father's death."

"It's possible. But would that cause Mayhew to drop everything and leave the cottage at a moment's notice?"

Jasper asked, "But you said a suitcase was found."

"Yes, and that does indicate either preparation to leave town . . . or an incredibly devious mind." I could feel Jasper looking at me as I said, "If I'm right, Mayhew didn't intend to depart that day. The whole 'departure' is a ruse to distract everyone, to put off the discovery of Mayhew's death. The person who killed Mayhew went back to the cottage and typed up some notes, one to Anna, telling her to continue with the manuscript, and others to the grocer and the milkman to cancel deliveries. I think that's what happened."

"Perhaps Mayhew was leaving to start over somewhere else, somewhere where she could live without a mask and without pretending to be a man."

I turned away from the water to the trees. "But Mayhew made no arrangements to move out of the cottage or close accounts." We plunged into the woods to go around the washed-out section of the path. "I know there's no solid evidence, yet I don't think Mayhew planned to leave."

"You *are* good at these intuitive leaps, I will give you that, but . . ."

"You think I'm jumping to conclusions," I said.

"I didn't say that. You have a way of putting together all sorts of things. You're good at reading people and assessing situations below the surface. You sense things others miss."

"I think that's quite the nicest thing you've said to me."

"I could say much nicer things to you than that, but I must leave you here." The windows of Blackburn Hall were dark. "How are you getting back in?"

"I wedged a coin into the lock of the library door. And if that fails, Zippy left the front door open."

"Of course he did."

Jasper walked with me up the steps to the terrace as I said, "I'll poke around and see if I can find out what Lady Holt was doing on Wednesday."

"I believe Grigsby might be able to help."

"Grigsby is here?" I hadn't seen Jasper's valet at all and assumed he'd stayed behind in London.

"He is now. He went to visit his sister in Canterbury for a few days, but he rejoined me today. I'm sure he and Bower would get along well. Lady Holt has invited me to stay at Blackburn Hall tomorrow evening after the dinner party. I'll bring Grigsby with me. Perhaps he can find a few moments to chat with Bower."

"Just don't tell Grigsby it's for me." Grigsby disapproved of me. The few times I'd met Grigsby, he'd behaved like an elderly chaperone trying to protect Jasper from an unwelcome suitor—me.

"I'll tell him it's one of my quirky inquiries," Jasper said.

"You have many of those?"

"Constantly. He'll take it in stride. I'll see you tomorrow morning."

"I may not be here. Serena arranged for us to play golf. She wants to introduce me to the game. I suppose it will be after lunch before we return."

"Tomorrow afternoon, then," Jasper said as I approached the door to the library. It opened easily, and I caught the half crown before it hit the terrace.

"Clever . . . and a bit devious," Jasper said.

"Thank you."

"Where did you learn a trick like that?"

"Boarding school provided quite a well-rounded education. Good night."

"Good night," Jasper said, then waited until I was inside the library before he melted into the shadows of the terrace. I made sure the door to the terrace was locked, then I listened for a moment before I crossed the library. The ticking of the clock on the mantelpiece was the only sound.

I used the torch to make my way through the library but switched it off when I left the room because the moonlight filtering through the windows above the landing lit up the entry hall. I crept by the stairs and kept going until I reached the morning room.

I went across to Lady Holt's desk with a little twinge of guilt. I switched on the torch, shining it on her calendar. It was a monthly calendar and lay open on the desk, thank goodness. It seemed less like snooping if I merely glanced at something on the desk rather than digging through the drawers.

On Wednesday of last week, a note in Lady Holt's penmanship read, "Bridge lunch." A few notes under the entry with instructions for preparations made it clear Lady Holt was hosting the bridge lunch at Blackburn Hall. As I returned to my room, I wondered how elaborate the lunch had been. Would preparations for it have taken all day, or would someone like Bower have been able to slip out and confront Mayhew?

I should've slept deeply after hiking around the countryside, but I spent most of the rest of the night plumping my pillow and shifting from one side to another. After what seemed like hours, the notes of a jaunty whistle drifted through the air. I turned my head toward the door. Had I been dreaming?

No, there it was again. The notes grew louder, then faded. Faintly, I heard a solid thud as a door closed. I'd wound my watch and put it on the bedside table before I'd crawled into bed, and now I tilted it so I could see the face. The hands and numbers picked out in radium glowed. Four in the morning. So Zippy had made it home no worse for wear.

It was only as sunlight began to press between the folds of the drapes that I felt my muscles begin to relax. The sheer exhaustion of going several hours without sleep finally overtook me, and I dropped into a deep, dreamless sleep.

I came awake when Janet entered my room with a cup of

hot chocolate. She opened the drapes and sunlight streamed into the room at an angle that indicated it was late morning. "Pardon me, Miss Belgrave," she said. "Bower sent me to tell you someone is here to see you."

I pushed my hair out of my eyes, squinted against the invading light, then struggled up on an elbow as I reached for the hot chocolate. "I told Jasper not to come until this afternoon."

"It's not Mr. Rimington, miss. It's Inspector Longly."

"Sorry to keep you waiting, Inspector," I said, wishing my heartbeat would calm down. It wasn't as if I'd done anything wrong. From Inspector Longly's point of view, I'm sure it looked as if I could be guilty of Pearce's death, but I *wasn't* guilty, and I shouldn't act like I was. I smoothed my features into an expression of polite interest.

"Good morning, Miss Belgrave." Longly gestured to a seat on a sofa opposite him, and I sat down. "I need to clarify a few points."

"Of course. I'll help in any way I can."

"Excellent." He consulted his notebook. "Tell me again what you and Mr. Pearce discussed when you met."

"I don't believe you asked about it."

He looked up. "Very good. No, I didn't, but I need to know now. What did you talk about?"

The hot chocolate suddenly wasn't settling well in my stomach, but I didn't let my expression slip. "I don't remember exactly. I do know I asked him if he came from the firm of Mercer, Blackthorne, and Thompkins. He confirmed that. And we talked about the Hartman debacle. He said he lost money too."

"What else?"

"That's all I recall." My heartbeat quickened again, and

my armpits grew damp. I hated lying, and I knew where these questions were leading.

Longly put his notebook on the cushion beside him and draped his arm across his leg. "Miss Belgrave, let's not dance around it any longer. I have statements from the other guests that you threatened Mr. Pearce."

"Threatened?"

"Yes." He pressed the notebook down into the cushion, tilting it so he could read from it. "'I'd like to wring his neck. I must get my revenge.'" Longly looked back at me. "Did you say that?"

I clapped my lips together for a moment, then said, "I believe I need to make a phone call before I say anything else."

A look of what seemed to be disappointment traced across Longly's face. He closed the notebook with a snap. "I suggest you do that." He scooted forward to the edge of the cushion but paused before he stood. He seemed to want to say something else.

I sat still. After a second, he said, "I'm not pleased with the direction the investigation has taken, but I must pursue it. I suggest you engage legal counsel at the earliest convenience." I opened my mouth, but he held up his hand. "No, don't say anything. I'm not speaking as an officer of the law now. I know how deeply your family cares for you, and I would hate to see *any* of them hurt because of your involvement in this situation."

It took me a moment to parse the plethora of words, but then I said, "You're worried about Gwen and how this will impact her."

A trace of pink suffused his cheeks. "I think I have a . . . friendship with your family—your extended family, that is. I say this out of concern for you . . . and them. I suggest you retain legal counsel at your earliest possible convenience."

My heartbeat skipped into an even faster pace, but I kept

my voice steady. "I don't see how I could have anything to worry about. Pearce's death and Mayhew's *must* to be linked somehow. And I was not even in Hadsworth when Mayhew died."

Longly shook his head. "It's a faulty conclusion that the two deaths are linked."

"How can they not be? Two deaths within such a short period of time in a small village? Surely they must be associated."

Longly stood. "There's no evidence Mayhew's death was anything other than an accident."

"But several people had a motive to want Mayhew dead—Dr. Finch and An—um—and Lady Holt, to name two."

His head came up. "Lady Holt?"

"You didn't know Lady Holt was afraid her son was visiting Mayhew at East Bank Cottage? That she thought that he might be . . . um . . . involved with Mayhew? It wasn't true," I added. I didn't want to start any rumors. "Zippy was sneaking out of the house to visit a barmaid in Sidlingham, but he let Lady Holt think he was doing something else to cover up his real destination."

Longly's eyes narrowed. "I wasn't aware of this. What's your source of information?"

"Zippy, but I heard it first from the servants." I didn't mention it was servants' gossip I'd been eavesdropping on, but Longly seemed to be turning things over in his mind. He knew as well as I did the servants were often better informed about everything that went on in a household than the owners.

"And you think Lady Holt did something to prevent this association from continuing?"

"No, probably not Lady Holt. But I wonder if she enlisted the help of someone else to do it for her . . . someone like Bower. Zippy says Bower would do anything for her."

Longly gave a little shake to his head as he closed his eyes for a second. "Miss Belgrave," he said, his tone one of someone who was dealing with a person who tried their patience. "Both Lady Holt as well as Bower's whereabouts on the morning of Mayhew's death have been accounted for." He held up a hand as I opened my mouth. "Multiple witnesses confirm both Lady Holt and Bower as well as the rest of the staff were fully occupied preparing for Lady Holt's bridge lunch last Wednesday. No one left Blackburn Hall that morning. I'm sure of it. Neither one could possibly be involved in Mayhew's death. And—again—we have no solid evidence Mayhew's death was anything other than an accident."

My confidence that I'd found a new angle on the situation deflated as Longly went on, "On the other hand, Mr. Pearce's death was unquestionably murder. I suggest you leave off these absurd theories and concentrate on locating a solicitor."

I swallowed and raised my chin, glad Longly couldn't know how hard my heart was pounding. "I have nothing to worry about related to Mr. Pearce."

"We have statements you threatened Mr. Pearce. We never take that lightly."

I fisted my hands. "I was frustrated and upset, but I didn't hurt him in any way."

"I advise you to retain a solicitor at your earliest convenience." Longly left the room, and a cocktail of anger and frustration swirled through me . . . along with fear. I hated to admit it, but I was frightened. Longly had been completely serious, and I doubted he usually urged suspects to get legal advice. He had a fondness for Gwen, and he'd spoken out of loyalty and concern for her.

Footsteps sounded, and my heart kicked. Was Longly returning to arrest me? But it was only Serena who walked past the door then backtracked when she caught sight of me. "There you are. We should leave soon."

I gave myself a mental shake as I registered that Serena was in golf clothes. "Um . . . yes." I'd completely forgotten about our plans. Golfing was the last thing I wanted to do. But a good houseguest doesn't abandon plans once one has committed to them. I'd have to mull things over on the course. "I need to make a telephone call and change clothes."

"Let's meet in the hall in a quarter of an hour."

∾

"We'll start on the back nine today," Serena said as we marched across the grass away from the clubhouse. "I thought we'd play nine holes. That'll give you a little introduction to the game and let me get back to work this afternoon."

My bag of borrowed golf clubs bumped against my hip with every step. "Good idea." Sun beamed down on us from a sky that was a broad swath of unbroken blue. It was a warm, lovely day.

I'd telephoned Uncle Leo and explained I needed a solicitor. Ringing him gave me a twisty, sick feeling. I hated to ask for help, but I had no money to pay for a solicitor and neither did Father. After the chat with Longly, it seemed to be a good idea to at least contact someone, and Uncle Leo was the only person I trusted to put me in touch with someone reliable.

As we strode across the grass, I was actually glad I was on the course with Serena. There was nothing more I could do at Blackburn Hall. Not one of my ideas had panned out. If Mayhew's death really was an accident—and I still couldn't quite make myself believe that was the case—then all my running around asking questions had been completely useless. I'd wasted a massive amount of time and mental energy. Getting out in the sunshine and walking around the golf course until I was exhausted was probably the best thing I could do. It would keep my mind off my other troubles, namely being a possible murder suspect.

It was a quiet morning on the course, and it was only

Serena and I playing together. Serena hit a beautiful drive down the middle of the course from the tee box. She waved for me to take her place. "Go ahead. Do it like we practiced, and don't think about it too much."

Serena had shown me the basics of how to swing at the golf ball before we set off on the course. For my first attempt, I positioned my feet apart and put the club behind the ball. I blew out a steadying breath, drew back the club, and whacked the ball. It sailed through the air. Unfortunately, it didn't go down the middle of the green. It ended up far off the course in the rough.

"Excellent," Serena said.

I dropped my arms, letting the club head fall to the ground. "If that was good, then I have several misconceptions about the game of golf."

"Nonsense. You did fine. I knew you wouldn't be one of those halfhearted, tentative players. Much better to get in there and give it a good thwack. Let's go find your ball. It's not too far off the fairway."

My ball was buried in a thick tuft of grass, but with Serena's coaching on how to approach the shot, I hit the ball back onto the fairway and completed the hole. I found putting to be much more challenging than driving off the tee. I finally managed to tap my ball into the hole and reached down to retrieve it. "At this rate, my score will be astronomical. Good thing we're only playing nine holes."

Serena lined up and tapped her ball in with ease. "No worries. You're learning, so the score doesn't really matter." She plucked her golf ball from the cup, and we moved on to the eleventh. I missed the fairway again. When I finally got in range of the hole, the ball was about forty yards short of the green.

"So what do I do here?" I asked as I approached the ball. "It's too far away to putt, but if I use a driver, I'll go far past the hole."

SARA ROSETT

Serena selected a club with an open face. "Keep your back-swing short and hinge your wrists." Serena demonstrated how to angle my wrists upward during the shortened back-swing. "Then be aggressive in the downswing and hit it sharply."

I imitated Serena's motions. The ball lofted through the air, dropped onto the green, and rolled almost to the edge of the hole. "It worked!"

"Of course it worked. You're a natural," Serena said.

"Beginner's luck, more likely," I said as we moved on to the twelfth. Instead of connecting with the ball squarely, I hit the top of it. My drive dribbled down the course. "At least I'm in the fairway this time." Serena laughed and teed off, sending her ball sailing far beyond mine. As we set off down the fairway, a gap in the trees drew my attention. I could see across the river to the path that ran along the grounds of Blackburn Hall. I slowed my steps. "Is this where you saw Mayhew walking on the path?"

Serena nodded and pointed with a club. "Right through that break in the trees. I saw a slash of red—the tie, you know. That's what caught my eye."

The distance wasn't that great. I could see how she would be able to spot someone on the path.

Serena said, "Mayhew gave me a jaunty little wave."

"Did she usually do that?" From everything I'd heard, Mayhew avoided people.

"No, but I suppose it was just a friendly gesture. After all, there was no way we could stop and talk, not with the river between us." Serena wiped a bit of grass from the head of her golf club before she returned it to her bag. "Our foursome walked on, and we didn't hear the bank collapse. Probably because the wind was so high that day. Quite a noisy thing, wind."

I stopped walking. "How did you say Mayhew waved?"

"Just a lift of a hand. She was holding her hat with the

other hand." Serena demonstrated, lifting her left hand in a single motion, then she let it drop back to her side. "It was a blustery day. We fought the wind all day." She shook her head. "It's terrible when I think about it. We were so focused on correcting for the strong wind, and a person was injured and dying on the other side of the river. We didn't know a thing about it."

I was barely listening to Serena. I was lost in my own churning thoughts.

"Olive?"

I blinked and realized Serena must have been walking as she spoke. I hadn't moved from the spot where I'd stopped.

"What is it?" Serena asked.

"Nothing. Sorry." I hurried to catch up with her.

We finished the hole, and Serena recorded our scores, her head bent. "It's interesting to play the course backward, as it were. Starting on the back nine gives it a whole new perspective."

Her words penetrated my fuzzy thoughts, then reverberated in my mind. "That's it," I said to myself. "I've been looking at it all wrong. I've been looking at it backward."

Serena looked up from the scoring card. "What did you say?"

"Just talking to myself. Sorry."

She put the card away and headed down the path to the next tee. "Don't be. I do it all the time. It's an excellent way to work out your thoughts."

I hurried to catch up with her, my thoughts spinning. "Yes, it is."

CHAPTER TWENTY-FOUR

$\mathcal{M}$y mind was not on golf for the rest of the game. We completed our nine holes, had a quick lunch at the clubhouse, and then Serena decided to stay on and work on her putting. I couldn't imagine she needed improvement in that area. She'd sunk every putt within two or three strokes, but she insisted her long putts were not as consistent as she'd like. I returned to Blackburn Hall, still mulling over what I'd discovered about Mayhew.

Bower opened the door for me. "Hello, Miss Belgrave. Did you enjoy your golf game?"

"Yes. I found it to be very productive."

"I'm glad to hear it. Will Miss Serena be returning soon?"

"No, she stayed on to work on her putting."

Bower said, "Very good. You may leave the clubs here." He glanced at a footman, who was walking across the hall. The footman changed course and took the clubs from me. "Mr. Rimington arrived a short while ago," Bower continued. "Shall I inform him that you have returned?"

"No, that's fine. I'll speak to him myself."

"He's in the library."

Jasper sat in one of the chairs by the window, but only his

well-tailored trousers and perfectly polished shoes were visible. The upper half of his body was hidden behind an open newspaper.

"Hello, Jasper. Don't let Lady Holt see you reading that. She has a phobia about the newspapers."

Jasper folded the paper. "Oh, I don't think she'd mind me reading about Mr. Carter's lecture to the Royal Geographical Society on King Tut's tomb. He predicts crowns and regalia still to be discovered, by the way. Surely Lady Holt wouldn't object to that. No local scandal reported."

"I wouldn't risk it. She's rabid about the newspapers. It's odd, though. Her etiquette column runs in a newspaper."

"I suppose she considers everything else besides her column disgraceful. No worries, I'll dispose of the evidence shortly. How was golf?"

"Surprisingly illuminating."

"I've heard golf described quite a few different ways but never like that. By the way, I just encountered Zippy a short time ago. It seems he made it home unscathed last night."

I perched on the arm of a chair. "I heard him whistling on his way back to his room during the early hours of this morning. How is he today?"

"He's sworn off drink forever. I expect that to last for"— Jasper checked his wristwatch—"a few more hours. Until cocktail hour tonight."

"You're probably right. You can call off Grigsby, by the way."

"Found out the information on your own?"

"In a way. Inspector Longly came to visit me this morning. I told him our suspicions. He informed me Lady Holt as well as Bower and the rest of the staff have alibis for the morning of Mayhew's death."

Jasper's eyebrows went up. "He came here to discuss the case with you?"

"No. He wanted to warn me to engage a solicitor. It

appears there will be an arrest soon. And I have the distinct feeling it will be me."

Jasper turned sharply to me. "And you spent the afternoon golfing?"

"I telephoned Uncle Leo. He's engaging a solicitor for me. But I don't think I'll need him." I slid off the arm of the chair. I was too excited to sit still. I walked to a table by the windows with a chessboard, the pieces lined up on each side of the board.

"You've solved the case?" Jasper asked.

I tilted my head to the left and right. "Maybe. I do think I'm finally on the right track." I picked up the black knight and moved it up two squares, then over one. "Serena and I played the back nine today. When we came to the hole where Serena spotted Mayhew, we talked about what she saw. And then she made a comment about playing the course backward —starting on the tenth instead of the first—and it all came together."

Jasper came over and leaned on the back of the chair across the table from me. "I know you're speaking English—I recognize the words—but you're not making sense."

"I'm about to explain it all. I think I've worked it out. I've been looking at it all wrong—backward. It's actually quite simple. Serena didn't see Mayhew on the path."

Jasper had leaned forward and was moving a white pawn up two spaces. He looked up at me, his hand still on the pawn. "What do you mean? Is it too far to see someone clearly?"

"No, it's not that. It's perfectly possible to see someone. It's not the distance that's the issue. The point is Serena didn't see *Mayhew*."

Jasper removed his hand from the pawn, crossed his arms, and leaned on the back of the chair. "How can you know that?"

"When Mayhew's body was discovered, Serena told

Calder she saw a man in a tweed jacket and a hat from the golf course. Today she said it was extremely windy that day. Mayhew was holding her hat with one hand while she waved to Serena with the other." I bounced on my toes. "Do you see? It *couldn't* have been Mayhew."

"I wish I could say I'm only playing the part of the rather dim sidekick to humor you, but I really don't see what you're getting at."

I picked up the knight, knocked over Jasper's pawn, and set the knight on that square. "The person Serena saw didn't have a suitcase."

Jasper's eyebrows flared. "Ah, yes. That does make all the difference."

"I knew you'd understand as soon as I described it." I put the pawn to one side of the board. "Serena demonstrated what 'Mayhew' did." I pressed my right hand to my head and lifted my left hand in a quick wave.

"So where was the suitcase?" Jasper asked, the excitement in his words matching mine.

"Exactly. One was found with the body."

"Could Serena be lying?"

"She was with a group of golfers."

"Yes, that's right," Jasper said. "At the inquest, Longly said the other golfers' testimony agreed with Serena's."

"You see what this means, don't you?" I leaned over the chessboard and lowered my voice. "It's most likely Mayhew was already dead at that point."

"And someone had dressed as Mayhew and appeared in public to confuse the timeline."

"Exactly. Anna said the postmortem estimated the time of death at five to seven days before Mayhew's body was discovered. Seven days before would be Tuesday, which was the day before Serena saw the imposter, so I think Mayhew must have been killed Tuesday, probably during the night, either at East Bank Cottage or during one of his nighttime strolls. Mayhew liked to go out at night, probably because she could roam in the darkness without wearing her mask."

"I suppose the bit about it happening at night is logical. You wouldn't want to be carting a body around during the day," Jasper said.

"And why would you imitate Mayhew if she were still alive? That doesn't make sense."

"Tuesday night, you think?" Jasper spoke slowly, testing the idea.

"And while it was dark, the murderer must have packed a suitcase for Mayhew to make it look as if Mayhew had left. The murderer dumped Mayhew's body over the edge of the riverbank at its weakest point and pitched the suitcase after the body. Then, either the bank collapsed and covered Mayhew, or the murderer helped it along, making sure the falling earth covered Mayhew's body. The murderer returned to Mayhew's cottage, typed up the notes, including the one to Anna, so Mayhew's disappearance wouldn't be noted straightaway. Once it was daylight on Wednesday, he—or she —put on one of Mayhew's tweed jackets and walked the path, making sure to draw the attention of a golfing party so 'Mayhew' would be seen that morning, establishing she was alive. It was far enough away that someone would recognize the clothes but not close enough to see the person's face well."

"Quite a thorough sort."

"Scarily so. I think the murderer even remembered to replicate Mayhew's bright tie. Serena said when she saw Mayhew on the path that morning, it was the red tie that drew her attention—a slash of red—those were her exact words, which makes me wonder . . . where was Mayhew's pocket square? She should have seen two bright splashes of red, not one. Several people mentioned Mayhew always wore a tie and matching pocket square in bright colors."

"It could have slipped down inside the pocket." Jasper

demonstrated, pushing his tasteful cream-colored pocket square down so it wasn't visible.

"Oh, don't do that. Grigsby will have heart palpitations if he sees you like that." I plucked it out and repositioned it.

"Indeed." Jasper checked the alignment of the pocket square and made a minor adjustment.

I crossed my arms and leaned against the chair by the chess set. "Or it could have been taken out of Mayhew's pocket before the murderer pitched Mayhew into the riverbed. Later, after the notes were typed, the murderer folded the red pocket square lengthwise and fixed it so that from a distance it would look like a tie. When Mayhew's body was discovered, I only saw a tie, not a pocket square."

Jasper frowned. "It could have been lost at some point, though. Perhaps the water swept it away."

"Perhaps. But there's still the suitcase. Mayhew was found with a suitcase, but the person Serena saw wasn't carrying a suitcase. The murderer must have packed Mayhew's suitcase so it would look as if Mayhew intended to travel, but once the suitcase was tipped over the edge of the bank, there wasn't another suitcase handy for the masquerade by the river. The murderer must have hoped no one would realize the suitcase was missing from the sighting. Or perhaps it was such a convoluted plan, they didn't realize the mistake."

Jasper said, "It's possible, but what's the connection between Mayhew's death and Pearce's? Why was Mayhew killed?"

"This is where the backward bit comes in. Who had a severe accident shortly before Mayhew died?"

"The local solicitor. But you think it wasn't an accident," Jasper said, spacing his words apart.

"Right." I dropped into the chair. "I've been looking at everything backward. I thought Mayhew's death was the first incident in a chain of events that led to Pearce's death. But what if Pearce's death was in the works from the beginning?

What if Pearce's fall—or botched attempt to kill Pearce by pushing him down the stairs—was the *start* of the chain, not the end?"

Jasper gave me a long look, then said, "And you think Mayhew somehow got mixed up in that?"

"Exactly," I said. "What if Mayhew knew something or saw something about a plan to kill Pearce?"

Jasper eased into the chair across from me. "Then our murderer would want Mayhew out of the way. Although, Mayhew wasn't exactly the chatty type."

"But if you planned to murder Pearce, you wouldn't want someone around who might inform the police of your plan. Or if you succeeded in killing Pearce, you wouldn't want someone to tell the police you'd thought about doing away with Pearce. You wouldn't—couldn't—take that chance."

"*I* wouldn't plan to murder anyone in the first place," Jasper said, then turned serious as he gazed at the chessboard. "Your theory does turn everything on its head."

"And raises the question of who wanted Pearce dead—besides me, of course."

Jasper rubbed his chin. "Let's run through your list of suspects for Mayhew's death. Are any of them connected with Pearce?"

I sighed. "I've been pondering that and can't come up with a motive or even a connection between Pearce and anyone I suspected might be involved in Mayhew's death."

Jasper leaned back in his typical languid manner, but his hooded gaze was sharp. "Talk me through it." He propped an elbow on the arm of the chair and cupped his fingers around his chin.

"All right." I began to shift the chess pieces back to their typical places on their respective sides of the board. "Operating on the theory that Mayhew's death was murder and that the same person committed both crimes, we can eliminate Anna and Dr. Finch."

Jasper flexed his fingers away from his lips as he spoke. "Neither of them were present after dinner when Pearce's coffee was poisoned. With the qualifiers you've set, that makes sense."

"Emily Pearce has to be at the top of the suspect list of course."

"Emily?"

"The spouse is always a suspect."

"Oh, undoubtedly. But what reason would she have to do away with Mayhew—or her husband—for that matter?"

"I don't know in either case. Her husband was older than her—at least a decade or two, don't you think? Perhaps she wanted to be free of him. She had opportunity. She was at the bridge table with us."

"But anyone could have taken one of the asthma cigarettes and emptied the contents of it into Pearce's cup while the card tables were arranged."

I slumped back against the chair. "I know. It was chaotic there for a few minutes as the tables were set up. And I haven't heard a whisper of scandal about Mrs. Pearce. Lady Holt says she was devoted to Mr. Pearce."

"Yet Mrs. Pearce seemed as skittish as a colt," Jasper said. "Of course, her husband took a tumble down the stairs and then was poisoned, so she has every reason to be nervy."

"Then there's Zippy," I said. "Originally, I wondered if he was hiding something, but now we know he wasn't putting on an act of nonchalance when Mayhew died. Zippy's so besotted with Lucy, I doubt he's even given Mayhew's death, not to mention Pearce's, more than a passing thought."

"It seems that way," Jasper said.

"And then we have Lady Holt and Serena. If I'm right and Mayhew was already dead when Serena spotted someone on the path, that wipes out both her alibi and Lady Holt's."

"Any connection between either of them and Pearce?"

"Nothing worth murdering someone over. At least, I

haven't uncovered anything like that in the time I've been here. The two families socialized, of course, but Serena said the Pearces were new acquaintances."

"Perhaps she's lying? Maybe she and Mr. Pearce were . . . involved." Jasper flared an eyebrow. "Perhaps she wanted him to divorce Mrs. Pearce and be with her?"

"You haven't been around Serena much, have you?"

"No. Why?"

"She's much more interested in her work—her scientific studies—than anything romantic. I can't see her carrying on an affair with a neighbor." I paused. "Her work, though. It centers on decay and decomposition."

"Rather macabre."

"Yes." I tilted the bishop playing piece back and forth. "I did wonder if she was somehow involved in Mayhew's death . . . if perhaps—oh, it sounds absurd."

"We're theorizing. No theory too strange."

I set the bishop down. "Well, this one is definitely on the gruesome side. Seeing Mayhew's body didn't faze Serena. In fact, she studied it—avidly, I thought. I had to insist we leave and notify the police."

"Ah, I see what you're thinking. Did she carry her interest in decomposition a little too far?"

"See, it does sound absurd. No one would murder someone just to study decay."

Jasper lifted a shoulder. "If they're unhinged, they might."

I shook my head. "Serena is practical and forthright. If she wanted to study human decomposition she'd—I don't know, request a cadaver from a medical school or some such thing."

"But would they give it to her?"

"Now you're just playing devil's advocate."

"Guilty." Jasper grinned briefly. "But you're the one who brought it up. What about Lord Holt?"

"He only seems to be interested in golf, but perhaps that's a front?"

"If it is, he should be on the stage. Golf seems to be his single focus."

"Even when the men stay behind in the drawing room?"

"Especially then." Jasper stared at the ceiling a moment, then shook his head. "No, can't say I've heard him mention anything else. And he didn't seem to be friendly with Pearce. They didn't have much interaction. What about Lady Holt? Perhaps she invested in Hartman Consolidated on Pearce's advice?"

"No, I don't think so. Lady Holt said she never bothers with anything to do with money. I'm sure she considers it vulgar." I looked out the window to the far side of the terrace, where the servants were positioning chairs and tables for this evening. "Funny how once you have plenty of money, you can pretend it's tawdry."

I gave myself a mental shake. It wouldn't do any good to succumb to jealousy. I had enough money to get by—at least for a little longer. "It sounds as if she and Lord Holt leave all that sort of thing to their estate steward," I added.

"I agree," Jasper said. "They don't seem to be the most involved land owners."

"Even if their steward did invest the money unwisely," I said, "I doubt Lady Holt would know about it."

"Perhaps *she* was having a torrid affair with Pearce."

"Be sensible. Can you really picture that?"

"I'd rather not. Don't frown at me like a school matron." Jasper levered himself higher in the chair. "I'll be serious. No, our hostess doesn't seem the type to indulge in dalliances of that sort. But you realize where that leaves us?"

"Yes. Back with one viable suspect—me."

CHAPTER TWENTY-FIVE

*D*espite Lady Holt's original plans to keep dinner simple, it turned out to be a long and elaborate meal with three more courses than usual. Emily Pearce smiled at all the appropriate times and participated in the conversation, but her manner was reserved. I was glad for Mrs. Shaw's presence and soothing demeanor. She and Lady Holt combined forces to carry us through dinner's stilted atmosphere. I think the tense atmosphere was because we were all on guard, making an effort not to refer to Pearce in any way. Mrs. Shaw's soothing murmur of conversation, which flowed as steadily as a slow-moving stream, provided a nice counterpoint to Lady Holt's dictatorial control of the dialogue around the table.

When Lady Holt led the ladies out of the dining room, she guided us to the entryway, around the stairs, down a short passage, and then out the French doors that opened onto the terrace, where tables and chairs were set up along with coffee and after-dinner drinks. It was warm, but it wasn't as muggy as it had been last night. A gentle breeze ruffled the leaves of the trees and made the paper lanterns strung up around the terrace bob.

I took a seat next to Emily Pearce in the hopes that I could guide the conversation and she'd reveal something about Pearce I hadn't uncovered. I'd been seated at the other end of the table from her and hadn't yet had the opportunity to talk with her.

"Hadsworth is such a picturesque village," I said.

Mrs. Pearce gave a perfunctory smile. "Yes."

"Have you lived here long?"

"Nearly a year." Her reply was perfectly polite but also conveyed she'd rather not chat about Hadsworth.

I tried another topic. "Were you originally from the area?"

"No. I'd lived in London all my life." She fell silent.

I stifled a sigh. This was hard going. If I could barely get her to talk about herself, how could I pry any information out of her about her husband? Had Emily Pearce come to dinner because Lady Holt insisted? Mrs. Pearce didn't appear to want to be here or to be enjoying the evening.

The men joined us at that point, and Mr. Busby strolled over, his hands in his pockets. I tensed, ready to parry a disparaging comment about either me or my work with Hightower Books, but he only said, "Lovely evening tonight."

So we were in a truce state—at least as long as we were in polite company. "Yes, it is," I said. "A perfect night to be outside."

"I believe I'll get a cup of coffee," Mr. Busby said. "Would you like one, Mrs. Pearce?"

She'd been staring out into the dark garden and turned her head when he said her name. "I'm sorry. What did you say?"

Mr. Busby jingled some coins in his pocket. "Care for a cup of coffee? I'm getting one for myself."

"Yes, thank you."

Mr. Busby looked to me. "I'm fine, thank you." I wasn't anxious to drink anything I hadn't poured myself.

Mr. Busby returned in a moment and handed Mrs.

Pearce her cup before he took a seat. He brought his own cup of coffee, which was full to the brim, to his lips. Mrs. Pearce's cup was half full, and the coffee was a pale taupe color. She put it down on the table without sipping it. Maybe Mrs. Pearce also felt cautious about her drinks. She adjusted the angle of the cup's handle in the saucer but didn't pick it up.

A little alarm bell clanged in my mind as I stared at her cup . . . something about coffee . . .

Then it came to me. After the last dinner party, when I went to get coffee for myself and Mrs. Shaw, Mrs. Pearce had been at the table in front of me. She'd only filled her coffee cup halfway before adding cream. And during the bridge game, when Pearce had brought her another cup of coffee, he'd also only filled her cup halfway.

My gaze pinged from her half-full cup of buff-colored coffee to Mr. Busby, to Mrs. Pearce, then back down to the coffee. At that moment, I thought of the list of names Jasper had copied out of the guest ledger at the Sidlingham pub. I didn't remember them all, but I knew one of them had been a Mr. Leighland. Had Mr. Busby, Mr. *Leland* Busby, been staying at the Sidlingham pub during the time Mayhew was killed? Had he registered under a variant spelling of his first name, Leland, instead of Mr. Busby?

Mrs. Pearce noticed I was looking at her untouched coffee. I glanced away and cast around for something to say. "Mr. Busby, have you finished reading the manuscript I gave you?"

"Yes. It's adequate. I'll have to edit some of it heavily, but I suppose the fans of the series will be pleased."

Mrs. Pearce stared at her coffee cup, a wrinkle between her eyebrows.

I pushed my chair back. "Excuse me, I've changed my mind. I think I will have coffee." As I stood, Mr. Busby half rose. He and Mrs. Pearce exchanged a glance that sent a jolt through me. It was a look that communicated things, and only people who knew each other well exchanged glances like that.

I poured a cup of black coffee, the spout clattering against the coffee cup, then ambled along the terrace until I was near the French doors to the house. I hadn't wanted to speak to Longly earlier in the evening, but now I wished he were here. I had to get in touch with him straightaway.

I slipped through the door and went down the short passage to the entry hall, where the telephone was positioned near the stairs. The deeply shadowed entry hall was silent. The dark paneling seemed to absorb any sounds from the rest of the house. The servants would be clearing the dining room, but they were on the other side of Blackburn Hall, and I couldn't hear them at all. My coffee cup rattled in the saucer as I put it down on the table beside the telephone. I perched on the edge of the wingback chair's cushion, picked up the handset and earpiece, and asked the operator to connect me to The Crown.

Was that a footfall on the parquet? I pulled the earpiece away and twisted around with a jerk.

Shadows filled the deepest corners of the short passageway leading to the terrace. The terrace doors stood open, but no one was in the doorway. The faint murmur of conversation drifted in from outside.

I swept my gaze around the entry hall, but it was empty too—what I could see of it. Electric sconces on the staircase only lit up the expensive runner on the steps and didn't penetrate the cavernous expanse of the entry hall.

Don't be a rabbit, I lectured myself. But I shifted around in the chair so I could keep an eye on the French doors. A blast of sound came out of the earpiece. I pressed it to my ear.

A gravelly voice said, "The Crown."

"Inspector Longly, please." I'd telephoned the pub after I'd talked with Jasper this afternoon, intending to tell Longly what I suspected about Mayhew and Pearce's death, but the inspector had been out. He hadn't returned my call before dinner. Surely he'd be in now.

A sharply drawn breath sounded behind me. I twisted and saw a flash of movement. Pain crashed through my head. I felt myself falling forward, but I couldn't seem to put my arms out to break my fall. Then, darkness.

The sibilant noise of whispered voices penetrated the dark tunnel I was in. My head felt as if it were the dinner gong and someone was enthusiastically pounding away, announcing dinner was served. At the same time, I had the definite sensation I was on a boat, complete with seasickness. But that couldn't be right. There was no smell of the sea, no breath of wind. I opened my eyes, but all was blackness. I was lying on my side on something cold and hard. The voices continued, and the discordant sounds sorted themselves into words.

". . . of course I'm sure. She knows."

"How could she? We've hardly spoken a word to each other in weeks." The second voice was deeper, masculine. I cautiously tilted my head. The pounding intensified. I went still, and the pain dropped a notch.

The higher-pitched voice of the woman answered. "It was the coffee. You only poured half a cup—that gave the game away. You should've poured me a full cup. Someone I'd met a few days ago couldn't know I only drink half a cup."

The mental fog cleared. A half-full cup of coffee, Emily Pearce, and Leland Busby. I stayed motionless, concentrating on the voices as the roiling sensation in my stomach subsided. The deeper voice, Mr. Busby's, said, "You're overreacting, Emily."

"I'm not." The pitch of Mrs. Pearce's voice went higher. "She *knows*. Don't argue with me. We don't have time."

I tilted my head slowly in an effort to prevent the gong-banging sensation from worsening. The pain stayed on the low-level pulse, not the bone-shattering crash I'd initially felt. The nauseous feeling didn't return, but a band seemed to tighten around my chest, the first sign of one of my asthma attacks. *Breathe. In. Out. Steady on.* I went through the words and actions that had calmed me so many times in the past. I turned my head and saw a strip of light at my eye level. I blinked and focused on the line of brightness, which high-lighted a parquet floor. The sight comforted me, although I couldn't work out why. My head felt mussy, but my breathing was easier.

"We have to do something." It was the woman's voice, Mrs. Pearce's, still shrill and edged with panic.

The brightness hurt. I closed my eyes and rubbed them, then I probed the back of my head. I had a huge lump at the base of my skull. I opened my eyes and squinted as I held my fingers to the light. They were dry. No blood.

"I could see it in her eyes when she looked at me," Mrs. Pearce said. "She knows what you did."

I had to move. They were talking about me. I couldn't stay here—wherever here was.

Mrs. Pearce continued, "What are we going to do? I can't believe this. If you hadn't been so rash, we wouldn't be in this situation."

I inched myself up. For a brief moment, I felt as if the darkness were about to spin around me. I held still, and the sensation faded.

"What do you mean? You wanted your husband gone, and we agreed to do it." Mr. Busby's voice was casual and not strained at all. "I saw an opportunity and took it."

I eased into a sitting position. It was fortunate I was moving slowly because my forehead bumped something solid. I stilled until the vibrations of pain tapered off. Thank goodness I'd been moving slowly. If I'd sat up quickly, I'd probably have knocked myself out again.

Mrs. Pearce continued, her tone high and angry. "But you did it with *me* there. After Mayhew, we agreed no more of that."

"You wanted to be rid of Pearce as much as I did," Mr. Busby said.

"Yes, but I didn't want you to do it in a room full of people —with me there. You put both of us under suspicion. I told you it was too soon after Mayhew."

So I'd been right—Mayhew and Pearce's deaths *were* linked. I would have enjoyed being vindicated more if I wasn't locked away in the dark, fighting down nausea after being bashed on the head.

Mr. Busby's voice was brisk. "Forget that. It doesn't matter now. What are we going to do with her? Why did you have to hit her on the head?"

"She was calling the inspector. I told you, she knows. I had to do something."

"You couldn't just disconnect the call?"

I reached out into the darkness around me. My fingers traced over the low ceiling. It was stair stepped, so I was in the closet under the stairs. That's why the parquet looked familiar. Part of my fuzzy brain had recognized the pattern of the wood. I knew where I was. At that thought, the tightness in my chest faded. I wasn't in a good situation, but at least I was still inside Blackburn Hall. I shifted closer to the strip of light and explored the edges of the door, looking for a latch.

"Oh, why does that even matter now?" Mrs. Pearce said. "What's done is done. Let's figure out what to do, how to . . . get rid of her."

I paused in my exploration. Get rid of me? I did *not* like the sound of that.

I ran my hands up and down, racing along the edge of the door, looking for a door handle, but I only found a tiny seam wide enough for a fingernail. Of course there wouldn't be a handle on the inside of a closet door.

If I screamed, would anyone hear me? I could only barely hear the voices of the conversation on the other side of the door. The thick wooden paneling on the walls of the entry hall and stairs would probably stifle most of the noise I could make. Screaming would only alert Mrs. Pearce and Mr. Busby that I was awake.

No, better to bide my time. I could make a racket when the door opened—that was a better plan.

"And you should have left well enough alone with Mayhew," Mrs. Pearce said, circling back to what was obviously a sore point with her. "Mayhew never spoke to anyone."

"You forget. He wrote books."

Mrs. Pearce went on as if Mr. Busby hadn't spoken. "I still think you overreacted. He might not have heard us at all. And you should have waited and not poisoned Don until this Olive person returned to London. She's been making a nuisance of herself all over the village. She's one of those tiresomely dogged females. She's not the type to give up, I can tell."

Dogged? Anger fired through me. Mrs. Pearce had attacked me then shut me in a closet, and she was calling me dogged? Right. Emily Pearce had no idea how determined I could be. I patted around the closet quietly to find something to defend myself with.

"It's not her we need to worry about," Mr. Busby countered. "It's the inspector. Mayhew's death is officially an accident, remember? So stop worrying about that. Now let's focus on what we need to do here. I overheard Miss Belgrave and Pearce arguing about some investment that went bad. Miss Belgrave had plenty of animosity toward Pearce. In fact, this actually may work out well—she dies, taking the blame for Pearce's death, which leaves us out of it. Yes, this may work out much better than I first thought. The only question is how we do it."

My fingers felt the scratch of wool—mittens or a scarf—and the slick rubber of boots. I touched an oblong shape made of canvas and traced my hand along the edges of it. A section of it lifted away. A strap, I realized. It was a bag of golf clubs, probably the one I'd taken with me to the course.

I let my fingers play across the clubs until I found a weighty one, then worked it out of the bag, making sure I didn't bang it against the stair-stepped ceiling.

Mrs. Pearce's voice was now almost at full volume, and the pitch was reaching into soprano territory. "It *must* look as if it were an accident. After what happened with Don, we can't have *any* questions—none at all! And we have to do it quickly. The servants are occupied in the dining room, but someone might come along here any minute."

"The servants are using the door at the far end of the terrace. They won't come through here. We have a few minutes before someone notices we haven't returned from our stroll in the gardens. Where's that doorstop you hit her with? Do you still have it?"

"Here."

I inched to the door and shifted to a standing position. I could stand up straight, but I had to tuck my head under one of the stair treads. My head whirled for a second, but I pressed my hand against the rough wood of the stairs. I clung there, deep breathing until my head cleared and I didn't feel as if I were about to spin off into the dark.

"Good. I think it'll have to be the stairs," Mr. Busby said. "There's nothing else we can do that will look like an accident. Can't strangle her. That would leave marks. And there's no way we could pawn off a knifing as purely accidental."

I took up the stance Serena had demonstrated this morning, my legs slightly apart. Mr. Busby said, "I'll carry her to the top of the stairs and drop her down. If she's still alive at the bottom, we'll use the doorstop again. You make sure nobody comes in from the terrace."

Footsteps tapped away.

My palms were slick on the shaft of the golf club, and my heart pounded. The latch clicked.

As the door opened, I pulled the club back, hinged my wrists, and swung through. The club connected with Mr. Busby's chin, and I let out a scream that set off the gong in my head again.

Mr. Busby collapsed, and I shoved the door open all the way. I stepped over him, the club at the ready in case Mrs. Pearce came at me with the doorstop. But she stood frozen in the doorway to the terrace, silhouetted against the faint light from the paper lanterns.

Jasper came into the entry hall, pushing her along in front of him. He reached out to steady her, but I noticed he didn't release her shoulder.

Jasper looked from me to Mr. Busby's crumpled form to Mrs. Pearce. I pointed the club from Mrs. Pearce to Mr. Busby. "They were in it together."

Mrs. Pearce stepped back, an attempt to disengage from Jasper, but he gripped her upper arm and steered her to the wingback chair by the telephone. "Better have a seat, Mrs. Pearce," Jasper said. "You look as if you've had a shock." He pushed her down into the chair and kept a firm hand on her shoulder as he turned to me. "Are you all right?"

"Never better."

"Rather nice to be proven right, I suppose," Jasper said.

"It almost makes the headache worthwhile. Almost."

Mr. Busby groaned and tried to roll onto his side. I put the club on his Adam's apple. "Don't move, Mr. Busby. I'm sure Inspector Longly will want to speak to you."

Mrs. Shaw appeared in the doorway. "Oh my," she said as she surveyed the scene, then turned back to the terrace and called, "Rodney, dear, it's just as I said. Inspector Longly won't need the warrant for Miss Belgrave's arrest. The clever girl has taken care of all of it for you."

CHAPTER TWENTY-SIX

"Good morning, Bower," I said as I entered the breakfast room the next morning. "Although, it's shockingly late. I could almost say 'good afternoon.'"

"Indeed," Bower said. "Shall I instruct cook to prepare your scrambled eggs?"

"No, thank you. Mr. Rimington and I plan to depart momentarily. I'll have a cup of coffee and wait for him on the terrace." I'd already instructed Janet to pack my bag and have a footman bring it down. I'd said a formal goodbye to Lady Holt, who'd murmured all the correct words about being glad to have me visit, but I knew she was thrilled to see me go. I'd taken one look at her face this morning and had to squash a surge of disappointment. She wouldn't sing my praises to other society matrons, so I had no hope of gaining any referrals from her.

Bower picked up a salver. "Mr. Rimington was called away." A cream-colored envelope with my name on it was centered on the tray. "He left this for you, to be given to you when you came downstairs."

I found it hard to believe Jasper had risen before me. It

had been the early hours of the morning before Longly had allowed us to retire. When we'd finally answered all of Longly's questions, Jasper asked if I'd give him a lift to London.

"He's left?" A curious sensation swept over me. Could it be . . . disappointment? No. Of course not. Jasper wasn't obligated to remain here until I left. But if he wanted to scamper away at daybreak, I wasn't going to waste a moment wondering where—or why he'd left so suddenly. The image in the newspaper of Jasper with the willowy Bebe Ravenna popped into my mind.

"He received a telephone call early this morning and left shortly afterwards," Bower said. "Shall I bring your coffee to the terrace?"

And Jasper said I was the one who flitted off impulsively. "Yes, thank you." I went out through the open doors, shaking off the irritated feeling.

The tables were still set up from last evening, and I chose one in the shade as I ripped open the envelope. Jasper may have written the note in a hurry, but his penmanship was as precise as ever.

Olive,

Sorry to leave you in the lurch, old girl. Hopefully Inspector Longly stays true to his word and doesn't have more questions for you—or me—seeing as I've been called away on urgent business. Jolly good show last night. Congratulations on getting your man—and woman. Chasing down clues with you was a delight . . . when you happened to remember you had a Watson, that is. I may be out of pocket for a while, but I'll be in touch soon.

Your partner in crime,
Jasper

As I read the last lines, Bower set down my coffee and melted away.

The coffee was scalding hot and had a bitter edge. Urgent business, indeed. What urgent business did Jasper have? Either it was the blonde or his tailor needed him for a final fitting.

Footsteps crunched across the gravel path in the garden at a quick pace. I shoved the note under the edge of the coffee cup's saucer and strained to see through the gaps in the shrubbery. Anna was racing across the garden, and when she saw I'd looked up, she ripped off her beret and waved it. "It's official," she called. "I'm to be an author."

I stood as she trotted up the steps. "But you're already an author."

She waved me back into my seat and collapsed into the chair near me. "But now it won't be a secret." She fanned herself with the beret. "Mr. Hightower"—she gulped some air —"he's here, in the village. He arrived this morning and came straight to Dad's surgery looking for me."

"Does he know about Mr. Busby?"

"Inspector Longly contacted him last night. Mr. High-tower set out immediately to come 'tidy things up,' as he phrased it."

"And there's quite a bit to clean up," I said.

"Yes, and I want to hear all about what happened last night."

Bower approached and offered Anna coffee.

"Oh, no. I'm much too hot. Perhaps a glass of lemonade?"

As Bower retreated, I asked, "Mr. Hightower offered you a contract?"

"He did," she said in the same way some women would speak about a man popping the question. She smiled widely and fell back into the chair, tossing her hat onto the table. "I still can't believe it. I told Inspector Longly about the ghost-writing, and Inspector Longly told Mr. Hightower."

"Oh no. I know you wanted it kept secret."

She bounced in her chair. "But it's a good thing. Mr. Hightower said he wants *Murder on the Ninth Green* squared away. He suggested my name go on the cover along with May's and"— she leaned forward—"he asked if I'd continue the series under my own name. He's got his solicitors working on it and says we can sign the paperwork in a few days."

"Brilliant! I'd wondered what would happen with the book series."

Bower returned with Anna's lemonade, and she gulped some before she continued. "Mr. Hightower owns the series characters and can commission anyone to write the next books. I've agreed to write two more Lady Eileen books, then I'd like to try my hand at something else. He's interested in seeing anything I write."

"That's wonderful. I'm so happy for you." I raised my coffee cup. "Congratulations."

She lifted her glass. "Thank you. It's a better outcome than any I dreamed of. All that worry about the manuscripts and the draft pages. But that's all sorted now, thank goodness." She plopped her lemonade down on the table and shifted in her chair so she faced me directly. "Now tell me everything that's happened. Is it true Mrs. Pearce tried to convince the inspector she didn't have anything to do with the deaths?"

"She did. Inspector Longly had barely gotten through the door before she turned on Mr. Busby, putting all the blame on him. Said he was deranged."

"But that's not what happened?"

"No, and Inspector Longly wasn't fooled. Mrs. Pearce and Mr. Busby were in it together from the beginning. The inspector separated Mrs. Pearce and Mr. Busby when he questioned them. Longly said they blamed each other and gave him enough information that he was able to piece together what happened."

"And what was that?" Anna propped her elbow on the table and put her chin in her hand. "I want all the details—for research, you know."

I grinned. "Of course. Mayhew wasn't the only person who liked to stroll after sunset. Mr. Busby would drive down from town most Fridays for a spot of golf, but he stayed in the pub in Sidlingham. He also liked to go on late evening rambles."

"As did Mrs. Pearce?"

"That's right. Lots of late-night walkers around here. Mr. Busby and Mrs. Pearce met on the deserted golf course. Mayhew overheard them discussing their first attempt to do away with Mr. Pearce."

Anna sat up straight. "First attempt? You don't mean his fall down the stairs?"

"Not a fall. A push."

"Was it Mrs. Pearce?"

"She says it was Mr. Busby. And I gather from what Inspector Longly says that Mr. Busby says it was Mrs. Pearce."

"Goodness," Anna said. "It's difficult to picture it. Emily Pearce always seemed such a timid little thing." Anna shook her head. "Amazing what they did. What will happen now?"

"The investigation into Mayhew's death will be reopened, for a start," I said. "And then with what I overheard . . ." I shrugged. "I'm sure Inspector Longly is busy building a case against them. I know he's got officers searching their homes and tracing their movements. I don't doubt he'll find enough evidence to go to trial."

Anna folded her arms across her chest as if she were cold. "I do find it hard to believe Mrs. Pearce and Mr. Busby knew each other. They certainly acted as if they'd never met before when Lady Holt introduced them at the dinner party."

"Inspector Longly said Mrs. Pearce told him they actually met earlier this year. Mr. Pearce was away on business, and Mrs. Pearce was staying in London alone. She attended an event Hightower Books hosted and met Mr. Busby. At some point after that, Mrs. Pearce and Mr. Busby decided to do away with Pearce and avoided being seen together publicly. It was Mayhew's misfortune that she got in the middle of their plans."

"Terribly unfortunate. And how are you feeling today?" Anna ran a critical eye over me. "It sounds as if Dad should've been called to examine you. I understand you were unconscious."

"I'm fine."

"Double vision? Nausea? You really should—"

I shook my head. "No. I'm fine. Nothing but a bump." I had no desire to spend any more time in Hadsworth.

"I'd argue with you, but I can see it would be useless."

The clock inside the drawing room chimed, and Anna looked at her wristwatch. "Noon already? I must fly. I told Dad I'd drive him to a house call after lunch." Anna drained her glass and set it down with a click. "And then I have pages to write." She squinted at the flowerbeds on the far side of the garden. "I must figure out a way to get one more suspect on the yacht . . ."

"Perhaps there's a stowaway."

"Oh, I like that . . ." she murmured as she settled her beret on her head and pushed back her chair.

I walked to the terrace steps with her. "Look me up next time you're in London. I'm sure you'll be up there quite often visiting Hightower Books."

"Yes, I suppose I will," Anna said as if the thought hadn't struck her until that moment. After we said goodbye, I picked up the note from Jasper and turned to go inside, but Bower came outside, escorting Mr. Hightower.

"Mr. Hightower, good afternoon. I just spoke with Anna.

In fact, she might still be on the grounds." I turned and scanned the garden. "No, she's already left. She's thrilled with the new arrangement."

"We are as well. Bower informed me you're leaving shortly. Do you have a few moments?"

"Yes, of course." I gestured for him to have a seat and returned to my chair. I asked Mr. Hightower if he'd like something to drink.

"Thank you, but no." Mr. Hightower settled in the chair. "When the inspector contacted me, I knew I had to come down immediately and speak to him as well as Miss Finch. Hightower Books needs to continue the series, and we're delighted Miss Finch will be able to write more Lady Eileen books."

"I understand. It's a mutually beneficial arrangement."

"Exactly. As was our arrangement." He removed an envelope from an inside pocket of his jacket and handed it to me. "I believe this will cover your expenses. There's a bonus as well. With the forthcoming books from Miss Finch, I assure you, the check will not bounce."

I tucked the envelope away in my pocket. "Thank you. I didn't think it would."

Mr. Hightower's expression turned somber. "I must apologize for the actions of Mr. Busby. I had no idea what Leland was involved in, and I hope you have completely recovered."

"Yes, I'm fine. Bit of a headache at first, but that's gone."

"Excellent. Glad to hear it." He cleared his throat. "I do hope that you don't hold any—ah—animosity toward Hightower Books."

"Of course not. Mr. Busby's actions were his own."

Mr. Hightower leaned back slightly and let out a barely disguised sigh of what seemed to be relief. "I'm happy to see you came through the ordeal relatively unscathed. I assure you, I'd never have sent you here if I'd known about Leland's horrible plans. To think he was the one who killed

Mayhew—it's astonishing. Hard to take it in, you know. It does explain why he kept asking if May's delayed manuscript had arrived, though." His voice dropped, and he spoke more to himself than to me as he said, "I should have picked up on that."

"Mr. Busby was looking for it?"

"Oh yes." Mr. Hightower's voice returned to full volume. "Leland's never shown much interest in May's books." He gazed out over the gardens. "He knew the publishing schedule, of course—it was no secret—so Leland was aware we needed the manuscript soon. However, Leland didn't know Mr. Pearce handled all of Mayhew's communication with Hightower Books. Leland didn't realize that causing Mr. Pearce an injury would delay the arrival of the manuscript."

"So Mr. Busby knew Mayhew was the author of the Lady Eileen books?"

Mr. Hightower shook his head. "No, I don't think so. The only people who knew Mayhew was the author of those books were myself and Mr. Pearce. The inspector asked if Mr. Pearce could have told Mrs. Pearce, but I don't think he would have. Mr. Pearce wasn't the type to share business confidences with his wife—or his secretary either. By the way, we finally received Mayhew's original manuscript. It arrived in the post on Saturday. Mr. Pearce sent it on with a cover letter apologizing for the delay. By that point, Leland was already here in Hadsworth."

I frowned, trying to work out the timing. "But Mr. Busby must have discovered Mayhew's identity as a Hightower Books author," I said.

"I believe so," Mr. Hightower said. "I understand Mr. Busby had access to Mayhew's cottage . . . ?"

"Yes, that must have been how Mr. Busby figured it out." I thought of the notes and manuscripts in Mayhew's desk. "He probably found something in Mayhew's desk that indicated Mayhew wrote the Lady Eileen books, so he used Mayhew's typewriter to type up notes to delay the discovery that Mayhew was missing."

"Yes, that seems to be the case," said Mr. Hightower. "At that point, Leland must have thought the manuscript for *Murder on the Ninth Green* was already on my desk. It must have given Leland a fright when he worked out exactly who Mayhew was and realized he'd killed off his livelihood."

"But then Mr. Busby must have sorted out that Anna was ghostwriting the books and sent off the note to her with instructions to keep at it," I said. "There was plenty of evidence of their collaboration in the drafts."

The distinctive tones of Lady Holt's voice drifted out of the open window of the drawing room. Mr. Hightower glanced over his shoulder, then picked up the pace of his words. "Shocking. The whole thing is dreadful. As I said, I know it's not possible to make up for what you've been through, but that envelope contains more than we agreed on." He glanced at my pocket. "I feel it's only fair we increase your remuneration, considering what happened."

"That's kind of you, and unexpected but greatly appreciated."

He pushed back his chair. "I should be getting on."

I stood and held out my hand. "It's been a pleasure doing business with you, Mr. Hightower."

He shook my hand. "If I have need of a discreet investigator in the future, I'll contact you."

"I'd be delighted."

As I walked with him into the entry hall, I asked, "What will happen with Lady Holt's etiquette book?"

"Oh, we'll publish it," Mr. Hightower said. "We signed the contract. Hightower Books follows through on its promises."

Lady Holt came striding across the entry hall, her long arms swinging. "Mr. Hightower! Delighted you could join us here at Blackburn Hall. You've no idea the mess your associate made of things. Such a disgrace. I'm afraid there's no way we'll be able to keep Blackburn Hall out of those ghastly gossip sheets. But I assure you it does not impact my feelings toward Hightower Books. I'm still determined to make the best of things and do everything possible to make sure the etiquette book is successful."

"Excellent. Glad to hear it." Mr. Hightower raised his eyebrows a fraction of an inch at Bower, who stood near the door with Mr. Hightower's hat. At the signal from Mr. Hightower, Bower began to make his way across the parquet floor. "It's a pleasure to see you, Lady Holt, but I cannot stay. I must—"

Lady Holt halted Bower with a flick of a wrist, then she clamped a hand on Mr. Hightower's arm. "You must stay for lunch. It's so fortunate you're here. I have a few small details that must be sorted."

Bower reversed course, and Lady Holt propelled Mr. Hightower into the library. He threw a last gaze over his shoulder. I raised a hand and mouthed, *good luck*. I hoped he escaped before dinner, otherwise Lady Holt would keep him at Blackburn Hall for days.

I returned to my room to gather my hat and gloves, but before I picked them up, I ripped open the envelope from Mr. Hightower. It contained a check for one hundred pounds.

I pressed the piece of paper to my chest. *One hundred pounds.* Mind-boggling. I could pay my rent for many, many months. And have actual meals for dinner instead of crumbly buns. And maybe even a winter coat.

I folded the check solemnly and tucked it away in my handbag. I put on my hat and gloves. I passed Serena's workroom on my way downstairs and stopped to tap on the door. She looked up from her seat at one of the tables and waved me in. "Look. I think I've done it." Her hands were covered in black smudges.

"Made a mess?"

"No. I've invented a new kind of pen. The felt works wonderfully well. Here, try it."

"It looks like a fountain pen without the nib."

"It is. But I modified it, and the ink is different. Better use this to hold it." She wrapped a rag around the inky exterior of the pen, then cleared pots of ink, scraps of fabric, and several dismantled pens out of the way. She pushed a stack of paper across the table to me. I signed my name. "Very nice."

"See how it evens out the flow of ink? It won't need a refill, and it dries quickly," Serena said. "Now I just have to fashion a cap for it so the pen doesn't dry out."

I touched one of the letters with a gloved fingertip. It came away clean. "That is an improvement. What will you call it?"

"I don't know. Perhaps a felt pen? The felt material worked the best."

I handed back the pen. "Congratulations."

"Thank you. And congratulations to you too. For exposing Mrs. Pearce and Mr. Busby. Who would've thought a passionate affair would be going on in our quiet village?" She began to put the lids back on the pots of ink. "Give me my predictable and methodical science. Nothing is ever as messy as human relationships."

Thinking of Jasper's early-morning disappearance, I had to agree. "Unfortunately, that's often true."

"What will you do now?" Serena asked.

"I don't know." Perhaps Jasper was right that I did focus too much on the moment and didn't think ahead. "Return to London and find a new client, I suppose." I'd have money in the bank, and I could be choosy about who I worked for—at least for a while.

"Well, let me know if you ever want to play another round of golf. You showed promise."

"Thank goodness for your lessons. They came in quite handy."

"Glad it was useful." She walked with me to the door.

"Where's Zippy this morning?" I asked. "I should say goodbye to him before I leave."

"He's in Sidlingham, and he's not keeping it a secret from Maria anymore. This morning at breakfast, he said if Blackburn Hall could survive the scandal of a double murder and a salacious affair, his interest in a barmaid should be completely innocuous."

"And how did Lady Holt react?" I asked as Serena came downstairs with me.

"She forbade him to go, of course. But Zippy stood up to her, wonder of wonders. He said he'd reached his majority and he could do whatever he liked. Of course Maria threatened to withdraw his allowance, and Zippy said that was fine, he'd sell his Bugatti so he would have funds to live on."

"Really? I thought he was fond of the car."

"Oh, he is. That gave Maria a bad turn. She was wise enough to stop there. Later, I told her to give it a few days. If she presses, I'm sure Zippy will dig in his heels. If she lets it go, he'll probably lose interest and move on to someone else. Half of the lure of a relationship like that is the thrill of the secrecy."

"That's probably true."

Serena lifted a shoulder as we reached the entry hall. "It's basic human nature. Messy, as I said, but often predictable."

Bower met us as we stepped off the last stair. He held a tray with a letter. "For you, Miss Belgrave."

Serena said, "I hope it's not bad news."

"When did it arrive?" I asked Bower, studying the envelope. It was addressed to the boarding house in London, but I recognized my landlady's left-handed script where she'd redirected the note here.

"By the morning post."

I ripped it open and felt my eyebrows shoot up when I read the signature. "It's from Lady Agnes Wells."

"The Egyptian curse," Bower breathed. Both Serena and I turned to look at him.

The usual impassive blankness was gone from his face. It was alive with curiosity, and he'd leaned forward to get a glimpse of the note. He cleared his throat and stepped back. "Pardon me."

"It's all right, Bower," I said. "What's this about a curse?"

"It's been in the newspapers. The—um—lower staff has been quite interested."

"Go on," I said. "What do the papers say about it?"

"As I understand it, Lord Mulvern, Lady Agnes's uncle, was an Egyptologist. He sponsored a dig and brought back antiquities."

"Including a mummy?" Serena asked.

Bower nodded. "Several, apparently."

"And now there's a curse?" I asked.

"That's what the newspapers say killed him."

"Good heavens." I skimmed the note.

Dear Miss Belgrave,

I am in a difficult spot, and my friend Sebastian Blakely suggested I contact you. He says you are a lady detective, and that is exactly what I need. You may have read about our family recently in the newspapers. I assure you the real story is not as lurid as they make out, but it is most disturbing. I would like to discuss the situation with you. Perhaps you could call at Mulvern House on Monday at ten o'clock in the morning.

Yours truly,
Agnes Curtis

"Sounds like you have a new case," Serena said. "If you're interested in curses and mummies and all that."

"Who isn't interested in Egyptology? It's fascinating." My gaze flew to the date at the top of the note. "Monday. That's tomorrow." I stuffed the letter in my handbag and turned to Bower. "Have my motor brought around immediately. I must get back to London."

Let's stay in touch! Sign up for Sara's Notes and News at SaraRosett.com/signup to get updates on new releases as well as exclusive content.

THE STORY BEHIND THE STORY

I hope you enjoyed Olive's second case. *Murder at Blackburn Hall* was a fun book to write. I always love delving into 1920s research, and with the added angles of ghostwriting and authorship as themes, I was one happy writer!

The list of female writers using male pen names is long and ranges from Victorian writers like George Elliot and all three Brontë sisters to modern authors like J.K. Rowling, who writes her mysteries under the name Robert Galbraith. One female author who was published in the 1920s actually did masquerade as a male to fool her publisher. I ran across the story in Martin Edwards's nonfiction book, *The Golden Age of Murder*. Author Lucy Beatrice Malleson thought she'd be taken more seriously if her publisher thought she was a man and submitted her manuscripts under male names, including Anthony Gilbert. When her publisher asked her for a publicity photo, she sent in a photo of herself "disguised as an old man with a beard," according to Edwards. Malleson wrote nearly seventy mysteries under the Gilbert pseudonym. Her short stories and novels were adapted for television and movies.

I used her story as inspiration for the character of Ronnie

Mayhew, but since Mayhew was so withdrawn from village life and used a tin mask to hide her appearance in the village itself, she needed an even bigger reason to hide her background. When I read an article about the Cottingley Fairies, I knew I'd found the inspiration for Mayhew's backstory.

In 1917, two young cousins, Elsie Wright and Frances Griffiths, photographed themselves with paper fairies that they'd traced from a book. They used a camera that belonged to Elise's father. Her father developed the pictures and recognized it was a prank—and he didn't lend his camera to the girls again. His wife, however, was interested in psychic phenomena and showed the pictures at a meeting of like-minded individuals. From there, interest in the fairy sightings spread and caught the attention of the public, including Sir Arthur Conan Doyle, who was a spiritualist. He wrote an article about the fairies for *The Strand* magazine, declaring the existence of the fairies would help people to believe in other psychic phenomena. The girls played along with the psychic phenomena investigators. In a 1983 interview, the cousins admitted they'd faked the photographs. Once Doyle was a part of the story, they felt they couldn't reveal the truth. According to the Wikipedia entry on the Cottingley Fairies, the girls said, "Two village kids and a brilliant man like Conan Doyle—well, we could only keep quiet."

I used the Cottingley story as a jumping-off point for Mayhew's backstory, changing it quite a bit and creating a situation where an unscrupulous parent was more concerned about money than his daughter, which caused Mayhew to bury herself in a quiet English village.

I was researching asthma and read an article about asthma cigarettes, which, as a mystery writer, I found incredibly intriguing. Mystery writers are always on the lookout for a good poison, and once I learned that the cigarettes contained belladonna and *datura stramonium* and anyone could buy them at a chemist, I knew I'd found the murder weapon for

Murder in Blackburn Hall. As strange as it sounds today, asthma cigarettes were a popular and accepted treatment for people who experienced breathing problems.

The character of Serena Shires was a fun one to write. I wanted her to be scientifically-minded and interested in innovation, but I had a hard time finding something for her to invent. Serena is a practical type and would be interested in something that would improve efficiency in the home or the workplace. I was surprised to learn that many of the inventions I assumed occurred in the early 1900s actually happened quite a bit earlier. For instance, paper clips, staplers, drinking straws, ball point pens, erasers, vacuums, clear tape, and refrigerators were all invented long before 1923. The felt-tip pen, however, wasn't, which is why Serena is so interested in pens and ink. The real inventor of the felt-tip pen was Walter J. De Groft, and he applied for a patent in 1944. Yukio Horie created the modern felt-tip pen in 1962.

Olive's next case is *The Egyptian Antiquities Murder*. If you'd like news about upcoming books, exclusive content, and members-only giveaways, sign up for my updates at SaraRosett.com/signup. I'd love to stay in touch with you!

ABOUT THE AUTHOR

USA Today bestselling author Sara Rosett writes fun mysteries. Her books are light-hearted escapes for readers who enjoy interesting settings, quirky characters, and puzzling mysteries. *Publishers Weekly* called Sara's books, "satisfying," "well-executed," and "sparkling."

Sara loves to get new stamps in her passport and considers dark chocolate a daily requirement. Find out more at Sara-Rosett.com.

Connect with Sara
www.SaraRosett.com

facebook.com/AuthorSaraRosett
twitter.com/SaraRosett

ALSO BY SARA ROSETT

This is Sara Rosett's complete library at the time of publication, but Sara has new books coming out all the time. Sign up for her updates at SaraRosett.com/signup to stay up to date on new releases.

High Society Lady Detective

Murder at Archly Manor

Murder at Blackburn Hall

The Egyptian Antiquities Murder

Murder on Location

Death in the English Countryside

Death in an English Cottage

Death in a Stately Home

Death in an Elegant City

Menace at the Christmas Market (novella)

Death in an English Garden

Death at an English Wedding

On the Run

Elusive

Secretive

Deceptive

Suspicious

Devious

Treacherous

Ellie Avery

Moving is Murder
Staying Home is a Killer
Getting Away is Deadly
Magnolias, Moonlight, and Murder
Mint Juleps, Mayhem, and Murder
Mimosas, Mischief, and Murder
Mistletoe, Merriment and Murder
Milkshakes, Mermaids, and Murder
Marriage, Monsters-in-law, and Murder
Mother's Day, Muffins, and Murder

CPSIA information can be obtained
at www.ICGtesting.com
Printed in the USA
BVHW081719070119
537200BV00001B/22/P